And Then There Were None

By Agatha Christie

Kodansha

AND THEN THERE WERE NONE Copyright ©1939 Agatha Christie Limited.
All rights reserved.
Published in Japan 2016 by Kodansha Ltd.

Agatha Christie and the Agatha Christie signature are registered trademarks
of Agatha Christie Limited in the UK and elsewhere.

Textbook rights arranged with Agatha Christie Ltd.
through Timo Associates, Inc.

Contents

Chapter 1 5
Chapter 2 21
Chapter 3 43
Chapter 4 62
Chapter 5 73
Chapter 6 87
Chapter 7 103
Chapter 8 116
Chapter 9 133
Chapter 10 160
Chapter 11 173
Chapter 12 188
Chapter 13 202
Chapter 14 216
Chapter 15 234
Chapter 16 251
Epilogue 260

A Manuscript Document Sent to Scotland Yard by the Master of the *Emma Jane* Fishing Trawler 273

Notes 288

Chapter 1

I

In the corner of a first-class smoking carriage, Mr. Justice Wargrave, lately retired from the bench, puffed at a cigar and ran an interested eye through the political news in *The Times*.

He laid the paper down and glanced out of the window. They were running now through Somerset. He glanced at his watch—another two hours to go.

He went over in his mind all that had appeared in the papers about Soldier Island. There had been its original purchase by an American millionaire who was crazy about yachting—and an account of the luxurious modern house he had built on this little island off the Devon coast. The unfortunate fact that the new third wife of the American millionaire was a bad sailor had led to the subsequent putting up of the house and island for sale. Various glowing advertisements of it had appeared in the papers. Then came the first bald statement that it had been bought—by a Mr. Owen. After that the rumours of the gossip writers had started. Soldier Island had really been bought by Miss Gabrielle Turl, the Hollywood film star! She wanted to spend some months there free from all publicity! *Busy Bee* had hinted delicately that it was to be an abode for Royalty??! *Mr. Merryweather* had had it whispered to him that it had been bought for a honeymoon—Young Lord L—had surrendered to Cupid at last! *Jonas* knew for a *fact* that it had been purchased by the Admiralty with a view to carrying out some very hush-hush experiments!

Definitely, Soldier Island was news!

From his pocket Mr. Justice Wargrave drew out a letter. The handwriting was practically illegible but words here and there stood out with unexpected clarity. *Dearest Lawrence . . . such years since I heard anything of you . . . must come to Soldier Island . . . the most enchanting place . . . so much to talk over . . . old days . . . communion with nature . . . bask in sunshine . . . 12:40 from Paddington . . . meet you at Oakbridge . . .* and his correspondent signed herself with a flourish his *ever Constance Culmington.*

Mr. Justice Wargrave cast back in his mind to remember when exactly he had last seen Lady Constance Culmington. It must be seven—no, eight years ago. She had then been going to Italy to bask in the sun and be at one with Nature and the *contadini.* Later, he had heard, she had proceeded to Syria where she proposed to bask in a yet stronger sun and live at one with Nature and the *bedouin.*

Constance Culmington, he reflected to himself, was exactly the sort of woman who *would* buy an island and surround herself with mystery! Nodding his head in gentle approval of his logic, Mr. Justice Wargrave allowed his head to nod...

He slept...

II

Vera Claythorne, in a third-class carriage with five other travellers in it, leaned her head back and shut her eyes. How hot it was travelling by train today! It would be nice to get to the sea! Really a great piece of luck getting this job. When you wanted a holiday post it nearly always meant looking after a swarm of children—secretarial holiday posts were much more difficult to get. Even the agency hadn't held out much hope.

And then the letter had come.

"I have received your name from the Skilled Women's Agency together with their recommendation. I understand they know you personally. I shall be glad to pay you the salary you ask and shall expect you to take up your duties on August 8th. The train is the 12:40 from Paddington and you will be met at Oakbridge station. I enclose five £1 notes for expenses.
Yours truly,
Una Nancy Owen."

And at the top was the stamped address, *Soldier Island, Sticklehaven, Devon*...

Soldier Island! Why, there had been nothing else in the papers lately! All sorts of hints and interesting rumours. Though probably they were mostly untrue. But the house had certainly been built by a millionaire and was said to be absolutely the last word in luxury.

Vera Claythorne, tired by a recent strenuous term at school, thought to herself, "Being a games mistress in a third-class school isn't much of a catch ... If only I could get a job at some *decent* school."

And then, with a cold feeling round her heart, she thought: "But I'm lucky to have even this. After all, people don't like a Coroner's Inquest, even if the Coroner *did* acquit me of all blame!"

He had even complimented her on her presence of mind and courage, she remembered. For an inquest it couldn't have gone better. And Mrs. Hamilton had been kindness itself to her—only Hugo—*but she wouldn't think of Hugo!*

Suddenly, in spite of the heat in the carriage she shivered and wished she wasn't going to the sea. A picture rose clearly before her mind. *Cyril's head, bobbing up and down, swimming to the rock* ... up and down—up and down ... and herself, swimming in easy practised strokes after him—cleaving her way through the water but knowing, only too surely, that she wouldn't be in time ...

The sea—its deep warm blue—mornings spent lying out on the sands—Hugo—Hugo who had said he loved her ...

She must *not* think of Hugo ...

She opened her eyes and frowned across at the man opposite her. A tall man with a brown face, light eyes set rather close together and an arrogant, almost cruel mouth.

She thought to herself:

I bet he's been to some interesting parts of the world and seen some interesting things...

I I I

Philip Lombard, summing up the girl opposite in a mere flash of his quick moving eyes thought to himself:

"Quite attractive—a bit schoolmistressy perhaps."

A cool customer, he should imagine—and one who could hold her own—in love or war. He'd rather like to take her on...

He frowned. No, cut out all that kind of stuff. This was business. He'd got to keep his mind on the job.

What exactly was up, he wondered? That little Jew had been damned mysterious.

"Take it or leave it, Captain Lombard."

He had said thoughtfully:

"A hundred guineas, eh?"

He had said it in a casual way as though a hundred guineas was nothing to him. *A hundred guineas* when he was literally down to his last square meal! He had fancied, though, that the little Jew had not been deceived—that was the damnable part about Jews, you couldn't deceive them about money—they *knew*!

He had said in the same casual tone:

"And you can't give me any further information?"

Mr. Isaac Morris had shaken his little bald head very positively.

"No, Captain Lombard, the matter rests there. It is understood by my client that your reputation is that of a good man in a tight place. I am empowered to hand you one hundred guineas in return for which you will travel to Sticklehaven, Devon. The nearest station is Oakbridge, you will be met there and motored to Sticklehaven where a motor launch will convey you to Soldier Island. There you will hold yourself at the disposal of my client."

Lombard had said abruptly:

"For how long?"

"Not longer than a week at most."

Fingering his small moustache, Captain Lombard said:

"You understand I can't undertake anything—illegal?"

He had darted a very sharp glance at the other as he had spoken. There had been a very faint smile on the thick Semitic lips of Mr. Morris as he answered gravely:

"If anything illegal is proposed, you will, of course, be at perfect liberty to withdraw."

Damn the smooth little brute, he had smiled! It was as though he knew very well that in Lombard's past actions legality had not always been a *sine qua non* ...

Lombard's own lips parted in a grin.

By Jove, he'd sailed pretty near the wind once or twice! But he'd always got away with it! There wasn't much he drew the line at really...

No, there wasn't much he'd draw the line at. He fancied that he was going to enjoy himself at Soldier Island...

IV

In a non-smoking carriage Miss Emily Brent sat very upright as was her custom. She was sixty-five and she did not approve of lounging. Her father, a Colonel of the old school, had been particular about deportment.

The present generation was shamelessly lax—in their carriage, *and in every other way*...

Enveloped in an aura of righteousness and unyielding principles, Miss Brent sat in her crowded third-class carriage and triumphed over its discomfort and its heat. Every one made such a fuss over things nowadays! They wanted injections before they had teeth pulled—they took drugs if they couldn't sleep—they wanted easy chairs and cushions and the girls allowed their figures to slop about anyhow and lay about half naked on the beaches in summer.

Miss Brent's lips set closely. She would like to make an example of certain people.

She remembered last year's summer holiday. This year, however, it would be quite different. Soldier Island...

Mentally she re-read the letter which she had already read so many times.

"Dear Miss Brent,

I do hope you remember me? We were together at Belhaven Guest House in August some years ago, and we seemed to have so much in common.

I am starting a guest house of my own on an island off the coast of Devon. I think there is really an opening for a place where there is good plain cooking and a nice old-fashioned type of person. None of this nudity and gramophones half the night. I shall be very glad if you could see your way to spending your summer holiday on Soldier Island—quite free—as my guest. Would early in August suit you? Perhaps the 8th.

Yours sincerely,
U. N. O.—"

What was the name? The signature was rather difficult to read. Emily Brent thought impatiently: "So many people write their signatures quite illegibly."

She let her mind run back over the people at Belhaven. She had been there two summers running. There had been that nice middle-aged woman—Miss—Miss—now what *was* her name?—her father had been a Canon. And there had been a Mrs. Olton—Ormen—No, surely it was *Oliver*! Yes—Oliver.

Soldier Island! There had been things in the paper about Soldier Island—something about a film star—or was it an American millionaire?

Of course often those places went very cheap—islands didn't suit everybody. They thought the idea was romantic but when they came to live there they realized the disadvantages and were only too glad to sell.

Emily Brent thought to herself: *"I shall be getting a free holiday at any rate."*

With her income so much reduced and so many dividends not being paid, that was indeed something to take into consideration. If only she could remember a little more about Mrs.—or was it Miss—Oliver?

V

General Macarthur looked out of the carriage window. The train was just coming into Exeter where he had to change. Damnable, these slow branch line trains! This place, Soldier Island, was really no distance at all as the crow flies.

He hadn't got it clear who this fellow Owen was. A friend of Spoof Leggard's, apparently—and of Johnny Dyer's.

"—One or two of your old cronies are coming—would like to have a talk over old times."

Well, he'd enjoy a chat about old times. He'd had a fancy lately that fellows were rather fighting shy of him. All owing to that damned rumour! By God, it was pretty hard—nearly thirty years ago now! Armitage had talked, he supposed. Damned young pup! What did *he* know about it? Oh, well, no good brooding about these things! One fancied things sometimes—fancied a fellow was looking at you queerly.

This Soldier Island, now, he'd be interested to see it. A lot of gossip flying about. Looked as though there might be something in the rumour that the Admiralty or the War Office or the Air Force had got hold of it ...

Young Elmer Robson, the American millionaire, had actually built the place. Spent thousands on it, so it was said. Every mortal luxury ...

Exeter! And an hour to wait! And he didn't want to wait. He wanted to get on ...

VI

Dr. Armstrong was driving his Morris across Salisbury Plain. He was very tired ... Success had its penalties. There had been a time when he had sat in his consulting room in

Harley Street, correctly apparelled, surrounded with the most up to date appliances and the most luxurious furnishings and waited—waited through the empty days for his venture to succeed or fail ...

Well, it had succeeded! He'd been lucky! Lucky *and* skilful of course. He was a good man at his job—but that wasn't enough for success. You had to have luck as well. And he'd had it! An accurate diagnosis, a couple of grateful women patients—women with money and position—and word had got about. "You ought to try Armstrong—*quite* a young man—but *so* clever—Pam had been to all sorts of people for *years* and he put his finger on the trouble at once!" The ball had started rolling.

And now Dr. Armstrong had definitely arrived. His days were full. He had little leisure. And so, on this August morning, he was glad that he was leaving London and going to be for some days on an island off the Devon coast. Not that it was exactly a holiday. The letter he had received had been rather vague in its terms, but there was nothing vague about the accompanying cheque. A whacking fee. These Owens must be rolling in money. Some little difficulty, it seemed, a husband who was worried about his wife's health and wanted a report on it without her being alarmed. She wouldn't hear of seeing a doctor. Her nerves—

Nerves! The doctor's eyebrows went up. These women and their nerves! Well, it was good for business, after all.

Half the women who consulted him had nothing the matter with them but boredom, but they wouldn't thank you for telling them so! And one could usually find something.

"A slightly uncommon condition of the (some long word) nothing at all serious—but it needs just putting right. A simple treatment."

Well, medicine was mostly faith-healing when it came to it. And he had a good manner—he could inspire hope and belief.

Lucky that he'd managed to pull himself together in time after that business ten—no, fifteen years ago. It had been a near thing, that! He'd been going to pieces. The shock had pulled him together. He'd cut out drink altogether. By Jove, it had been a near thing, though ...

With a devastating ear-splitting blast on the horn an enormous Super-Sports Dalmain car rushed past him at eighty miles an hour. Dr. Armstrong nearly went into the hedge. One of these young fools who tore round the country. He hated them. That had been a near shave, too. Damned young fool!

VII

Tony Marston, roaring down into Mere, thought to himself:

"The amount of cars crawling about the roads is frightful. Always something blocking your way. *And* they will drive in the middle of the road! Pretty hopeless driving in England, anyway ... Not like France where you really *could* let out ..."

Should he stop here for a drink, or push on? Heaps of time! Only another hundred miles and a bit to go. He'd have a gin and ginger beer. Fizzing hot day!

This island place ought to be rather good fun—if the weather lasted. Who *were* these Owens, he wondered? Rich and stinking, probably. Badger was rather good at nosing people like that out. Of course, he *had* to, poor old chap, with no money of his own ...

Hope they'd do one well in drinks. Never knew with these fellows who'd made their money and weren't born to it. Pity that story about Gabrielle Turl having bought Soldier Island wasn't true. He'd like to have been in with that film star crowd.

Oh, well, he supposed there'd be a few girls there ...

Coming out of the hotel, he stretched himself, yawned, looked up at the blue sky and climbed into the Dalmain.

Several young women looked at him admiringly—his six feet of well-proportioned body, his crisp hair, tanned face, and intensely blue eyes.

He let in the clutch with a roar and leapt up the narrow street. Old men and errand boys jumped for safety. The latter looked after the car admiringly.

Anthony Marston proceeded on his triumphal progress.

VIII

Mr. Blore was in the slow train from Plymouth. There was only one other person in his carriage, an elderly seafaring gentleman with a bleary eye. At the present moment he had dropped off to sleep.

Mr. Blore was writing carefully in a little notebook.

"That's the lot," he muttered to himself. "Emily Brent, Vera Claythorne, Dr. Armstrong, Anthony Marston, old Justice Wargrave, Philip Lombard, General Macarthur, C.M.G., D.S.O. Manservant and wife: Mr. and Mrs. Rogers."

He closed the notebook and put it back in his pocket. He glanced over at the corner and the slumbering man.

"Had one over the eight," diagnosed Mr. Blore accurately.

He went over things carefully and conscientiously in his mind.

"Job ought to be easy enough," he ruminated. "Don't see how I can slip up on it. Hope I look all right."

He stood up and scrutinized himself anxiously in the glass. The face reflected there was of a slightly military cast with a moustache. There was very little expression in it. The eyes were grey and set rather close together.

"Might be a Major," said Mr. Blore. "No, I forgot. There's

that old military gent. He'd spot me at once.

"South Africa," said Mr. Blore, "that's my line! None of these people have anything to do with South Africa, and I've just been reading that travel folder so I can talk about it all right."

Fortunately there were all sorts and types of colonials. As a man of means from South Africa, Mr. Blore felt that he could enter into any society unchallenged.

Soldier Island. He remembered Soldier Island as a boy... Smelly sort of rock covered with gulls—stood about a mile from the coast.

Funny idea to go and build a house on it! Awful in bad weather! But millionaires were full of whims!

The old man in the corner woke up and said:

"You can't never tell at sea—never!"

Mr. Blore said soothingly, "That's right. You can't."

The old man hiccuped twice and said plaintively:

"There's a squall coming."

Mr. Blore said:

"No, no, mate, it's a lovely day."

The old man said angrily:

"There's a squall ahead. I can *smell* it."

"Maybe you're right," said Mr. Blore pacifically.

The train stopped at a station and the old fellow rose unsteadily.

"Thish where I get out." He fumbled with the window. Mr. Blore helped him.

The old man stood in the doorway. He raised a solemn hand and blinked his bleary eyes.

"Watch and pray," he said. "Watch and pray. The day of judgement is at hand."

He collapsed through the doorway on to the platform. From a recumbent position he looked up at Mr. Blore and said with immense dignity:

"I'm talking to *you*, young man. The day of judgment is very close at hand."

Subsiding on to his seat Mr. Blore thought to himself: He's nearer the day of judgment than I am!

But there, as it happens, he was wrong ...

Chapter 2

I

Outside Oakbridge station a little group of people stood in momentary uncertainty. Behind them stood porters with suitcases. One of these called, "Jim!"

The driver of one of the taxis stepped forward.

"You'm for Indian Island, maybe?" he asked in a soft Devon voice. Four voices gave assent—and then immediately afterwards gave quick surreptitious glances at each other.

The driver said, addressing his remarks to Mr. Justice Wargrave as the senior member of the party:

"There are two taxis here, sir. One of them must wait till the slow train from Exeter gets in—a matter of five minutes—there's one gentleman coming by that. Perhaps one of you wouldn't mind waiting? You'd be more comfortable that way."

Vera Claythorne, her own secretarial position clear in her mind, spoke at once.

"I'll wait," she said, "if you will go on?" She looked at the other three, her glance and voice had that slight suggestion of command in it that comes from having occupied a position of authority. She might have been directing which tennis sets the girls were to play in.

Miss Brent said stiffly, "Thank you," bent her head and entered one of the taxis, the door of which the driver was holding open.

Mr. Justice Wargrave followed her.

Captain Lombard said:

"I'll wait with Miss—"

"Claythorne," said Vera.

"My name is Lombard, Philip Lombard."

The porters were piling luggage on the taxi. Inside, Mr. Justice Wargrave said with due legal caution:

"Beautiful weather we are having."

Miss Brent said:

"Yes, indeed."

A very distinguished old gentleman, she thought to herself. Quite unlike the usual type of man in seaside guest houses. Evidently Mrs. or Miss Oliver had good connections . . .

Mr. Justice Wargrave inquired:

"Do you know this part of the world well?"

"I have been to Cornwall and to Torquay, but this is my first visit to this part of Devon."

The judge said:

"I also am unacquainted with this part of the world."

The taxi drove off.

The driver of the second taxi said:

"Like to sit inside while you're waiting?"

Vera said decisively:

"Not at all."

Captain Lombard smiled. He said:

"That sunny wall looks more attractive. Unless you'd rather go inside the station?"

"No, indeed. It's so delightful to get out of that stuffy train."

He answered:

"Yes, travelling by train *is* rather trying in this weather."

Vera said conventionally:

"I do hope it lasts—the weather, I mean. Our English summers are so treacherous."

With a slight lack of originality Lombard asked:

"Do you know this part of the world well?"

"No, I've never been here before." She added quickly, conscientiously determined to make her position clear at once, "I haven't even seen my employer yet."

"Your employer?"

"Yes, I'm Mrs. Owen's secretary."

"Oh, I see." Just imperceptibly his manner changed. It was slightly more assured—easier in tone. He said: "Isn't that rather unusual?"

Vera laughed.

"Oh, no, I don't think so. Her own secretary was suddenly taken ill and she wired to an agency for a substitute and they sent me."

"So that was it. And suppose you don't like the post when you've got there?"

Vera laughed again.

"Oh, it's only temporary—a holiday post. I've got a permanent job at a girls' school. As a matter of fact, I'm frightfully thrilled at the prospect of seeing Soldier Island. There's been such a lot about it in the papers. Is it really very fascinating?"

Lombard said:

"I don't know. I haven't seen it."

"Oh, really? The Owens are frightfully keen on it, I suppose. What are they like? Do tell me."

Lombard thought: Awkward, this—am I supposed to have met them or not? He said quickly:

"There's a wasp crawling up your arm. No—keep quite still." He made a convincing pounce. "There. It's gone!"

"Oh, thank you. There are a lot of wasps about this summer."

"Yes, I suppose it's the heat. Who are we waiting for, do you know?"

"I haven't the least idea."

The loud drawn-out scream of an approaching train was heard. Lombard said:

"That will be the train now."

It was a tall soldierly old man who appeared at the exit from the platform. His grey hair was clipped close and he had a neatly trimmed white moustache.

His porter, staggering slightly under the weight of the solid leather suitcase, indicated Vera and Lombard.

Vera came forward in a competent manner. She said:

"I am Mrs. Owen's secretary. There is a car here waiting." She added: "This is Mr. Lombard."

The faded blue eyes, shrewd in spite of their age, sized up Lombard. For a moment a judgement showed in them—had there been any one to read it.

"Good-looking fellow. Something just a little wrong about him..."

The three of them got into the waiting taxi. They drove through the sleepy streets of little Oakbridge and continued about a mile on the main Plymouth road. Then they plunged into a maze of cross-country lanes, steep, green and narrow.

General Macarthur said:

"Don't know this part of Devon at all. My little place is in East Devon—just on the borderline of Dorset."

Vera said:

"It really is lovely here. The hills and the red earth and everything so green and luscious-looking."

Philip Lombard said critically:

"It's a bit shut in... I like open country myself. Where you can see what's coming.."

General Macarthur said to him:

"You've seen a bit of the world, I fancy?"

Lombard shrugged his shoulders disparagingly.

"I've knocked about here and there, sir."

He thought to himself: "He'll ask me now if I was old enough to be in the War. These old boys always do."

But General Macarthur did not mention the War.

II

They came up over a steep hill and down a zigzag track to Sticklehaven—a mere cluster of cottages with a fishing boat or two drawn up on the beach.

Illuminated by the setting sun, they had their first glimpse of Soldier Island jutting up out of the sea to the south.

Vera said, surprised:

"It's a long way out."

She had pictured it differently, close to shore, crowned with a beautiful white house. But there was no house visible, only the boldly silhouetted rock with its faint resemblance to a giant head. There was something sinister about it. She shivered faintly.

Outside a little inn, the Seven Stars, three people were sitting. There was the hunched elderly figure of the judge, the upright form of Miss Brent, and a third man—a big bluff man who came forward and introduced himself.

"Thought we might as well wait for you," he said. "Make one trip of it. Allow me to introduce myself. Name's Davis.

Natal, South Africa's my natal spot, ha, ha!"

He laughed breezily.

Mr. Justice Wargrave looked at him with active malevolence. He seemed to be wishing that he could order the court to be cleared. Miss Emily Brent was clearly not sure if she liked Colonials.

"Any one care for a little nip before we embark?" asked Mr. Davis hospitably.

Nobody assenting to this proposition, Mr. Davis turned and held up a finger.

"Mustn't delay, then. Our good host and hostess will be expecting us," he said.

He might have noticed that a curious constraint came over the other members of the party. It was as though the mention of their host and hostess had a curiously paralysing effect upon the guests.

In response to Davis's beckoning finger, a man detached himself from a nearby wall against which he was leaning and came up to them. His rolling gait proclaimed him a man of the sea. He had a weather-beaten face and dark eyes with a slightly evasive expression. He spoke in his soft Devon voice.

"Will you be ready to be starting for the island, ladies and gentlemen? The boat's waiting. There's two gentlemen coming by car but Mr. Owen's orders was not to wait for them as they might arrive at any time."

The party got up. Their guide led them along a small

stone jetty. Alongside it a motorboat was lying.

Emily Brent said:

"That's a very small boat."

The boat's owner said persuasively:

"She's a fine boat that, Ma'am. You could go to Plymouth in her as easy as winking."

Mr. Justice Wargrave said sharply:

"There are a good many of us."

"She'd take double the number, sir."

Philip Lombard said in his pleasant easy voice:

"It's quite all right. Glorious weather—no swell."

Rather doubtfully, Miss Brent permitted herself to be helped into the boat. The others followed suit. There was as yet no fraternizing among the party. It was as though each member of it was puzzled by the other members.

They were just about to cast loose when their guide paused, boat-hook in hand.

Down the steep track into the village a car was coming. A car so fantastically powerful, so superlatively beautiful that it had all the nature of an apparition. At the wheel sat a young man, his hair blown back by the wind. In the blaze of the evening light he looked, not a man, but a young God, a Hero God out of some Northern Saga.

He touched the horn and a great roar of sound echoed from the rocks of the bay.

It was a fantastic moment. In it, Anthony Marston seemed to be something more than mortal. Afterwards more than one of those present remembered that moment.

III

Fred Narracott sat by the engine thinking to himself that this was a queer lot. Not at all his idea of what Mr. Owen's guests were likely to be. He'd expected something altogether more classy. Togged up women and gentlemen in yachting costume and all very rich and important looking.

Not at all like Mr. Elmer Robson's parties. A faint grin came to Fred Narracott's lips as he remembered the millionaire's guests. That had been a party if you like—and the drink they'd got through!

This Mr. Owen must be a very different sort of gentleman. Funny, it was, thought Fred, that he'd never yet set eyes on Owen—or his Missus either. Never been down here yet he hadn't. Everything ordered and paid for by that Mr. Morris. Instructions always very clear and payment prompt, but it was odd, all the same. The papers said there was some mystery about Owen. Mr. Narracott agreed with them.

Perhaps after all, it *was* Miss Gabrielle Turl who had bought the island. But that theory departed from him as he surveyed his passengers. Not this lot—none of them looked likely to have anything to do with a film star.

He summed them up dispassionately.

One old maid—the sour kind—he knew them well enough. She was a tartar he could bet. Old military gentleman—real Army look about him. Nice-looking young lady—but the ordinary kind, not glamourous—no Hollywood touch about her. That bluff cheery gent—*he* wasn't a real gentleman. Retired tradesman, that's what he is, thought Fred Narracott. The other gentleman, the lean hungry-looking gentleman with the quick eyes, he was a queer one, he was. Just possible he *might* have something to do with the pictures.

No, there was only one satisfactory passenger in the boat. The last gentleman, the one who had arrived in the car (and what a car! A car such as had never been seen in Sticklehaven before. Must have cost hundreds and hundreds, a car like that). He was the right kind. Born to money, he was. If the party had been all like him . . . he'd understand it . . .

Queer business when you came to think of it—the whole thing was queer—very queer . . .

IV

The boat churned its way round the rock. Now at last the house came into view. The south side of the island was quite different. It shelved gently down to the sea. The house was there facing south—low and square and modern looking with rounded windows letting in all the light.

An exciting house—a house that lived up to expectation!

Fred Narracott shut off the engine, they nosed their way gently into a little natural inlet between rocks.

Philip Lombard said sharply:

"Must be difficult to land here in dirty weather."

Fred Narracott said cheerfully:

"Can't land on Soldier Island when there's a southeasterly. Sometimes 'tis cut off for a week or more."

Vera Claythorne thought:

"The catering must be very difficult. That's the worst of an island. All the domestic problems are so worrying."

The boat grated against the rocks. Fred Narracott jumped out and he and Lombard helped the others to alight. Narracott made the boat fast to a ring in the rock. Then he led the way up steps cut in the cliff.

General Macarthur said:

"Ha! delightful spot!"

But he felt uneasy. Damned odd sort of place.

As the party ascended the steps and came out on a terrace above, their spirits revived. In the open doorway of the house a correct butler was awaiting them, and something about his gravity reassured them. And then the house itself was really most attractive, the view from the terrace magnificent...

The butler came forward bowing slightly. He was a tall lank man, grey-haired and very respectable. He said:

"Will you come this way, please."

In the wide hall drinks stood ready. Rows of bottles. Anthony Marston's spirits cheered up a little. He'd just been thinking this was a rum kind of show. None of *his* lot! What could old Badger have been thinking about to let him in for this? However, the drinks were all right. Plenty of ice, too.

What was it the butler chap was saying?

Mr. Owen—unfortunately delayed—unable to get here till tomorrow. Instructions—everything they wanted—if they would like to go to their rooms? ... dinner would be at eight o'clock ...

V

Vera had followed Mrs. Rogers upstairs. The woman had thrown open a door at the end of a passage and Vera had walked into a delightful bedroom with a big window that opened wide upon the sea and another looking east. She uttered a quick exclamation of pleasure.

Mrs. Rogers was saying:

"I hope you've got everything you want, Miss?"

Vera looked round. Her luggage had been brought up and had been unpacked. At one side of the room a door stood open into a pale blue-tiled bathroom.

She said quickly:

"Yes, everything, I think."

"You'll ring the bell if you want anything, Miss?"

Mrs. Rogers had a flat monotonous voice. Vera looked at her curiously. What a white bloodless ghost of a woman! Very respectable-looking, with her hair dragged back from her face and her black dress. Queer light eyes that shifted the whole time from place to place.

Vera thought:

"She looks frightened of her own shadow."

Yes, that was it—frightened!

She looked like a woman who walked in mortal fear...

A little shiver passed down Vera's back. What on earth was the woman afraid of?

She said pleasantly:

"I'm Mrs. Owen's new secretary. I expect you know that."

Mrs. Rogers said:

"No, Miss, I don't know anything. Just a list of the ladies and gentlemen and what rooms they were to have."

Vera said:

"Mrs. Owen didn't mention me?"

Mrs. Rogers' eyelashes flickered.

"I haven't seen Mrs. Owen—not yet. We only came here two days ago."

Extraordinary people, these Owens, thought Vera. Aloud she said:

"What staff is there here?"

"Just me and Rogers, Miss."

Vera frowned. Eight people in the house—ten with the host and hostess—and only one married couple to do for them.

Mrs. Rogers said:

"I'm a good cook and Rogers is handy about the house. I didn't know, of course, that there was to be such a large party."

Vera said:

"But you can manage?"

"Oh, yes, Miss, I can manage. If there's to be large parties often perhaps Mrs. Owen could get extra help in."

Vera said, "I expect so."

Mrs. Rogers turned to go. Her feet moved noiselessly over the ground. She drifted from the room like a shadow.

Vera went over to the window and sat down on the window seat. She was faintly disturbed. Everything—somehow—was a little queer. The absence of the Owens, the pale ghostlike Mrs. Rogers. And the guests! Yes, the guests were queer, too. An oddly assorted party.

Vera thought:

"I wish I'd seen the Owens . . . I wish I knew what they were like."

She got up and walked restlessly about the room.

A perfect bedroom decorated throughout in the modern style. Off-white rugs on the gleaming parquet floor—faintly tinted walls—a long mirror surrounded by lights. A mantelpiece bare of ornaments save for an enormous block of white marble shaped like a bear, a piece of modern sculpture in which was inset a clock. Over it, in a gleaming chromium frame, was a big square of parchment—a poem.

She stood in front of the fireplace and read it. It was the old nursery rhyme that she remembered from her childhood days.

Ten little soldier boys went out to dine;
One choked his little self and then there were Nine.

Nine little soldier boys sat up very late;
One overslept himself and then there were Eight.

Eight little soldier boys travelling in Devon;
One said he'd stay there and then there were Seven.

Seven little soldier boys chopping up sticks;
One chopped himself in halves and then there were Six.

Six little soldier boys playing with a hive;
A bumble bee stung one and then there were Five.

Five little soldier boys going in for law;
One got in Chancery and then there were Four.

Four little soldier boys going out to sea;
A red herring swallowed one and then there were Three.

Three little soldier boys walking in the Zoo;
A big bear hugged one and then there were Two.

Two little soldier boys sitting in the sun;
One got frizzled up and then there was One.

One little soldier boy left all alone;
He went and hanged himself and then there were None.

Vera smiled. Of course! This was Soldier Island!

She went and sat again by the window looking out to sea.

How big the sea was! From here there was no land to be seen anywhere—just a vast expanse of blue water rippling in the evening sun.

The sea ... So peaceful today—sometimes so cruel ... The sea that dragged you down to its depths. Drowned ... Found drowned ... Drowned at sea ... Drowned—drowned—drowned ...

No, she wouldn't remember ... She would *not* think of it! All that was over ...

VI

Dr. Armstrong came to Soldier Island just as the sun was sinking into the sea. On the way across he had chatted to the boatman—a local man. He was anxious to find out a little about these people who owned Soldier Island, but the man Narracott seemed curiously ill-informed, or perhaps unwilling to talk.

So Dr. Armstrong chatted instead of the weather and of fishing.

He was tired after his long motor drive. His eyeballs ached. Driving west you were driving against the sun.

Yes, he was very tired. The sea and perfect peace—that was what he needed. He would like, really, to take a long holiday. But he couldn't afford to do that. He could afford it financially, of course, but he couldn't afford to drop out. You were soon forgotten nowadays. No, now that he had arrived, he must keep his nose to the grindstone.

He thought:

"All the same, this evening, I'll imagine to myself that I'm not going back—that I've done with London and Harley Street and all the rest of it."

There was something magical about an island—the mere word suggested fantasy. You lost touch with the world—an island was a world of its own. A world, perhaps, from which you might never return.

He thought:

"I'm leaving my ordinary life behind me."

And, smiling to himself, he began to make plans, fantastic plans for the future. He was still smiling when he walked up the rock-cut steps.

In a chair on the terrace an old gentleman was sitting and the sight of him was vaguely familiar to Dr. Armstrong. Where had he seen that frog-like face, that tortoise-like neck, that hunched up attitude—yes and those pale shrewd little eyes? Of course—old Wargrave. He'd given evidence once before him. Always looked half asleep, but was shrewd as could be when it came to a point of law. Had great power with a jury—it was said he could make their minds up for them any day of the week. He'd got one or two unlikely convictions out of them. A hanging judge, some people said.

Funny place to meet him . . . here—out of the world.

VII

Mr. Justice Wargrave thought to himself:

"Armstrong? Remember him in the witness-box. Very correct and cautious. All doctors are damned fools. Harley Street ones are the worst of the lot." And his mind dwelt malevolently on a recent interview he had had with a suave personage in that very street.

Aloud he grunted:

"Drinks are in the hall."

Dr. Armstrong said:

"I must go and pay my respects to my host and hostess."

Mr. Justice Wargrave closed his eyes again, looking

decidedly reptilian, and said:

"You can't do that."

Dr. Armstrong was startled.

"Why not?"

The judge said:

"No host and hostess. Very curious state of affairs. Don't understand this place."

Dr. Armstrong stared at him for a minute. When he thought the old gentleman had actually gone to sleep, Wargrave said suddenly:

"D'you know Constance Culmington?"

"Er—no, I'm afraid I don't."

"It's of no consequence," said the judge. "Very vague woman—and practically unreadable handwriting. I was just wondering if I'd come to the wrong house."

Dr. Armstrong shook his head and went on up to the house.

Mr. Justice Wargrave reflected on the subject of Constance Culmington. Undependable like all women.

His mind went on to the two women in the house, the tight-lipped old maid and the girl. He didn't care for the girl, cold-blooded young hussy. No, three women, if you counted the Rogers woman. Odd creature, she looked scared to death. Respectable pair and knew their job.

Rogers coming out on the terrace that minute, the judge asked him:

"Is Lady Constance Culmington expected, do you

know?"

Rogers stared at him.

"No, sir, not to my knowledge."

The judge's eyebrows rose. But he only grunted.

He thought:

"Soldier Island, eh? There's a fly in the ointment."

VIII

Anthony Marston was in his bath. He luxuriated in the steaming water. His limbs had felt cramped after his long drive. Very few thoughts passed through his head. Anthony was a creature of sensation—and of action.

He thought to himself:

"Must go through with it, I suppose," and thereafter dismissed everything from his mind.

Warm steaming water—tired limbs—presently a shave—a cocktail—dinner.

And after—?

IX

Mr. Blore was tying his tie. He wasn't very good at this sort of thing.

Did he look all right? He supposed so.

Nobody had been exactly cordial to him... Funny the way they all eyed each other—as though they *knew*...

Well, it was up to him.

He didn't mean to bungle his job.

He glanced up at the framed nursery rhyme over the mantelpiece.

Neat touch, having that there!

He thought:

Remember this island when I was a kid. Never thought I'd be doing this sort of a job in a house here. Good thing, perhaps, that one can't foresee the future.

X

General Macarthur was frowning to himself.
Damn it all, the whole thing was deuced odd! Not at all what he'd been led to expect...

For two pins he'd make an excuse and get away... Throw up the whole business...

But the motorboat had gone back to the mainland.

He'd have to stay.

That fellow Lombard now, he was a queer chap.

Not straight. He'd swear the man wasn't straight.

XI

As the gong sounded, Philip Lombard came out of his room and walked to the head of the stairs. He moved like a panther, smoothly and noiselessly. There was something of the panther about him altogether. A beast of prey—pleasant to the eye.

He was smiling to himself.

A week—eh?

He was going to enjoy that week.

XII

In her bedroom, Emily Brent, dressed in black silk ready for dinner, was reading her Bible.

Her lips moved as she followed the words:

"The heathen are sunk down in the pit that they made: in the net which they hid is their own foot taken. The Lord is known by the judgment which he executeth: the wicked is snared in the work of his own hands. The wicked shall be turned into hell."

Her tight lips closed. She shut the Bible.

Rising, she pinned a cairngorm brooch at her neck, and went down to dinner.

Chapter 3

I

Dinner was drawing to a close.

The food had been good, the wine perfect. Rogers waited well.

Every one was in better spirits. They had begun to talk to each other with more freedom and intimacy.

Mr. Justice Wargrave, mellowed by the excellent port, was being amusing in a caustic fashion, Dr. Armstrong and Tony Marston were listening to him. Miss Brent chatted to General Macarthur, they had discovered some mutual friends. Vera Claythorne was asking Mr. Davis intelligent questions about South Africa. Mr. Davis was quite fluent on the subject. Lombard listened to the conversation. Once or twice he looked up quickly, and his eyes narrowed. Now and then his eyes played round the table, studying the others.

Anthony Marston said suddenly:

"Quaint, these things, aren't they?"

In the centre of the round table, on a circular glass stand, were some little china figures.

"Soldiers," said Tony. "Soldier Island. I suppose that's the idea."

Vera leaned forward.

"I wonder. How many are there? Ten?"

"Yes—ten there are."

Vera cried:

"What fun! They're the ten little soldier boys of the nursery rhyme, I suppose. In my bedroom the rhyme is framed and hung up over the mantelpiece."

Lombard said:

"In my room, too."

"And mine."

"And mine."

Everybody joined in the chorus. Vera said:

"It's an amusing idea, isn't it?"

Mr. Justice Wargrave grunted:

"Remarkably childish," and helped himself to port.

Emily Brent looked at Vera Claythorne. Vera Claythorne looked at Miss Brent. The two women rose.

In the drawing room the French windows were open on to the terrace and the sound of the sea murmuring against the rocks came up to them.

Emily Brent said, "Pleasant sound."

Vera said sharply, "I hate it."

Miss Brent's eyes looked at her in surprise. Vera flushed. She said, more composedly:

"I don't think this place would be very agreeable in a storm."

Emily Brent agreed.

"I've no doubt the house is shut up in winter," she said. "You'd never get servants to stay here for one thing."

Vera murmured:

"It must be difficult to get servants anyway."

Emily Brent said:

"Mrs. Oliver has been lucky to get these two. The woman's a good cook."

Vera thought:

"Funny how elderly people always get names wrong."

She said:

"Yes, I think Mrs. Owen has been very lucky indeed."

Emily Brent had brought a small piece of embroidery out of her bag. Now, as she was about to thread her needle, she paused.

She said sharply:

"Owen? Did you say Owen?"

"Yes."

Emily Brent said sharply:

"I've never met anyone called Owen in my life."

Vera stared.

"But surely—"

She did not finish her sentence. The door opened and the men joined them. Rogers followed them into the room with the coffee tray.

The judge came and sat down by Emily Brent. Armstrong came up to Vera. Tony Marston strolled to the open window. Blore studied with naïve surprise a statuette in brass—wondering perhaps if its bizarre angularities were really supposed to be the female figure. General Macarthur stood with his back to the mantelpiece. He pulled at his little white moustache. That had been a damned good dinner! His spirits were rising. Lombard turned over the pages of *Punch* that lay with other papers on a table by the wall.

Rogers went round with the coffee tray. The coffee was good—really black and very hot.

The whole party had dined well. They were satisfied with themselves and with life. The hands of the clock pointed to twenty minutes past nine. There was a silence—a comfortable replete silence.

Into that silence came The Voice. Without warning, inhuman, penetrating ...

"Ladies and gentlemen! Silence please!"

Everyone was startled. They looked round—at each other, at the walls. Who was speaking?

The Voice went on—a high clear voice:

"You are charged with the following indictments:

"Edward George Armstrong, that you did upon the 14th day of March, 1925, cause the death of Louisa Mary Clees.

"Emily Caroline Brent, that upon the 5th of November, 1931, you were responsible for the death of Beatrice Taylor.

"William Henry Blore, that you brought about the death of James Stephen Landor on October 10th, 1928.

"Vera Elizabeth Claythorne, that on the 11th day of August,

1935, you killed Cyril Ogilvie Hamilton.

"Philip Lombard, that upon a date in February, 1932, you were guilty of the death of twenty-one men, members of an East African tribe.

"John Gordon Macarthur, that on the 4th of January, 1917, you deliberately sent your wife's lover, Arthur Richmond, to his death.

"Anthony James Marston, that upon the 14th day of November last, you were guilty of the murder of John and Lucy Combes.

"Thomas Rogers and Ethel Rogers, that on the 6th of May, 1929, you brought about the death of Jennifer Brady.

"Lawrence John Wargrave, that upon the 10th day of June, 1930, you were guilty of the murder of Edward Seton.

"Prisoners at the bar, have you anything to say in your defence?"

II

The voice had stopped.

There was a moment's petrified silence and then a resounding crash! Rogers had dropped the coffee tray!

At the same moment, from somewhere outside the room there came a scream and the sound of a thud.

Lombard was the first to move. He leapt to the door and flung it open. Outside, lying in a huddled mass, was Mrs. Rogers.

Lombard called:

"Marston."

Anthony sprang to help him. Between them, they lifted up the woman and carried her into the drawing room.

Dr. Armstrong came across quickly. He helped them to lift her on to the sofa and bent over her. He said quickly:

"It's nothing. She's fainted, that's all. She'll be round in a minute."

Lombard said to Rogers:

"Get some brandy."

Rogers, his face white, his hands shaking, murmured:

"Yes, sir," and slipped quickly out of the room.

Vera cried out:

"*Who was that speaking?* Where was he? It sounded—it sounded—"

General Macarthur spluttered out:

"What's going on here? What kind of a practical joke was that?"

His hand was shaking. His shoulders sagged. He looked suddenly ten years older.

Blore was mopping his face with a handkerchief.

Only Mr. Justice Wargrave and Miss Brent seemed comparatively unmoved. Emily Brent sat upright, her head held high. In both cheeks was a spot of hard colour. The judge sat in his habitual pose, his head sunk down into his neck. With one hand he gently scratched his ear. Only his eyes were active, darting round and round the room, puzzled, alert with intelligence.

Again it was Lombard who acted. Armstrong being busy with the collapsed woman, Lombard was free once more to take the initiative.

He said:

"That voice? It sounded as though it were in the room."

Vera cried:

"*Who was it?* Who was it? It wasn't one of us."

Like the judge, Lombard's eyes wandered slowly round the room. They rested a minute on the open window, then he shook his head decisively. Suddenly his eyes lighted up. He moved forward swiftly to where a door near the fireplace led into an adjoining room.

With a swift gesture, he caught the handle and flung the door open. He passed through and immediately uttered an exclamation of satisfaction.

He said:

"Ah, here we are."

The others crowded after him. Only Miss Brent remained alone sitting erect in her chair.

Inside the second room a table had been brought up close to the wall which adjoined the drawing room. On the table was a gramophone—an old-fashioned type with a large trumpet attached. The mouth of the trumpet was against the wall, and Lombard, pushing it aside indicated where two or three small holes had been unobtrusively bored through the wall.

Adjusting the gramophone he replaced the needle on the record and immediately they heard again *"You are charged with the following indictments—"*

Vera cried:

"Turn it off! Turn it off! It's horrible!"

Lombard obeyed.

Dr. Armstrong said, with a sigh of relief:

"A disgraceful and heartless practical joke, I suppose."

The small clear voice of Mr. Justice Wargrave murmured:

"So you think it's a joke, do you?"

The doctor stared at him.

"What else could it be?"

The hand of the judge gently stroked his upper lip.

He said:

"At the moment I'm not prepared to give an opinion."

Anthony Marston broke in. He said:

"Look here, there's one thing you've forgotten. Who the devil turned the thing on and set it going?"

Wargrave murmured:

"Yes, I think we must inquire into that."

He led the way back into the drawing room. The others followed.

Rogers had just come in with a glass of brandy. Miss Brent was bending over the moaning form of Mrs. Rogers.

Adroitly Rogers slipped between the two women.

"Allow me, Madam, I'll speak to her. Ethel—Ethel—it's all right. All right, do you hear? Pull yourself together."

Mrs. Rogers' breath came in quick gasps. Her eyes, staring frightened eyes, went round and round the ring of faces. There was urgency in Rogers' tone.

"Pull yourself together, Ethel."

Dr. Armstrong spoke to her soothingly:

"You'll be all right now, Mrs. Rogers. Just a nasty turn."

She said:

"Did I faint, sir?"

"Yes."

"It was the voice—that awful voice—*like a judgment*—"

Her face turned green again, her eyelids fluttered.

Dr. Armstrong said sharply:

"Where's that brandy?"

Rogers had put it down on a little table. Some one handed it to the doctor and he bent over the gasping woman with it.

"Drink this, Mrs. Rogers."

She drank, choking a little and gasping. The spirit did her good. The colour returned to her face. She said:

"I'm all right now. It just gave me a turn."

Rogers said quickly:

"Of course it did. It gave me a turn, too. Fair made me drop that tray. Wicked lies, it was! I'd like to know—"

He was interrupted. It was only a cough—a dry little cough but it had the effect of stopping him in full cry. He stared at Mr. Justice Wargrave and the latter coughed again. Then he said:

"Who put that record on the gramophone? Was it you, Rogers?"

Rogers cried:

"I didn't know what it was. Before God, I didn't know what it was, sir. If I had I'd never have done it."

The judge said dryly:

"That is probably true. But I think you'd better explain, Rogers."

The butler wiped his face with a handkerchief. He said earnestly:

"I was just obeying orders, sir, that's all."

"Whose orders?"

"Mr. Owen's."

Mr. Justice Wargrave said:

"Let me get this quite clear. Mr. Owen's orders were—what exactly?"

Rogers said:

"I was to put a record on the gramophone. I'd find the record in the drawer and my wife was to start the gramophone when I'd gone into the drawing room with the coffee tray."

The judge murmured:

"A very remarkable story."

Rogers cried:

"It's the truth, sir. I swear to God it's the truth. I didn't know what it was—not for a moment. It had a name on it—I thought it was just a piece of music."

Wargrave looked at Lombard.

"Was there a title on it?"

Lombard nodded. He grinned suddenly, showing his white pointed teeth. He said:

"Quite right, sir. It was entitled *Swan Song*..."

III

General Macarthur broke out suddenly. He exclaimed:

"The whole thing is preposterous—preposterous! Slinging accusations about like this! Something must be done about it. This fellow Owen whoever he is—"

Emily Brent interrupted. She said sharply:

"That's just it, who is he?"

The judge interposed. He spoke with the authority that a lifetime in the courts had given him. He said:

"That is exactly what we must go into very carefully. I should suggest that you get your wife to bed first of all, Rogers. Then come back here."

"Yes, sir."

Dr. Armstrong said:

"I'll give you a hand, Rogers."

Leaning on the two men, Mrs. Rogers tottered out of the room. When they had gone Tony Marston said:

"Don't know about you, sir, but I could do with a drink."

Lombard said:

"I agree."

Tony said:

"I'll go and forage."

He went out of the room.

He returned a second or two later.

"Found them all waiting on a tray outside ready to be brought in."

He set down his burden carefully. The next minute or two was spent in dispensing drinks. General Macarthur had a stiff whiskey and so did the judge. Every one felt the need of a stimulant. Only Emily Brent demanded and obtained a glass of water.

Dr. Armstrong reentered the room.

"She's all right," he said. "I've given her a sedative to take. What's that, a drink? I could do with one."

Several of the men refilled their glasses. A moment or two later Rogers reentered the room.

Mr. Justice Wargrave took charge of the proceedings. The room became an impromptu court of law.

The judge said:

"Now then, Rogers, we must get to the bottom of this. Who is this Mr. Owen?"

Rogers stared.

"He owns this place, sir."

"I am aware of that fact. What I want you to tell me is what you yourself know about the man."

Rogers shook his head.

"I can't say, sir. You see, I've never seen him."

There was a faint stir in the room.

General Macarthur said:

"You've never seen him? What d'yer mean?"

"We've only been here just under a week, sir, my wife and I. We were engaged by letter, through an agency. The Regina Agency in Plymouth."

Blore nodded.

"Old established firm," he volunteered.

Wargrave said:

"Have you got that letter?"

"The letter engaging us? No, sir. I didn't keep it."

"Go on with your story. You were engaged, as you say, by letter."

"Yes, sir. We were to arrive on a certain day. We did. Everything was in order here. Plenty of food in stock and everything very nice. Just needed dusting and that."

"What next?"

"Nothing, sir. We got orders—by letter again—to prepare the rooms for a house party, and then yesterday by the afternoon post I got another letter from Mr. Owen. It said he and Mrs. Owen were detained and to do the best we could, and it gave the instructions about dinner and coffee and putting on the gramophone record."

The judge said sharply:

"Surely you've got that letter?"

"Yes, sir, I've got it here."

He produced it from a pocket. The judge took it.

"H'm," he said. "Headed Ritz Hotel and typewritten."

With a quick movement Blore was beside him.

He said:

"If you'll just let me have a look."

He twitched it out of the other's hand, and ran his eye over it. He murmured:

"Coronation machine. Quite new—no defects. Ensign paper—the most widely used make. You won't get anything out of that. Might be fingerprints, but I doubt it."

Wargrave stared at him with sudden attention.

Anthony Marston was standing beside Blore looking over his shoulder. He said:

"Got some fancy Christian names, hasn't he? Ulick Norman Owen. Quite a mouthful."

The old judge said with a slight start:

"I am obliged to you, Mr. Marston. You have drawn my attention to a curious and suggestive point."

He looked round at the others and thrusting his neck forward like an angry tortoise, he said:

"I think the time has come for us all to pool our information. It would be well, I think, for everybody to come forward with all the information they have regarding the owner of this house." He paused and then went on: "We are all his guests. I think it would be profitable if each one of us were to explain exactly how that came about."

There was a moment's pause and then Emily Brent

spoke with decision.

"There's something very peculiar about all this," she said. "I received a letter with a signature that was not very easy to read. It purported to be from a woman I had met at a certain summer resort two or three years ago. I took the name to be either Ogden or Oliver. I am acquainted with a Mrs. Oliver and also with a Miss Ogden. I am quite certain that I have never met, or become friendly with, any one of the name of Owen."

Mr. Justice Wargrave said:

"You have that letter, Miss Brent?"

"Yes, I will fetch it for you."

She went away and returned a minute later with the letter.

The judge read it. He said:

"I begin to understand . . . Miss Claythorne?"

Vera explained the circumstances of her secretarial engagement.

The judge said:

"Marston?"

Anthony said:

"Got a wire. From a pal of mine. Badger Berkeley. Surprised me at the time because I had an idea the old horse had gone to Norway. Told me to roll up here."

Again Wargrave nodded. He said:

"Dr. Armstrong?"

"I was called in professionally."

"I see. You had no previous acquaintanceship with the family?"

"No. A colleague of mine was mentioned in the letter."

The judge said:

"To give verisimilitude . . . Yes, and that colleague, I presume, was momentarily out of touch with you?"

"Well—er—yes."

Lombard, who had been staring at Blore, said suddenly:

"Look here, I've just thought of something—"

The judge lifted a hand.

"In a minute—"

"But I—"

"We will take one thing at a time, Mr. Lombard. We are at present inquiring into the causes which have resulted in our being assembled here tonight. General Macarthur?"

Pulling at his moustache, the General muttered:

"Got a letter—from this fellow Owen—mentioned some old pals of mine who were to be here—hoped I'd excuse informal invitation. Haven't kept the letter, I'm afraid."

Wargrave said: "Mr. Lombard?"

Lombard's brain had been active. Was he to come out in the open, or not? He made up his mind.

"Same sort of thing," he said. "Invitation, mention of mutual friends—I fell for it all right. I've torn up the letter."

Mr. Justice Wargrave turned his attention to Mr. Blore. His forefinger stroked his upper lip and his voice was dangerously polite.

He said:

"Just now we had a somewhat disturbing experience. An apparently disembodied voice spoke to us all by name, uttering certain precise accusations against us. We will deal with those accusations presently. At the moment I am interested in a minor point. Amongst the names recited was that of William Henry Blore. But as far as we know there is no one named Blore amongst us. The name of Davis was *not* mentioned. What have you to say about that, Mr. Davis?"

Blore said sulkily:

"Cat's out of the bag, it seems. I suppose I'd better admit that my name isn't Davis."

"You are William Henry Blore?"

"That's right."

"I will add something," said Lombard. "Not only are you here under a false name, Mr. Blore, but in addition I've noticed this evening that you're a first-class liar. You claim to have come from Natal, South Africa. I know South Africa and Natal and I'm prepared to swear that you've never set foot in South Africa in your life."

All eyes were turned on Blore. Angry suspicious eyes. Anthony Marston moved a step nearer to him. His fists clenched themselves.

"Now then, you swine," he said. "Any explanation?"

Blore flung back his head and set his square jaw.

"You gentlemen have got me wrong," he said. "I've got my credentials and you can see them. I'm an ex-CID man. I run a detective agency in Plymouth. I was put on this job."

Mr. Justice Wargrave asked:

"By whom?"

"This man Owen. Enclosed a handsome money order for expenses and instructed me as to what he wanted done. I was to join the house party, posing as a guest. I was given all your names. I was to watch you all."

"Any reason given?"

Blore said bitterly:

"Mrs. Owen's jewels. Mrs. Owen my foot! I don't believe there's any such person."

Again the forefinger of the judge stroked his lip, this time appreciatively.

"Your conclusions are, I think, justified," he said. "Ulick Norman Owen! In Miss Brent's letter, though the signature of the surname is a mere scrawl the Christian names are reasonably clear—Una Nancy—in either case you notice, the same initials. Ulick Norman Owen—Una Nancy Owen—each time, that is to say, U.N. Owen. Or by a slight stretch of fancy, UNKNOWN!"

Vera cried:

"But this is fantastic—mad!"

The judge nodded gently.

He said:

"Oh, yes. I've no doubt in my own mind that we have been invited here by a madman—probably a dangerous homicidal lunatic."

Chapter 4

I

There was a moment's silence—a silence of dismay and bewilderment. Then the judge's small clear voice took up the thread once more.

"We will now proceed to the next stage of our inquiry. First however, I will just add my own credentials to the list."

He took a letter from his pocket and tossed it onto the table.

"This purports to be from an old friend of mine, Lady Constance Culmington. I have not seen her for some years. She went to the East. It is exactly the kind of vague incoherent letter she would write, urging me to join her here and referring to her host and hostess in the vaguest of terms. The same technique, you will observe. I only mention it because it agrees with the other evidence—from all of which emerges one interesting point. *Whoever it was who enticed us here, that person knows or has taken the trouble to find out a good deal about us all.* He, whoever he may be, is aware of my friendship for Lady Constance—and is familiar with her epistolary style. He knows something about Dr. Armstrong's colleagues and their present whereabouts. He knows the nickname of Mr. Marston's friend and the kind of telegrams he sends. He knows exactly where Miss Brent was two years ago for her holiday and the kind of people she met there. He knows all about General Macarthur's old cronies."

He paused. Then he said:

"*He knows, you see, a good deal.* And out of his knowledge concerning us, he has made certain definite accusations."

Immediately a babel broke out.

General Macarthur shouted:

"A pack of dam' lies! Slander!"

Vera cried out:

"It's iniquitous!" Her breath came fast. "Wicked!"

Rogers said hoarsely:

"A lie—a wicked lie . . . we never did—neither of us . . ."

Anthony Marston growled:

"Don't know what the damned fool was getting at!"

The upraised hand of Mr. Justice Wargrave calmed the tumult.

He said, picking his words with care:

"I wish to say this. Our unknown friend accuses me of the murder of one Edward Seton. I remember Seton perfectly well. He came up before me for trial in June of the year 1930. He was charged with the murder of an elderly woman. He was very ably defended and made a good impression on the jury in the witness-box.

Nevertheless, on the evidence, he was certainly guilty. I summed up accordingly, and the jury brought in a verdict of Guilty. In passing sentence of death I concurred with the verdict. An appeal was lodged on the grounds of misdirection. The appeal was rejected and the man was duly executed. I wish to say before you all that my conscience is perfectly clear on the matter. I did my duty and nothing more. I passed sentence on a rightly convicted murderer."

Armstrong was remembering now. The Seton case! The verdict had come as a great surprise. He had met Matthews, K.C., on one of the days of the trial dining at a restaurant. Matthews had been confident. "Not a doubt of the verdict. Acquittal practically certain." And then afterwards he had heard comments: "Judge was dead against him. Turned the jury right round and they brought him in guilty. Quite legal, though. Old Wargrave knows his law. It was almost as though he had a private down on the fellow."

All these memories rushed through the doctor's mind. Before he could consider the wisdom of the question he had asked impulsively:

"Did you know Seton at all? I mean previous to the case."

The hooded reptilian eyes met his. In a clear cold voice the judge said:

"I knew nothing of Seton previous to the case."

Armstrong said to himself:

"The fellow's lying—I know he's lying."

I I

Vera Claythorne spoke in a trembling voice.

She said:

"I'd like to tell you. About that child—Cyril Hamilton. I was nursery governess to him. He was forbidden to swim out far. One day, when my attention was distracted, he started off. I swam after him ... I couldn't get there in time ... It was awful ... But it wasn't my fault. At the inquest the Coroner exonerated me. And his mother—she was so kind. If even she didn't blame me, why should—why should this awful thing be said? It's not fair—not fair ..."

She broke down, weeping bitterly.

General Macarthur patted her shoulder.

He said:

"There there, my dear. Of course it's not true. Fellow's a madman. A madman! Got a bee in his bonnet! Got hold of the wrong end of the stick all round."

He stood erect, squaring his shoulders. He barked out:

"Best really to leave this sort of thing unanswered. However, feel I ought to say—no truth—no truth whatever in what he said about—er—young Arthur Richmond. Richmond was one of my officers. I sent him on a reconnaissance. He was killed. Natural course of events in wartime. Wish to say resent very much—slur on my wife. Best woman in the world. Absolutely—Caesar's wife!"

General Macarthur sat down. His shaking hand pulled at his moustache. The effort to speak had cost him a good deal.

Lombard spoke. His eyes were amused. He said:

"About those natives—"

Marston said:

"What about them?"

Philip Lombard grinned.

"Story's quite true! I left 'em! Matter of self-preservation. We were lost in the bush. I and a couple of other fellows took what food there was and cleared out."

General Macarthur said sternly:

"You abandoned your men—left them to starve?"

Lombard said:

"Not quite the act of a *pukka sahib*, I'm afraid. But self-preservation's a man's first duty. And natives don't mind dying, you know. They don't feel about it as Europeans do."

Vera lifted her face from her hands. She said, staring at him:

"You left them—to *die*?"

Lombard answered:

"I left them to die."

His amused eyes looked into her horrified ones.

Anthony Marston said in a slow puzzled voice:

"I've just been thinking—John and Lucy Combes. Must have been a couple of kids I ran over near Cambridge. Beastly bad luck."

Mr. Justice Wargrave said acidly:

"For them, or for you?"

Anthony said:

"Well, I was thinking—for me—but of course, you're right, sir, it was damned bad luck on them. Of course it was a pure accident. They rushed out of some cottage or other. I had my licence suspended for a year. Beastly nuisance."

Dr. Armstrong said warmly:

"This speeding's all wrong—all wrong! Young men like you are a danger to the community."

Anthony shrugged his shoulders. He said:

"Speed's come to stay. English roads are hopeless, of course. Can't get up a decent pace on them."

He looked round vaguely for his glass, picked it up off a table and went over to the side table and helped himself to another whiskey and soda. He said over his shoulder:

"Well, anyway it wasn't my fault. Just an accident!"

III

The manservant, Rogers, had been moistening his lips and twisting his hands. He said now in a low deferential voice:

"If I might just say a word, sir."

Lombard said:

"Go ahead, Rogers."

Rogers cleared his throat and passed his tongue once

more over his dry lips.

"There was a mention, sir, of me and Mrs. Rogers. And of Miss Brady. There isn't a word of truth in it, sir. My wife and I were with Miss Brady till she died. She was always in poor health, sir, always from the time we came to her. There was a storm, sir, that night—the night she was taken bad. The telephone was out of order. We couldn't get the doctor to her. I went for him, sir, on foot. But he got there too late. We'd done everything possible for her, sir. Devoted to her, we were. Any one will tell you the same. There was never a word said against us. Not a word."

Lombard looked thoughtfully at the man's twitching face, his dry lips, the fright in his eyes. He remembered the crash of the falling coffee tray. He thought, but did not say: "Oh, yeah?"

Blore spoke—spoke in his hearty bullying official manner.

He said:

"Came into a little something at her death, though? Eh?"

Rogers drew himself up. He said stiffly:

"Miss Brady left us a legacy in recognition of our faithful services. And why not, I'd like to know?"

Lombard said:

"What about yourself, Mr. Blore?"

"What about me?"

"Your name was included in the list."

Blore went purple.

"Landor, you mean? That was the bank robbery—London and Commercial."

Mr. Justice Wargrave stirred. He said:

"I remember. It didn't come before me, but I remember the case. Landor was convicted on your evidence. You were the police officer in charge of the case?"

Blore said:

"I was."

"Landor got penal servitude for life and died on Dartmoor a year later. He was a delicate man."

Blore said:

"He was a crook. It was he who knocked out the night watchman. The case was quite clear against him."

Wargrave said slowly:

"You were complimented, I think, on your able handling of the case."

Blore said sulkily:

"I got my promotion."

He added in a thick voice.

"I was only doing my duty."

Lombard laughed—a sudden ringing laugh. He said:

"What a duty-loving law-abiding lot we all seem to be! Myself excepted. What about you, doctor—and your little professional mistake? Illegal operation, was it?"

Emily Brent glanced at him in sharp distaste and drew herself away a little.

Dr. Armstrong, very much master of himself, shook his

head good-humouredly.

"I'm at a loss to understand the matter," he said. "The name meant nothing to me when it was spoken. What was it—Clees? Close? I really can't remember having a patient of that name, or being connected with a death in any way. The thing's a complete mystery to me. Of course, it's a long time ago. It might possibly be one of my operation cases in hospital. They come too late, so many of these people. Then, when the patient dies, they always consider it's the surgeon's fault."

He sighed, shaking his head.

He thought:

Drunk—that's what it was—drunk . . . And I operated! Nerves all to pieces—hands shaking. I killed her all right. Poor devil—elderly woman—simple job if I'd been sober. Lucky for me there's loyalty in our profession. The Sister knew, of course—but she held her tongue. God, it gave me a shock! Pulled me up. But who could have known about it—after all these years?

IV

There was a silence in the room. Everybody was looking, covertly or openly, at Emily Brent. It was a minute or two before she became aware of the expectation. Her eyebrows rose on her narrow forehead. She said:

"Are you waiting for me to say something? I have

nothing to say."

The judge said: "Nothing, Miss Brent?"

"Nothing."

Her lips closed tightly.

The judge stroked his face. He said mildly:

"You reserve your defence?"

Miss Brent said coldly:

"There is no question of defence. I have always acted in accordance with the dictates of my conscience. I have nothing with which to reproach myself."

There was an unsatisfied feeling in the air. But Emily Brent was not one to be swayed by public opinion. She sat unyielding.

The judge cleared his throat once or twice. Then he said: "Our inquiry rests there. Now Rogers, who else is there on this island besides ourselves and you and your wife?"

"Nobody, sir. Nobody at all."

"You're sure of that?"

"Quite sure, sir."

Wargrave said:

"I am not yet clear as to the purpose of our Unknown host in getting us to assemble here. But in my opinion this person, whoever he may be, is not sane in the accepted sense of the word.

"He may be dangerous. In my opinion it would be well for us to leave this place as soon as possible. I suggest that we leave tonight."

Rogers said:

"I beg your pardon, sir, but there's no boat on the island."

"No boat at all?"

"No, sir."

"How do you communicate with the mainland?"

"Fred Narracott, he comes over every morning, sir. He brings the bread and the milk and the post, and takes the orders."

Mr. Justice Wargrave said:

"Then in my opinion it would be well if we all left tomorrow morning as soon as Narracott's boat arrives."

There was a chorus of agreement with only one dissentient voice. It was Anthony Marston who disagreed with the majority.

"A bit unsporting, what?" he said. "Ought to ferret out the mystery before we go. Whole thing's like a detective story. Positively thrilling."

The judge said acidly:

"At my time of life, I have no desire for 'thrills' as you call them."

Anthony said with a grin:

"The legal life's narrowing! I'm all for crime! Here's to it."

He picked up his drink and drank it off at a gulp.

Too quickly, perhaps. He choked—choked badly. His face contorted, turned purple. He gasped for breath—then slid down off his chair, the glass falling from his hand.

Chapter 5

I

It was so sudden and so unexpected that it took every one's breath away. They remained stupidly staring at the crumpled figure on the ground.

Then Dr. Armstrong jumped up and went over to him, kneeling beside him. When he raised his head his eyes were bewildered.

He said in a low awe-struck whisper:

"My God! he's dead."

They didn't take it in. Not at once.

Dead? *Dead*? That young Norse God in the prime of his health and strength. Struck down all in a moment. Healthy young men didn't die like that, choking over a whiskey and soda...

No, they couldn't take it in.

Dr. Armstrong was peering into the dead man's face. He sniffed at the blue twisted lips. Then he picked up the glass from which Anthony Marston had been drinking.

General Macarthur said:

"Dead? D'you mean the fellow just choked and—and died?"

The physician said:

"You can call it choking if you like. He died of asphyxiation right enough."

He was sniffing now at the glass. He dipped a finger into the dregs and very cautiously just touched the finger with the tip of his tongue.

His expression altered.

General Macarthur said:

"Never knew a man could die like that—just of a choking fit!"

Emily Brent said in a clear voice:

"In the midst of life we are in death."

Dr. Armstrong stood up. He said brusquely:

"No, a man doesn't die of a mere choking fit. Marston's death wasn't what we call a natural death."

Vera said almost in a whisper:

"Was there—something—in the whiskey?"

Armstrong nodded.

"Yes. Can't say exactly. Everything points to one of the cyanides. No distinctive smell of Prussic Acid, probably Potassium Cyanide. It acts pretty well instantaneously."

The judge said sharply:

"It was in his glass?"

"Yes."

The doctor strode to the table where the drinks were. He removed the stopper from the whiskey and smelt and tasted it. Then he tasted the soda water. He shook his head.

"They're both all right."

Lombard said:

"You mean—he must have put the stuff in his glass *himself?*"

Armstrong nodded with a curiously dissatisfied expression. He said:

"Seems like it."

Blore said:

"Suicide, eh? That's a queer go."

Vera said slowly:

"You'd never think that *he* would kill himself. He was so alive. He was—oh—enjoying himself! When he came down the hill in his car this evening he looked—he looked—oh, I can't *explain!*"

But they knew what she meant. Anthony Marston, in the height of his youth and manhood, had seemed like a being who was immortal. And now, crumpled and broken, he lay on the floor.

Dr. Armstrong said:

"Is there any possibility other than suicide?"

Slowly every one shook his head. There could be no other explanation. The drinks themselves were untampered with. They had all seen Anthony Marston go across and help himself. It followed therefore that any cyanide in the drink must have been put there by Anthony Marston himself.

And yet—why should Anthony Marston commit suicide?

Blore said thoughtfully:

"You know, doctor, it doesn't seem right to me. I shouldn't have said Mr. Marston was a suicidal type of gentleman."

Armstrong answered:

"I agree."

II

They had left it like that. What else was there to say?

Together Armstrong and Lombard had carried the inert body of Anthony Marston to his bedroom and had laid him there covered over with a sheet.

When they came downstairs again, the others were standing in a group, shivering a little, though the night was not cold.

Emily Brent said:

"We'd better go to bed. It's late."

It was past twelve o'clock. The suggestion was a wise one—yet every one hesitated. It was as though they clung to each other's company for reassurance.

The judge said:

"Yes, we must get some sleep."

Rogers said:

"I haven't cleared yet—in the dining room."

Lombard said curtly:

"Do it in the morning."

Armstrong said to him:

"Is your wife all right?"

"I'll go and see, sir."

He returned a minute or two later.

"Sleeping beautiful, she is."

"Good," said the doctor. "Don't disturb her."

"No, sir. I'll just put things straight in the dining room and make sure everything's locked up right, and then I'll turn in."

He went across the hall into the dining room.

The others went upstairs, a slow unwilling procession.

If this had been an old house, with creaking wood, and dark shadows, and heavily panelled walls, there might have been an eerie feeling. But this house was the essence of modernity. There were no dark corners—no possible sliding panels—it was flooded with electric light—everything was new and bright and shining. There was nothing hidden in this house, nothing concealed. It had no atmosphere about it.

Somehow, that was the most frightening thing of all...

They exchanged good-nights on the upper landing. Each of them went into his or her own room, and each of them automatically, almost without conscious thought, locked the door...

III

In his pleasant softly tinted room, Mr. Justice Wargrave removed his garments and prepared himself for bed.

He was thinking about Edward Seton.

He remembered Seton very well. His fair hair, his blue eyes, his habit of looking you straight in the face with a pleasant air of straightforwardness. That was what had made so good an impression on the jury.

Llewellyn, for the Crown, had bungled it a bit. He had been overvehement, had tried to prove too much.

Matthews, on the other hand, for the Defence, had been good. His points had told. His cross-examinations had been deadly. His handling of his client in the witness-box had been masterly.

And Seton had come through the ordeal of cross-examination well. He had not got excited or over-vehement. The jury had been impressed. It had seemed to Matthews, perhaps, as though everything had been over bar the shouting.

The judge wound up his watch carefully and placed it by the bed.

He remembered exactly how he had felt sitting there—listening, making notes, appreciating everything, tabulating every scrap of evidence that told against the prisoner.

He'd enjoyed that case! Matthews' final speech had been first-class. Llewellyn, coming after it, had failed to remove the good impression that the defending counsel had made.

And then had come his own summing up...

Carefully, Mr. Justice Wargrave removed his false teeth and dropped them into a glass of water. The shrunken lips fell in. It was a cruel mouth now, cruel and predatory.

Hooding his eyes, the judge smiled to himself.

He'd cooked Seton's goose all right!

With a slightly rheumatic grunt, he climbed into bed and turned out the electric light.

IV

Downstairs in the dining-room, Rogers stood puzzled.

He was staring at the china figures in the centre of the table.

He muttered to himself:

"That's a rum go! I could have sworn there were ten of them."

V

General Macarthur tossed from side to side.

Sleep would not come to him.

In the darkness he kept seeing Arthur Richmond's face.

He'd liked Arthur—he'd been damned fond of Arthur.

He'd been pleased that Leslie liked him too.

Leslie was so capricious. Lots of good fellows that Leslie would turn up her nose at and pronounce dull. "Dull!" Just like that.

But she hadn't found Arthur Richmond dull. They'd got on well together from the beginning. They'd talked of plays and music and pictures together. She'd teased him, made fun of him, ragged him. And he, Macarthur, had been delighted at the thought that Leslie took quite a motherly interest in the boy.

Motherly indeed! Damn fool not to remember that Richmond was twenty-eight to Leslie's twenty-nine.

He'd loved Leslie. He could see her now. Her heart-shaped face, and her dancing deep grey eyes, and the brown curling mass of her hair. He'd loved Leslie and he'd believed in her absolutely.

Out there in France, in the middle of all the hell of it, he'd sat thinking of her, taken her picture out of the breast pocket of his tunic.

And then—he'd found out!

It had come about exactly in the way things happened in books. The letter in the wrong envelope. She'd been writing to them both and she'd put her letter to Richmond in the envelope addressed to her husband. Even now, all these years after, he could feel the shock of it—the pain . . .

God, it had hurt!

And the business had been going on some time. The

letter made that clear. Weekends! Richmond's last leave ...

Leslie—Leslie and Arthur!

God damn the fellow! Damn his smiling face, his brisk "Yes, sir." Liar and hypocrite! Stealer of another man's wife!

It had gathered slowly—that cold murderous rage.

He'd managed to carry on as usual—to show nothing. He'd tried to make his manner to Richmond just the same.

Had he succeeded? He thought so. Richmond hadn't suspected. Inequalities of temper were easily accounted for out there, where men's nerves were continually snapping under the strain.

Only young Armitage had looked at him curiously once or twice. Quite a young chap, but he'd had perceptions, that boy.

Armitage, perhaps, had guessed—when the time came.

He'd sent Richmond deliberately to death. Only a miracle could have brought him through unhurt. That miracle didn't happen. Yes, he'd sent Richmond to his death and he wasn't sorry. It had been easy enough. Mistakes were being made all the time, officers being sent to death needlessly. All was confusion, panic. People might say afterwards "Old Macarthur lost his nerve a bit, made some colossal blunders, sacrificed some of his best men." They couldn't say more.

But young Armitage was different. He'd looked at his commanding officer very oddly. He'd known, perhaps, that Richmond was being deliberately sent to death.

(And after the War was over—had Armitage talked?)

Leslie hadn't known. Leslie had wept for her lover (he supposed) but her weeping was over by the time he'd come back to England. He'd never told her that he'd found her out. They'd gone on together—only, somehow, she hadn't seemed very real any more. And then, three or four years later she'd got double pneumonia and died.

That had been a long time ago. Fifteen years—sixteen years?

And he'd left the Army and come to live in Devon—bought the sort of little place he'd always meant to have. Nice neighbours—pleasant part of the world. There was a bit of shooting and fishing. He'd gone to church on Sundays. (But not the day that the lesson was read about David putting Uriah in the forefront of the battle. Somehow he couldn't face that. Gave him an uncomfortable feeling.)

Everybody had been very friendly. At first, that is. Later, he'd had an uneasy feeling that people were talking about him behind his back. They eyed him differently, somehow. As though they'd heard something—some lying rumour ...

(Armitage? Supposing Armitage had talked?)

He'd avoided people after that—withdrawn into himself. Unpleasant to feel that people were discussing you.

And all so long ago. So—so purposeless now. Leslie had faded into the distance and Arthur Richmond too. Nothing of what had happened seemed to matter any more.

It made life lonely, though. He'd taken to shunning his old Army friends.

(If Armitage had talked, they'd know about it.)

And now—this evening—a hidden voice had blared out that old hidden story.

Had he dealt with it all right? Kept a stiff upper lip? Betrayed the right amount of feeling—indignation, disgust—but no guilt, no discomfiture? Difficult to tell.

Surely nobody could have taken the accusation seriously. There had been a pack of other nonsense, just as far-fetched. That charming girl—the voice had accused her of drowning a child! Idiotic! Some madman throwing crazy accusations about!

Emily Brent, too—actually a niece of old Tom Brent of the Regiment. It had accused *her* of murder! Any one could see with half an eye that the woman was as pious as could be—the kind that was hand and glove with parsons.

Damned curious business the whole thing! Crazy, nothing less.

Ever since they had got there—when was that? Why, damn it, it was only this afternoon! Seemed a good bit longer than that.

He thought: "I wonder when we shall get away again."

Tomorrow, of course, when the motorboat came from the mainland.

Funny, just this minute he didn't want much to get away from the island . . . To go back to the mainland, back to his little house, back to all the troubles and worries. Through the open window he could hear the waves breaking on the rocks—a little louder now than earlier in the evening. Wind was getting up, too.

He thought: Peaceful sound. Peaceful place...

He thought: Best of an island is once you get there—you can't go any further...you've come to the end of things...

He knew, suddenly, that he didn't want to leave the island.

VI

Vera Claythorne lay in bed, wide awake, staring up at the ceiling.

The light beside her was on. She was frightened of the dark.

She was thinking:

"Hugo...Hugo...Why do I feel you're so near to me tonight?...Somewhere quite close...

"Where is he really? I don't know. I never shall know. He just went away—right away—out of my life."

It was no good trying not to think of Hugo. He was close to her. She *had* to think of him—to remember...

Cornwall...

The black rocks, the smooth yellow sand. Mrs. Hamilton, stout, good-humoured. Cyril, whining a little always, pulling at her hand.

"I want to swim out to the rock, Miss Claythorne. Why can't I swim out to the rock?"

Looking up—meeting Hugo's eyes watching her.

The evenings after Cyril was in bed...

"Come out for a stroll, Miss Claythorne."

"I think perhaps I will."

The decorous stroll down to the beach. The moonlight—the soft Atlantic air.

And then, Hugo's arms round her.

"I love you. I love you. You know I love you, Vera?"

Yes, she knew.

(Or thought she knew.)

"I can't ask you to marry me. I've not got a penny. It's all I can do to keep myself. Queer, you know, once, for three months I had the chance of being a rich man to look forward to. Cyril wasn't born until three months after Maurice died. If he'd been a girl..."

If the child has been a girl, Hugo would have come into everything. He'd been disappointed, he admitted.

"I hadn't built on it, of course. But it was a bit of a knock. Oh well, luck's luck! Cyril's a nice kid. I'm awfully fond of him." And he was fond of him, too. Always ready to play games or amuse his small nephew. No rancour in Hugo's nature.

Cyril wasn't really strong. A puny child—no stamina. The kind of child, perhaps, who wouldn't live to grow up...

And then—?

"Miss Claythorne, why can't I swim to the rock?"

Irritating whiney repetition.

"It's too far, Cyril."

"But, Miss Claythorne..."

Vera got up. She went to the dressing table and swallowed three aspirins.

She thought:

"I wish I had some proper sleeping stuff."

She thought:

"If *I* were doing away with myself I'd take an overdose of veronal—something like that—not cyanide!"

She shuddered as she remembered Anthony Marston's convulsed purple face.

As she passed the mantelpiece, she looked up at the framed doggerel.

"Ten little soldier boys went out to dine;
One choked his little self and then there were Nine."

She thought to herself:

"It's horrible—*just like us this evening*..."

Why had Anthony Marston wanted to die?

She didn't want to die.

She couldn't imagine wanting to die...

Death was for—the other people...

Chapter 6

I

Dr. Armstrong was dreaming ...

It was very hot in the operating room ...

Surely they'd got the temperature too high? The sweat was rolling down his face. His hands were clammy. Difficult to hold the scalpel firmly ...

How beautifully sharp it was ...

Easy to do a murder with a knife like that. And of course he *was* doing a murder ...

The woman's body looked different. It had been a large unwieldy body. This was a spare meagre body. And the face was hidden.

Who was it that he had to kill?

He couldn't remember. But he *must* know! Should he ask Sister?

Sister was watching him. No, he couldn't ask her. She was suspicious, he could see that.

But who was it on the operating table?

They shouldn't have covered up the face like that ...

If he could only see the face ...

Ah! that was better. A young probationer was pulling off

the handkerchief.

Emily Brent, of course. It was Emily Brent that he had to kill. How malicious her eyes were! Her lips were moving. What was she saying?

"*In the midst of life we are in death...*"

She was laughing now. No, nurse, don't put the handkerchief back. I've got to see. I've got to give the anaesthetic. Where's the ether? I must have brought the ether with me. What have you done with the ether, Sister? Châteauneuf-du-Pape? Yes, that will do quite as well.

Take the handkerchief away, nurse.

Of course! I knew it all the time! *It's Anthony Marston!* His face is purple and convulsed. But he's not dead—he's laughing. I tell you he's laughing! He's shaking the operating table.

Look out, man, look out. Nurse, steady it—steady it—

With a start Dr. Armstrong woke up. It was morning. Sunlight was pouring into the room.

And some one was leaning over him—shaking him. It was Rogers. Rogers, with a white face, saying: "Doctor—doctor!"

Dr. Armstrong woke up completely.

He sat up in bed. He said sharply:

"What is it?"

"It's the wife, doctor. *I can't get her to wake.* My God! I can't get her to wake. And—and she don't look right to me."

Dr. Armstrong was quick and efficient. He wrapped himself in his dressing gown and followed Rogers.

He bent over the bed where the woman was lying peacefully on her side. He lifted the cold hand, raised the eyelid. It was some few minutes before he straightened himself and turned from the bed.

Rogers whispered:

"Is—she—is she—?"

He passed a tongue over dry lips.

Armstrong nodded.

"Yes, she's gone."

His eyes rested thoughtfully on the man before him. Then they went to the table by the bed, to the washstand, then back to the sleeping woman.

Rogers said:

"Was it—was it—'er 'eart, doctor?"

Dr. Armstrong was a minute or two before replying. Then he said:

"What was her health like normally?"

Rogers said:

"She was a bit rheumaticky."

"Any doctor been attending her recently?"

"Doctor?" Rogers stared. "Not been to a doctor for years—neither of us."

"You'd no reason to believe she suffered from heart trouble?"

"No, doctor. I never knew of anything."

Armstrong said:

"Did she sleep well?"

Now Rogers' eyes evaded his. The man's hands came together and turned and twisted uneasily. He muttered:

"She didn't sleep extra well—no."

The doctor said sharply:

"Did she take things to make her sleep?"

Rogers stared at him, surprised.

"Take things? To make her sleep? Not that I knew of. I'm sure she didn't."

Armstrong went over to the washstand.

There were a certain number of bottles on it. Hair lotion, lavender water, cascara, glycerine of cucumber for the hands, a mouthwash, toothpaste and some Elliman's.

Rogers helped by pulling out the drawers of the dressing-table. From there they moved on to the chest of drawers. But there was no sign of sleeping draughts or tablets.

Rogers said:

"She didn't have nothing last night, sir, except what you gave her..."

I I

When the gong sounded for breakfast at nine o'clock it found every one up and awaiting the summons.

General Macarthur and the judge had been pacing the terrace outside, exchanging desultory comments on the political situation.

Vera Claythorne and Philip Lombard had been up to the summit of the island behind the house. There they had discovered William Henry Blore, standing staring at the mainland.

He said:

"No sign of that motorboat yet. I've been watching for it."

Vera said smiling:

"Devon's a sleepy county. Things are usually late."

Philip Lombard was looking the other way, out to sea.

He said abruptly:

"What d'you think of the weather?"

Glancing up at the sky, Blore remarked:

"Looks all right to me."

Lombard pursed up his mouth into a whistle.

He said:

"It will come on to blow before the day's out."

Blore said:

"Squally—eh?"

From below them came the boom of a gong.

Philip Lombard said:

"Breakfast? Well, I could do with some."

As they went down the steep slope Blore said to Lombard in a ruminating voice:

"You know, it beats me—why that young fellow wanted to do himself in! I've been worrying about it all night."

Vera was a little ahead. Lombard hung back slightly. He said:

"Got any alternative theory?"

"I'd want some proof. Motive, to begin with. Well-off I should say he was."

Emily Brent came out of the drawing room window to meet them.

She said sharply:

"Is the boat coming?"

"Not yet," said Vera.

They went in to breakfast. There was a vast dish of eggs and bacon on the sideboard and tea and coffee.

Rogers held the door open for them to pass in, then shut it from the outside.

Emily Brent said:

"That man looks ill this morning."

Dr. Armstrong, who was standing by the window, cleared his throat. He said:

"You must excuse any—er—shortcomings this morning. Rogers has had to do the best he can for breakfast single-handed. Mrs. Rogers has—er—not been able to carry on this morning."

Emily Brent said sharply:

"What's the matter with the woman?"

Dr. Armstrong said easily:

"Let us start our breakfast. The eggs will be cold. Afterwards, there are several matters I want to discuss with you all."

They took the hint. Plates were filled, coffee and tea was

poured. The meal began.

Discussion of the island was, by mutual consent, tabooed. They spoke instead in a desultory fashion of current events. The news from abroad, events in the world of sport, the latest reappearance of the Loch Ness monster.

Then, when plates were cleared, Dr. Armstrong moved back his chair a little, cleared his throat importantly and spoke.

He said:

"I thought it better to wait until you had had your breakfast before telling you of a sad piece of news. Mrs. Rogers died in her sleep."

There were startled and shocked ejaculations.

Vera exclaimed:

"How awful! Two deaths on this island since we arrived!"

Mr. Justice Wargrave, his eyes narrowed, said in his small precise clear voice:

"H'm—very remarkable—what was the cause of death?"

Armstrong shrugged his shoulders.

"Impossible to say offhand."

"There must be an autopsy?"

"I certainly couldn't give a certificate. I have no knowledge whatsoever of the woman's state of health."

Vera said:

"She was a very nervous-looking creature. And she had a shock last night. It might have been heart failure, I suppose?"

Dr. Armstrong said dryly:

"Her heart certainly failed to beat—but what caused it to fail is the question."

One word fell from Emily Brent. It fell hard and clear into the listening group.

"Conscience!" she said.

Armstrong turned to her.

"What exactly do you mean by that, Miss Brent?"

Emily Brent, her lips tight and hard, said:

"You all heard. She was accused, together with her husband, of having deliberately murdered her former employer—an old lady."

"And you think?"

Emily Brent said:

"I think that the accusation was true. You all saw her last night. She broke down completely and fainted. The shock of having her wickedness brought home to her was too much for her. She literally died of fear."

Dr. Armstrong shook his head doubtfully.

"It is a possible theory," he said. "One cannot adopt it without more exact knowledge of her state of health. If there was cardiac weakness—"

Emily Brent said quietly:

"Call it if you prefer, an Act of God."

Every one looked shocked. Mr. Blore said uneasily:

"That's carrying things a bit far, Miss Brent."

She looked at them with shining eyes. Her chin went up.

She said:

"You regard it as impossible that a sinner should be struck down by the wrath of God! I do not!"

The judge stroked his chin. He murmured in a slightly ironic voice:

"My dear lady, in my experience of ill-doing, Providence leaves the work of conviction and chastisement to us mortals—and the process is often fraught with difficulties. There are no short cuts."

Emily Brent shrugged her shoulders.

Blore said sharply:

"What did she have to eat and drink last night after she went up to bed?"

Armstrong said:

"Nothing."

"She didn't take anything? A cup of tea? A drink of water? I'll bet you she had a cup of tea. That sort always does."

"Rogers assures me she had nothing whatsoever."

"Ah," said Blore. "But he *might* say so!"

His tone was so significant that the doctor looked at him sharply.

Philip Lombard said:

"So that's your idea?"

Blore said aggressively:

"Well, why not? We all heard that accusation last night. May be sheer moonshine—just plain lunacy! On the other hand, it may not. Allow for the moment that it's true. Rogers and his Missus polished off that old lady. Well, where does that get you? They've been feeling quite safe and happy about it—"

Vera interrupted. In a low voice she said:

"No, I don't think Mrs. Rogers ever felt safe."

Blore looked slightly annoyed at the interruption.

"Just like a woman," his glance said.

He resumed:

"That's as may be. Anyway there's no active danger to them as far as they know. Then, last night, some unknown lunatic spills the beans. What happens? The woman cracks—she goes to pieces. Notice how her husband hung over her as she was coming round. Not all husbandly solicitude! Not on your life! He was like a cat on hot bricks. Scared out of his life as to what she might say.

"And there's the position for you! They've done a murder and got away with it. But if the whole thing's going to be raked up, what's going to happen? Ten to one, the woman will give the show away. She hasn't got the nerve to stand up and brazen it out. She's a living danger to her husband, that's what she is. He's all right. *He'll* lie with a straight face till kingdom comes—but he can't be sure of *her*! And if *she* goes to pieces, his neck's in danger! So he slips something into a cup of tea and makes sure that her mouth is shut permanently."

Armstrong said slowly:

"There was no empty cup by her bedside—there was nothing there at all. I looked."

Blore snorted.

"Of course there wouldn't be! First thing he'd do when she'd drunk it would be to take that cup and saucer away and wash it up carefully."

There was a pause. Then General Macarthur said doubtfully:

"It may be so. But I should hardly think it possible that a man would do that—to his wife."

Blore gave a short laugh.

He said:

"When a man's neck's in danger, he doesn't stop to think too much about sentiment."

There was a pause. Before any one could speak, the door opened and Rogers came in.

He said, looking from one to the other:

"Is there anything more I can get you?"

Mr. Justice Wargrave stirred a little in his chair. He asked:

"What time does the motorboat usually come over?"

"Between seven and eight, sir. Sometimes it's a bit after eight. Don't know what Fred Narracott can be doing this morning. If he's ill he'd send his brother."

Philip Lombard said:

"What's the time now?"

"Ten minutes to ten, sir."

Lombard's eyebrows rose. He nodded slowly to himself.

Rogers waited a minute or two.

General Macarthur spoke suddenly and explosively.

"Sorry to hear about your wife, Rogers. Doctor's just been telling us."

Rogers inclined his head.

"Yes, sir. Thank you, sir."

He took up the empty bacon dish and went out.

Again there was silence.

III

On the terrace outside Philip Lombard said:

"About this motorboat—"

Blore looked at him.

Blore nodded his head.

He said:

"I know what you're thinking, Mr. Lombard. I've asked myself the same question. Motorboat ought to have been here nigh on two hours ago. It hasn't come? Why?"

"Found the answer?" asked Lombard.

"*It's not an accident*—that's what I say. It's part and parcel of the whole business. It's all bound up together."

Philip Lombard said:

"It won't come, you think?"

A voice spoke behind him—a testy impatient voice.

"The motorboat's not coming," he said.

Blore turned his square shoulder slightly and viewed the last speaker thoughtfully.

"You think not too, General?"

General Macarthur said sharply:

"Of course it won't come. We're counting on the motorboat to take us off the island. That's the meaning of the whole business. *We're not going to leave the island* . . . None of us will ever leave . . . It's the end, you see—the end of everything . . ."

He hesitated, then he said in a low strange voice:

"That's peace—real peace. To come to the end—not to have to go on . . . Yes, peace . . ."

He turned abruptly and walked away. Along the terrace, then down the slope towards the sea—obliquely—to the end of the island where loose rocks went out into the water.

He walked a little unsteadily, like a man who was only half awake.

Blore said:

"There goes another one who's barmy! Looks as though it'll end with the whole lot going that way."

Philip Lombard said:

"I don't fancy *you* will, Blore."

The ex-Inspector laughed.

"It would take a lot to send me off my head." He added dryly: "And I don't think you'll be going that way either, Mr. Lombard."

Philip Lombard said:
"I feel quite sane at the minute, thank you."

IV

Dr. Armstrong came out on to the terrace. He stood there hesitating. To his left were Blore and Lombard. To his right was Wargrave, slowly pacing up and down, his head bent down.

Armstrong, after a moment of indecision, turned towards the latter.

But at that moment Rogers came quickly out of the house.

"Could I have a word with you, sir, please?"

Armstrong turned.

He was startled at what he saw.

Rogers' face was working. Its colour was greyish green. His hands shook.

It was such a contrast to his restraint of a few minutes ago that Armstrong was quite taken aback.

"Please sir, if I could have a word with you. Inside, sir."

The doctor turned back and reentered the house with the frenzied butler. He said:

"What's the matter, man, pull yourself together."

"In here, sir, come in here."

He opened the dining room door. The doctor passed in.

Rogers followed him and shut the door behind him.

"Well," said Armstrong, "what is it?"

The muscles of Rogers' throat were working. He was swallowing. He jerked out:

"There's things going on, sir, that I don't understand."

Armstrong said sharply:

"Things? What things?"

"You'll think I'm crazy, sir. You'll say it isn't anything. But it's got to be explained, sir. It's got to be explained. Because it doesn't make any sense."

"Well, man, tell me what it is. Don't go on talking in riddles."

Rogers swallowed again.

He said:

"It's those little figures, sir. In the middle of the table. The little china figures. Ten of them, there were. I'll swear to that, ten of them."

Armstrong said:

"Yes, ten. We counted them last night at dinner."

Rogers came nearer.

"That's just it, sir. Last night, when I was clearing up, there wasn't but nine, sir. I noticed it and thought it queer. But that's all I thought. And now, sir, this morning. I didn't notice when I laid the breakfast. I was upset and all that.

"But now, sir, when I came to clear away. See for yourself if you don't believe me.

"There's only eight, sir! Only eight! It doesn't make sense, does it? *Only eight..."*

Chapter 7

I

After breakfast, Emily Brent had suggested to Vera Claythorne that they should walk up to the summit again and watch for the boat. Vera had acquiesced.

The wind had freshened. Small white crests were appearing on the sea. There were no fishing boats out—and no sign of the motor boat.

The actual village of Sticklehaven could not be seen, only the hill above it, a jutting out cliff of red rock concealed the actual little bay.

Emily Brent said:

"The man who brought us out yesterday seemed a dependable sort of person. It is really very odd that he should be so late this morning."

Vera did not answer. She was fighting down a rising feeling of panic.

She said to herself angrily:

"You must keep cool. This isn't like you. You've always had excellent nerves."

Aloud she said after a minute or two:

"I wish he would come. I—I want to get away."

Emily Brent said dryly:

"I've no doubt we all do."

Vera said:

"It's all so extraordinary ... There seems no—no meaning in it all."

The elderly woman beside her said briskly:

"I'm very annoyed with myself for being so easily taken in. Really that letter is absurd when one comes to examine it. But I had no doubts at the time—none at all."

Vera murmured mechanically: "I suppose not."

"One takes things for granted too much," said Emily Brent.

Vera drew a deep shuddering breath.

She said:

"Do you really think—what you said at breakfast?"

"Be a little more precise, my dear. To what in particular are you referring?"

Vera said in a low voice:

"Do you really think that Rogers and his wife did away with that old lady?"

Emily Brent gazed thoughtfully out to sea. Then she said:

"Personally, I am quite sure of it. What do you think?"

"I don't know what to think."

Emily Brent said:

"Everything goes to support the idea. The way the woman fainted. And the man dropped the coffee tray, remember. Then the way he spoke about it—it didn't ring true. Oh, yes, I'm afraid they did it."

Vera said:

"The way she looked—scared of her own shadow! I've never seen a woman look so frightened ... She must have been always haunted by it ..."

Miss Brent murmured:

"I remember a text that hung in my nursery as a child. *Be sure thy sin will find thee out.* It's very true, that. *Be sure thy sin will find thee out.*"

Vera scrambled to her feet. She said:

"But, Miss Brent—Miss Brent—in that case—"

"Yes, my dear?"

"The others? What about the others?"

"I don't quite understand you."

"All the other accusations—they—*they* weren't true? But if it's true about the Rogerses—" She stopped, unable to make her chaotic thought clear.

Emily Brent's brow, which had been frowning perplexedly, cleared.

She said:

"Ah, I understand you now. Well, there is that Mr. Lombard. He admits to having abandoned twenty men to their deaths."

Vera said: "They were only natives ..."

Emily Brent said sharply:

"Black or white, they are our brothers."

Vera thought:

"Our black brothers—our black brothers. Oh, I'm going to laugh. I'm hysterical. I'm not myself..."

Emily Brent continued thoughtfully:

"Of course, some of the other accusations were very farfetched and ridiculous. Against the judge, for instance, who was only doing his duty in his public capacity. And the ex-Scotland Yard man. My own case, too."

She paused and then went on:

"Naturally, considering the circumstances, I was not going to say anything last night. It was not a fit subject to discuss before gentlemen."

"No?"

Vera listened with interest. Miss Brent continued serenely.

"Beatrice Taylor was in service with me. *Not a nice girl*—as I found out too late. I was very much deceived in her. She had nice manners and was very clean and willing. I was very pleased with her. Of course all that was the sheerest hypocrisy! She was a loose girl with no morals. Disgusting! It was some time before I found out that she was what they call 'in trouble.'" She paused, her delicate nose wrinkling itself in distaste. "It was a great shock to me. Her parents were decent folk, too, who had brought her up very strictly. I'm glad to say they did not condone her behaviour."

Vera said, staring at Miss Brent:

"What happened?"

"Naturally I did not keep her an hour under my roof. No

one shall ever say that I condoned immorality."

Vera said in a lower voice:

"What happened—to her?"

Miss Brent said:

"The abandoned creature, not content with having one sin on her conscience, committed a still graver sin. She took her own life."

Vera whispered, horror-struck:

"She killed herself?"

"Yes, she threw herself into the river."

Vera shivered.

She stared at the calm delicate profile of Miss Brent. She said:

"What did you feel like when you knew she'd done that? Weren't you sorry? Didn't you blame yourself?"

Emily Brent drew herself up.

"I? I had nothing with which to reproach myself."

Vera said:

"But if your—hardness—drove her to it."

Emily Brent said sharply:

"Her own action—her own sin—that was what drove her to it. If she had behaved like a decent modest young woman none of this would have happened."

She turned her face to Vera. There was no self-reproach, no uneasiness in those eyes. They were hard and self-righteous. Emily Brent sat on the summit of Soldier Island, encased in her own armour of virtue.

The little elderly spinster was no longer slightly ridiculous to Vera.

Suddenly—she was terrible.

II

Dr. Armstrong came out of the dining room and once more came out on the terrace.

The judge was sitting in a chair now, gazing placidly out to sea.

Lombard and Blore were over to the left, smoking but not talking.

As before, the doctor hesitated for a moment His eye rested speculatively on Mr. Justice Wargrave. He wanted to consult with someone. He was conscious of the judge's acute logical brain. But nevertheless he wavered. Mr. Justice Wargrave might have a good brain but he was an elderly man. At this juncture, Armstrong felt what was needed was a man of action.

He made up his mind.

"Lombard, can I speak to you for a minute?"

Philip started.

"Of course."

The two men left the terrace. They strolled down the slope towards the water. When they were out of earshot Armstrong said:

"I want a consultation."

Lombard's eyebrows went up. He said:

"My dear fellow, I've no medical knowledge."

"No, no, I mean as to the general situation."

"Oh, that's different."

Armstrong said:

"Frankly, what do you think of the position?"

Lombard reflected a minute. Then he said:

"It's rather suggestive, isn't it?"

"What are your ideas on the subject of that woman? Do you accept Blore's theory?"

Philip puffed smoke into the air. He said:

"It's perfectly feasible—taken alone."

"Exactly."

Armstrong's tone sounded relieved. Philip Lombard was no fool.

The latter went on:

"That is, accepting the premise that Mr. and Mrs. Rogers have successfully got away with murder in their time. And I don't see why they shouldn't. What do you think they did exactly? Poisoned the old lady?"

Armstrong said slowly:

"It might be simpler than that. I asked Rogers this morning what this Miss Brady had suffered from. His answer was enlightening. I don't need to go into medical details, but in a certain form of cardiac trouble, amyl nitrite is used. When an attack comes on an ampoule of amyl nitrite is broken and it is inhaled. If amyl nitrite were withheld—well, the consequences might easily be fatal."

Philip Lombard said thoughtfully:

"As simple as that. It must have been—rather tempting."

The doctor nodded.

"Yes, no positive action. No arsenic to obtain and administer—nothing definite—just—negation! And Rogers hurried through the night to fetch a doctor and they both felt confident that no one could ever know."

"And even if any one knew, nothing could ever be proved against them," added Philip Lombard.

He frowned suddenly.

"Of course—that explains a good deal."

Armstrong said, puzzled:

"I beg your pardon."

Lombard said:

"I mean—it explains Soldier Island. There are crimes that cannot be brought home to their perpetrators. Instance the Rogerses'. Another instance, old Wargrave, who committed his murder strictly within the law."

Armstrong said sharply: "You believe that story?"

Philip Lombard smiled.

"Oh, yes, I believe it. Wargrave murdered Edward Seton all right, murdered him as surely as if he'd stuck a stiletto through him! But he was clever enough to do it from the judge's seat in wig and gown. So in the ordinary way you can't bring his little crime home to him."

A sudden flash passed like lightning through Armstrong's mind.

"*Murder in Hospital. Murder on the Operating table. Safe—yes, safe as houses!*"

Philip Lombard was saying:

"Hence—Mr. Owen—hence—Soldier Island!"

Armstrong drew a deep breath.

"Now we're getting down to it. What's the real purpose of getting us all here?"

Philip Lombard said:

"What do *you* think?"

Armstrong said abruptly:

"Let's go back a minute to this woman's death. What are the possible theories? Rogers killed her because he was afraid she would give the show away. Second possibility: She lost her nerve and took an easy way out herself."

Philip Lombard said:

"Suicide, eh?"

"What do you say to that?"

Lombard said:

"It could have been—yes—*if it hadn't been for Marston's death*. Two suicides within twelve hours is a little *too* much to swallow! And if you tell me that Anthony Marston, a young bull with no nerves and precious little brains, got the wind up over having mowed down a couple of kids and deliberately put himself out of the way—well, the idea's laughable! And anyway, how did he get hold of the stuff?

From all I've ever heard, potassium cyanide isn't the kind of stuff you take about with you in your waistcoat pocket. But that's your line of country."

Armstrong said:

"Nobody in their senses carries potassium cyanide. It might be done by someone who was going to take a wasps' nest."

"The ardent gardener or landowner, in fact? Again, not Anthony Marston. It strikes me that that cyanide is going to need a bit of explaining. Either Anthony Marston meant to do away with himself before he came here, and therefore came prepared—or else—"

Armstrong prompted him.

"Or else?"

Philip Lombard grinned.

"Why make me say it? When it's on the tip of your own tongue. *Anthony Marston was murdered, of course.*"

III

Dr. Armstrong drew a deep breath.

"And Mrs. Rogers?"

Lombard said slowly:

"I could believe in Anthony's suicide (with difficulty) if it weren't for Mrs. Rogers. I could believe in Mrs. Rogers' suicide (easily) if it weren't for Anthony Marston. I can believe that Rogers put his wife out of the way—if it were not for the unexpected death of Anthony Marston. But what we need is a theory to explain two deaths following rapidly on each other."

Armstrong said:

"I can perhaps give you some help towards that theory."

And he repeated the facts that Rogers had given him about the disappearance of the two little china figures.

Lombard said:

"Yes, little china figures... There were certainly ten last night at dinner. And now there are eight, you say?"

Dr. Armstrong recited:

*"Ten little soldier boys going out to dine;
One went and choked himself and then there were Nine.*

*"Nine little soldier boys sat up very late;
One overslept himself and then there were Eight."*

The two men looked at each other. Philip Lombard grinned and flung away his cigarette.

"Fits too damned well to be a coincidence! Anthony Marston dies of asphyxiation or choking last night after dinner, and Mother Rogers oversleeps herself with a vengeance."

"And therefore?" said Armstrong.

Lombard took him up.

"And therefore another kind of soldier. The Unkonwn

Soldier! X! Mr. Owen! U.N. Owen! One Unknown Lunatic at Large!"

"Ah!" Armstrong breathed a sigh of relief. "You agree. But you see what it involves? Rogers swore that there was no one but ourselves and he and his wife on the island."

"Rogers is wrong! Or possibly Rogers is lying!"

Armstrong shook his head.

"I don't think he's lying. The man's scared. He's scared nearly out of his senses."

Philip Lombard nodded.

He said:

"No motorboat this morning. That fits in. Mr. Owen's little arrangements again to the fore. Soldier Island is to be isolated until Mr. Owen has finished his job."

Armstrong had gone pale. He said:

"You realize—the man must be a raving maniac!"

Philip Lombard said, and there was a new ring in his voice:

"There's one thing Mr. Owen didn't realize."

"What's that?"

"This island's more or less a bare rock. We shall make short work of searching it. We'll soon ferret out U.N. Owen, Esq."

Dr. Armstrong said warningly:

"He'll be dangerous."

Philip Lombard laughed.

"Dangerous? Who's afraid of the big bad wolf? *I'*ll be

dangerous when I get hold of him!"

He paused and said:

"We'd better rope in Blore to help us. He'll be a good man in a pinch. Better not tell the women. As for the others, the General's ga-ga, I think, and old Wargrave's forte is masterly inactivity. The three of us can attend to this job."

Chapter 8

I

Blore was easily roped in. He expressed immediate agreement with their arguments.

"What you've said about those china figures, sir, makes all the difference. That's crazy, that is! There's only one thing. You don't think this Owen's idea might be to do the job by proxy, as it were?"

"Explain yourself, man."

"Well, I mean like this. After the racket last night this young Marston gets the wind up and poisons himself. And Rogers, *he* gets the wind up too and bumps off his wife! All according to U.N.O.'s plan."

Armstrong shook his head. He stressed the point about the cyanide. Blore agreed.

"Yes, I'd forgotten that. Not a natural thing to be carrying about with you. But how did it get into his drink, sir?"

Lombard said:

"I've been thinking about that. Marston had several drinks that night. Between the time he had his last one and the time he finished the one before it, there was quite a gap. During that time his glass was lying about on some table or other. I think—though I can't be sure, it was on the little table near the window. The window was open. Somebody could have slipped a dose of the cyanide into the glass."

Blore said unbelievingly:

"Without our all seeing him, sir?"

Lombard said dryly:

"We were all—rather concerned elsewhere."

Armstrong said slowly:

"That's true. We'd all been attacked. We were walking about, moving about the room. Arguing, indignant, intent on our own business. I think it *could* have been done . . ."

Blore shrugged his shoulders.

"Fact is, it must have been done! Now then, gentlemen, let's make a start. Nobody's got a revolver, by any chance? I suppose that's too much to hope for."

Lombard said:

"I've got one." He patted his pocket.

Blore's eyes opened very wide. He said in an overcasual tone:

"Always carry that about with you, sir?"

Lombard said:

"Usually. I've been in some tight places, you know."

"Oh," said Blore and added: "Well, you've probably never been in a tighter place than you are today! If there's a lunatic hiding on this island, he's probably got a young arsenal on him—to say nothing of a knife or dagger or two."

Armstrong coughed.

"You may be wrong there, Blore. Many homicidal lunatics are very quiet unassuming people. Delightful fellows."

Blore said:

"I don't feel this one is going to be of that kind, Dr. Armstrong."

II

The three men started on their tour of the island.

It proved unexpectedly simple. On the northwest side, towards the coast, the cliffs fell sheer to the sea below, their surface unbroken.

On the rest of the island there were no trees and very little cover. The three men worked carefully and methodically, beating up and down from the highest point to the water's edge, narrowly scanning the least irregularity in the rock which might point to the entrance to a cave. But there were no caves.

They came at last, skirting the water's edge, to where General Macarthur sat looking out to sea. It was very peaceful here with the lap of the waves breaking over the rocks. The old man sat very upright, his eyes fixed on the horizon.

He paid no attention to the approach of the searchers.

His oblivion of them made one at least faintly uncomfortable.

Blore thought to himself:

"'Tisn't natural—looks as though he'd gone into a trance or something."

He cleared his throat and said in a would-be conversational tone:

"Nice peaceful spot you've found for yourself, sir."

The General frowned. He cast a quick look over his shoulder. He said:

"There is so little time—so little time. I really must insist that no one disturbs me."

Blore said genially:

"We won't disturb you. We're just making a tour of the island so to speak. Just wondered, you know, if someone might be hiding on it."

The General frowned and said:

"You don't understand—you don't understand at all. Please go away."

Blore retreated. He said, as he joined the other two:

"He's crazy . . . It's no good talking to him."

Lombard asked with some curiosity:

"What did he say?"

Blore shrugged his shoulders.

"Something about there being no time and that he didn't want to be disturbed."

Dr. Armstrong frowned.

He murmured:

"I wonder now..."

III

The search of the island was practically completed. The three men stood on the highest point looking over towards the mainland. There were no boats out. The wind was freshening.

Lombard said:

"No fishing boats out. There's a storm coming. Damned nuisance you can't see the village from here. We could signal or do something."

Blore said:

"We might light a bonfire tonight."

Lombard said, frowning:

"The devil of it is that that's all probably been provided for."

"In what way, sir?"

"How do I know? Practical joke, perhaps. We're to be marooned here, no attention is to be paid to signals, etc. Possibly the village has been told there's a wager on. Some damn fool story anyway."

Blore said dubiously:

"Think they'd swallow that?"

Lombard said dryly:

"It's easier of belief than the truth! If the village were told that the island was to be isolated until Mr. Unknown Owen had quietly murdered all his guests—do you think they'd believe that?"

Dr. Armstrong said:

"There are moments when I can't believe it myself. And yet—"

Philip Lombard, his lips curling back from his teeth said:

"*And yet*—that's just it! You've said it, doctor!"

Blore was gazing down into the water.

He said:

"Nobody could have clambered down here, I suppose?"

Armstrong shook his head.

"I doubt it. It's pretty sheer. And where could he hide?"

Blore said:

"There might be a hole in the cliff. If we had a boat now, we could row round the island."

Lombard said:

"If we had a boat, we'd all be halfway to the mainland by now!"

"True enough, sir."

Lombard said suddenly:

"We can make sure of this cliff. There's only one place where there *could* be a recess—just a little to the right below here. If you fellows can get hold of a rope, you can let me down to make sure."

Blore said:

"Might as well *be* sure. Though it seems absurd—on the face of it! I'll see if I can get hold of something."

He started off briskly down to the house.

Lombard stared up at the sky. The clouds were beginning to mass themselves together. The wind was increasing.

He shot a sideways look at Armstrong. He said:

"You're very silent, doctor. What are you thinking?"

Armstrong said slowly:

"I was wondering exactly how mad old Macarthur was..."

IV

Vera had been restless all the morning. She had avoided Emily Brent with a kind of shuddering aversion.

Miss Brent herself had taken a chair just round the corner of the house so as to be out of the wind. She sat there knitting.

Every time Vera thought of her she seemed to see a pale drowned face with seaweed entangled in the hair... A face that had once been pretty—impudently pretty perhaps—and which was now beyond the reach of pity or terror.

And Emily Brent, placid and righteous, sat knitting.

On the main terrace, Mr. Justice Wargrave sat huddled in a porter's chair. His head was poked down well into his neck.

When Vera looked at him, she saw a man standing in

the dock—a young man with fair hair and blue eyes and a bewildered frightened face. Edward Seton. And in imagination she saw the judge's old hands put the black cap on his head and begin to pronounce sentence...

After a while Vera strolled slowly down to the sea. She walked along towards the extreme end of the island where an old man sat staring out to the horizon.

General Macarthur stirred at her approach. His head turned—there was a queer mixture of questioning and apprehension in his look. It startled her. He stared intently at her for a minute or two.

She thought to herself:

"How queer. It's almost as though he *knew*..."

He said:

"Ah! it's you! You've come..."

Vera sat down beside him. She said:

"Do you like sitting here looking out to sea?"

He nodded his head gently.

"Yes," he said. "It's pleasant. It's a good place, I think, to wait."

"To wait?" said Vera sharply. "What are you waiting for?"

He said gently:

"The end. But I think you know that, don't you? It's true, isn't it? We're all waiting for the end."

She said unsteadily:

"What do you mean?"

General Macarthur said gravely:

"*None of us are going to leave the island.* That's the plan. You know it, of course, perfectly. What, perhaps, you can't understand is the relief!"

Vera said wonderingly:

"The relief?"

He said:

"Yes. Of course, you're very young... you haven't got to that yet. But it does come! The blessed relief when you know that you've done with it all—that you haven't got to carry the burden any longer. You'll feel that too, some day..."

Vera said hoarsely:

"I don't understand you."

Her fingers worked spasmodically. She felt suddenly afraid of this quiet old soldier.

He said musingly:

"You see, I loved Leslie. I loved her very much..."

Vera said questioningly:

"Was Leslie your wife?"

"Yes, my wife... I loved her—and I was very proud of her. She was so pretty—and so gay."

He was silent for a minute or two, then he said:

"Yes, I loved Leslie. That's why I did it."

Vera said:

"You mean—" and paused.

General Macarthur nodded his head gently.

"It's not much good denying it now—not when we're all going to die. *I sent Richmond to his death.* I suppose, in a way, it was murder. Curious. *Murder*—and I've always been such a law-abiding man! But it didn't seem like that at the time. I had no regrets. 'Serves him damned well right!'—that's what I thought. But afterwards—"

In a hard voice, Vera said:

"Well, afterwards?"

He shook his head vaguely. He looked puzzled and a little distressed.

"I don't know. I—don't know. It was all different, you see. I don't know if Leslie ever guessed . . . I don't think so. But you see, I didn't know about her anymore. She'd gone far away where I couldn't reach her. And then she died—and I was alone . . ."

Vera said:

"Alone—alone—" and the echo of her voice came back to her from the rocks.

General Macarthur said:

"You'll be glad, too, when the end comes."

Vera got up. She said sharply:

"I don't know what you mean!"

He said:

"I *know*, my child, I *know* . . ."

"You don't. You don't understand at all . . ."

General Macarthur looked out to sea again. He seemed unconscious of her presence behind him.

He said very gently and softly:

"Leslie . . . ?"

V

When Blore returned from the house with a rope coiled over his arm, he found Armstrong where he had left him staring down into the depths.

Blore said breathlessly:

"Where's Mr. Lombard?"

Armstrong said carelessly:

"Gone to test some theory or other. He'll be back in a minute. Look here, Blore, I'm worried."

"I should say we were all worried."

The doctor waved an impatient hand.

"Of course—of course. I don't mean it that way. I'm thinking of old Macarthur."

"What about him, sir?"

Dr. Armstrong said grimly:

"What we're looking for is a madman. *What price Macarthur?*"

Blore said incredulously:

"You mean he's homicidal?"

Armstrong said doubtfully:

"I shouldn't have said so. Not for a minute. But, of course, I'm not a specialist in mental diseases. I haven't really had any conversation with him—I haven't studied him from that point of view."

Blore said doubtfully:

"Ga-ga, yes! But I wouldn't have said—"

Armstrong cut in with a slight effort as of a man who pulls himself together.

"You're probably right! Damn it all, there *must* be someone hiding on the island! Ah! here comes Lombard."

They fastened the rope carefully.

Lombard said:

"I'll help myself all I can. Keep a lookout for a sudden strain on the rope."

After a minute or two, while they stood together watching Lombard's progress, Blore said:

"Climbs like a cat, doesn't he?"

There was something odd in his voice.

Dr. Armstrong said:

"I should think he must have done some mountaineering in his time."

"Maybe."

There was a silence and the ex-Inspector said:

"Funny sort of cove altogether. D'you know what I think?"

"What?"

"He's a wrong 'un!"

Armstrong said doubtfully:

"In what way?"

Blore grunted. Then he said:

"I don't know—exactly. But I wouldn't trust him a yard."

Dr. Armstrong said:

"I suppose he's led an adventurous life."

Blore said:

"I bet some of his adventures have had to be kept pretty dark." He paused and then went on: "Did you happen to bring a revolver along with you, doctor?"

Armstrong stared.

"Me? Good Lord, no. Why should I?"

Blore said:

"*Why did Mr. Lombard?*"

Armstrong said doubtfully:

"I suppose—habit."

Blore snorted.

A sudden pull came on the rope. For some moments they had their hands full. Presently, when the strain relaxed, Blore said:

"There are habits *and* habits! Mr. Lombard takes a revolver to out of the way places, right enough, *and* a primus and a sleeping-bag and a supply of bug powder no doubt! But habit wouldn't make him bring the whole outfit down here! It's only in books people carry revolvers around as a matter of course."

Dr. Armstrong shook his head perplexedly.

They leaned over and watched Lombard's progress. His search was thorough and they could see at once that it was futile. Presently he came up over the edge of the cliff. He wiped the perspiration from his forehead.

"Well," he said. "We're up against it. It's the house or nowhere."

VI

The house was easily searched. They went through the few outbuildings first and then turned their attention to the building itself. Mrs. Rogers' yard measure discovered in the kitchen dresser assisted them. But there were no hidden spaces left unaccounted for. Everything was plain and straightforward, a modern structure devoid of concealments. They went through the ground floor first. As they mounted to the bedroom floor, they saw through the landing window Rogers carrying out a tray of cocktails to the terrace.

Philip Lombard said lightly:

"Wonderful animal, the good servant. Carries on with an impassive countenance."

Armstrong said appreciatively:

"Rogers is a first-class butler, I'll say that for him!"

Blore said:

"His wife was a pretty good cook, too. That dinner—last night—"

They turned in to the first bedroom.

Five minutes later they faced each other on the landing. No one hiding—no possible hiding place.

Blore said:

"There's a little stair here."

Dr. Armstrong said:

"It leads up to the servants' room."

Blore said:

"There must be a place under the roof—for cisterns, water tank, etc. It's the best chance—and the only one!"

And it was then, as they stood there, that they heard the sound from above. A soft furtive footfall overhead.

They all heard it. Armstrong grasped Blore's arm. Lombard held up an admonitory finger.

"Quiet—listen."

It came again—someone moving softly, furtively, overhead.

Armstrong whispered:

"He's actually in the bedroom itself. The room where Mrs. Rogers' body is."

Blore whispered back:

"Of course! Best hiding place he could have chosen! Nobody likely to go there. Now then—quiet as you can."

They crept stealthily upstairs.

On the little landing outside the door of the bedroom they paused again. Yes, someone was in the room. There was a faint creak from within.

Blore whispered:

"Now."

He flung open the door and rushed in, the other two close behind him.

Then all three stopped dead.

Rogers was in the room, his hands full of garments.

VII

Blore recovered himself first. He said:

"Sorry—er—Rogers. Heard someone moving about in here, and thought—well—"

He stopped.

Rogers said:

"I'm sorry, gentlemen. I was just moving my things. I take it there will be no objection if I take one of the vacant guest chambers on the floor below? The smallest room."

It was to Armstrong that he spoke and Armstrong replied:

"Of course. Of course. Get on with it."

He avoided looking at the sheeted figure lying on the bed.

Rogers said:

"Thank you, sir."

He went out of the room with his arm full of belongings and went down the stairs to the floor below.

Armstrong moved over to the bed and, lifting the sheet, looked down on the peaceful face of the dead woman. There was no fear there now. Just emptiness.

Armstrong said:

"Wish I'd got my stuff here. I'd like to know what drug it was."

Then he turned to the other two.

"Let's get finished. I feel it in my bones we're not going

to find anything."

Blore was wrestling with the bolts of a low manhole.

He said:

"That chap moves damned quietly. A minute or two ago we saw him in the garden. None of us heard him come upstairs."

Lombard said:

"I suppose that's why we assumed it must be a stranger moving about up here."

Blore disappeared into a cavernous darkness. Lombard pulled a torch from his pocket and followed.

Five minutes later three men stood on an upper landing and looked at each other. They were dirty and festooned with cobwebs and their faces were grim.

There was no one on the island but their eight selves.

Chapter 9

I

Lombard said slowly:

"So we've been wrong—wrong all along! Built up a nightmare of superstition and fantasy all because of the coincidence of two deaths!"

Armstrong said gravely:

"And yet, you know, the argument holds. Hang it all, I'm a doctor, I know something about suicides. Anthony Marston wasn't a suicidal type."

Lombard said doubtfully:

"It couldn't, I suppose, have been an accident?"

Blore snorted, unconvinced.

"Damned queer sort of accident," he grunted.

There was a pause, then Blore said:

"About the woman—" and stopped.

"Mrs. Rogers?"

"Yes. It's possible, isn't it, that that might have been an accident?"

Philip Lombard said:

"An accident? In what way?"

Blore looked slightly embarrassed. His red-brick face

grew a little deeper in hue. He said, almost blurting out the words:

"Look here, doctor, you did give her some dope, you know."

Armstrong stared at him.

"Dope? What do you mean?"

"Last night. You said yourself you'd give her something to make her sleep."

"Oh that, yes. A harmless sedative."

"What was it exactly?"

"I gave her a mild dose of trional. A perfectly harmless preparation."

Blore grew redder still. He said:

"Look here—not to mince matters—you didn't give her an overdose, did you?"

Dr. Armstrong said angrily:

"I don't know what you mean."

Blore said:

"It's possible, isn't it, that you may have made a mistake? These things do happen once in a while."

Armstrong said sharply:

"I did nothing of the sort. The suggestion is ridiculous." He stopped and added in a cold biting tone: "Or do you suggest that I gave her an overdose on purpose?"

Philip Lombard said quickly:

"Look here, you two, got to keep our heads. Don't let's start slinging accusations about."

Blore said sullenly:

"I only suggested the doctor had made a mistake."

Dr. Armstrong smiled with an effort. He said, showing his teeth in a somewhat mirthless smile:

"Doctors can't afford to make mistakes of that kind, my friend."

Blore said deliberately:

"It wouldn't be the first you've made—if that gramophone record is to be believed!"

Armstrong went white. Philip Lombard said quickly and angrily to Blore:

"What's the sense of making yourself offensive? We're all in the same boat. We've got to pull together. What about your own pretty little spot of perjury?"

Blore took a step forward, his hands clenched. He said in a thick voice:

"Perjury, be damned! That's a foul lie! You may try and shut me up, Mr. Lombard, but there's things I want to know—and one of them is about *you*!"

Lombard's eyebrows rose.

"About me?"

"Yes. I want to know why you brought a revolver down here on a pleasant social visit?"

Lombard said:

"You do, do you?"

"Yes, I do, Mr. Lombard."

Lombard said unexpectedly:

"You know, Blore, you're not nearly such a fool as you look."

"That's as may be. What about that revolver?"

Lombard smiled.

"I brought it because I expected to run into a spot of trouble."

Blore said suspiciously:

"You didn't tell us that last night."

Lombard shook his head.

"You were holding out on us?" Blore persisted.

"In a way, yes," said Lombard.

"Well, come on, out with it."

Lombard said slowly:

"I allowed you all to think that I was asked here in the same way as most of the others. That's not quite true. As a matter of fact I was approached by a little Jew-boy—Morris his name was. He offered me a hundred guineas to come down here and keep my eyes open—said I'd got a reputation for being a good man in a tight place."

"Well?" Blore prompted impatiently.

Lombard said with a grin:

"That's all."

Dr. Armstrong said:

"But surely he told you more than that?"

"Oh no, he didn't. Just shut up like a clam. I could take it or leave it—those were his words. I was hard up. I took it."

Blore looked unconvinced. He said:

"Why didn't you tell us all this last night?"

"My dear man—" Lombard shrugged eloquent shoulders. "How was I to know that last night wasn't exactly the eventuality I was here to cope with? I lay low and told a noncommittal story."

Dr. Armstrong said shrewdly:

"But now—you think differently?"

Lombard's face changed. It darkened and hardened. He said:

"Yes, I believe now that I'm in the same boat as the rest of you. That hundred guineas was just Mr. Owen's little bit of cheese to get me into the trap along with the rest of you."

He said slowly:

"*For we are in a trap*—I'll take my oath on that! Mrs. Rogers' death! Tony Marston's! The disappearing soldier boys on the dinner table! Oh yes, Mr. Owen's hand is plainly seen—*but where the devil is Mr. Owen himself?*"

Downstairs the gong pealed a solemn call to lunch.

II

Rogers was standing by the dining room door. As the three men descended the stairs he moved a step or two forward. He said in a low anxious voice:

"I hope lunch will be satisfactory. There is cold ham and cold tongue, and I've boiled some potatoes. And there's cheese and biscuits, and some tinned fruits."

Lombard said:

"Sounds all right. Stores are holding out, then?"

"There is plenty of food, sir—of a tinned variety. The larder is very well stocked. A necessity, that, I should say, sir, on an island where one may be cut off from the mainland for a considerable period."

Lombard nodded.

Rogers murmured as he followed the three men into the dining room:

"It worries me that Fred Narracott hasn't been over today. It's peculiarly unfortunate, as you might say."

"Yes," said Lombard, "peculiarly unfortunate describes it very well."

Miss Brent came into the room. She had just dropped a ball of wool and was carefully rewinding the end of it.

As she took her seat at table she remarked:

"The weather is changing. The wind is quite strong and there are white horses on the sea."

Mr. Justice Wargrave came in. He walked with a slow measured tread. He darted quick looks from under his bushy eyebrows at the other occupants of the dining-room. He said:

"You have had an active morning."

There was a faint malicious pleasure in his voice.

Vera Claythorne hurried in. She was a little out of breath. She said quickly:

"I hope you didn't wait for me. Am I late?"

Emily Brent said:

"You're not the last. The General isn't here yet."

They sat round the table.

Rogers addressed Miss Brent.

"Will you begin, Madam, or will you wait?"

Vera said:

"General Macarthur is sitting right down by the sea. I don't expect he would hear the gong there and anyway"—she hesitated—"he's a little vague today, I think."

Rogers said quickly:

"I will go down and inform him luncheon is ready."

Dr. Armstrong jumped up.

"I'll go," he said. "You others start lunch."

He left the room. Behind him he heard Rogers' voice.

"Will you take cold tongue or cold ham, Madam?"

III

The five people sitting round the table seemed to find conversation difficult. Outside, sudden gusts of wind came up and died away.

Vera shivered a little and said:

"There is a storm coming."

Blore made a contribution to the discourse. He said conversationally:

"There was an old fellow in the train from Plymouth yesterday. *He* kept saying a storm was coming. Wonderful how they know weather, these old salts."

Rogers went round the table collecting the meat plates.

Suddenly, with the plates held in his hands, he stopped. He said in an odd scared voice:

"There's somebody running..."

They could all hear it—running feet along the terrace.

In that minute, they knew—knew without being told...

As by common accord, they all rose to their feet. They stood looking towards the door.

Dr. Armstrong appeared, his breath coming fast.

He said:

"General Macarthur—"

"Dead!" The voice burst from Vera explosively.

Armstrong said:

"Yes, he's dead..."

There was a pause—a long pause.

Seven people looked at each other and could find no words to say.

IV

The storm broke just as the old man's body was borne in through the door.

The others were standing in the hall.

There was a sudden hiss and roar as the rain came down.

As Blore and Armstrong passed up the stairs with their burden, Vera Claythorne turned suddenly and went into the deserted dining room.

It was as they had left it. The sweet course stood ready on the sideboard untasted.

Vera went up to the table. She was there a minute or two later when Rogers came softly into the room.

He started when he saw her. Then his eyes asked a question.

He said:

"Oh, Miss, I—I just came to see..."

In a loud harsh voice that surprised herself Vera said:

"You're quite right, Rogers. Look for yourself. *There are only seven*..."

V

General Macarthur had been laid on his bed.

After making a last examination Armstrong left the room and came downstairs. He found the others assembled in the drawing room.

Miss Brent was knitting. Vera Claythorne was standing by the window looking out at the hissing rain. Blore was sitting squarely in a chair, his hands on his knees. Lombard was walking restlessly up and down. At the far end of the room Mr. Justice Wargrave was sitting in a grandfather chair. His eyes were half closed.

They opened as the doctor came into the room. He said in a clear penetrating voice:

"Well, doctor?"

Armstrong was very pale. He said:

"No question of heart failure or anything like that. Macarthur was hit with a life preserver or some such thing on the back of the head."

A little murmur went round, but the clear voice of the judge was raised once more.

"Did you find the actual weapon used?"

"No."

"Nevertheless you are sure of your facts?"

"I am quite sure."

Mr. Justice Wargrave said quietly:

"We know now exactly where we are."

There was no doubt now who was in charge of the situation. This morning Wargrave had sat huddled in his chair on the terrace refraining from any overt activity. Now he assumed command with the ease born of a long habit of authority. He definitely presided over the court.

Clearing his throat, he once more spoke.

"This morning, gentlemen, whilst I was sitting on the terrace, I was an observer of your activities. There could be little doubt of your purpose. You were searching the island for an unknown murderer?"

"Quite right, sir," said Philip Lombard.

The judge went on.

"You had come, doubtless, to the same conclusion that I had—namely that the deaths of Anthony Marston and Mrs. Rogers were neither accidental nor were they suicides. No doubt you also reached a certain conclusion as to the purpose of Mr. Owen in enticing us to this island?"

Blore said hoarsely:

"He's a madman! A loony."

The judge coughed.

"That almost certainly. But it hardly affects the issue. Our main preoccupation is this—to save our lives."

Armstrong said in a trembling voice:

"There's no one on the island, I tell you. *No one!*"

The judge stroked his jaw.

He said gently:

"In the sense you mean, no. I came to that conclusion early this morning. I could have told you that your search would be fruitless. Nevertheless I am strongly of the opinion that 'Mr. Owen' (to give him the name he himself has adopted) *is* on the island. Very much so. Given the scheme in question which is neither more nor less than the execution of justice upon certain individuals for offences which the law cannot touch, *there is only one way in which that scheme could be accomplished.* Mr. Owen could only come to the island in one way.

"It is perfectly clear. *Mr. Owen is one of us...*"

VI

"Oh, no, no, no..."

It was Vera who burst out—almost in a moan. The judge turned a keen eye on her.

He said:

"My dear young lady, this is no time for refusing to look facts in the face. We are all in grave danger. One of us is U.N. Owen. And we do not know which of us. Of the ten people who came to this island three are definitely cleared. Anthony Marston, Mrs. Rogers, and General Macarthur have gone beyond suspicion. There are seven of us left. Of those seven, one is, if I may so express myself, a bogus little soldier boy."

He paused—and looked round.

"Do I take it that you all agree?"

Armstrong said:

"It's fantastic—but I suppose you're right."

Blore said:

"Not a doubt of it. And if you ask me, I've a very good idea—"

A quick gesture of Mr. Justice Wargrave's hand stopped him. The judge said quietly:

"We will come to that presently. At the moment all I wish to establish is that we are in agreement on the facts."

Emily Brent, still knitting, said:

"Your argument seems logical. I agree that one of us is possessed by a devil."

Vera murmured:

"I can't believe it ... I can't ..."

Wargrave said:

"Lombard?"

"I agree, sir, absolutely."

The judge nodded his head in a satisfied manner. He said:

"Now let us examine the evidence. To begin with, is there any reason for suspecting one particular person? Mr. Blore, you have, I think, something to say."

Blore was breathing hard. He said:

"Lombard's got a revolver. He didn't tell the truth—last night. He admits it."

Philip Lombard smiled scornfully.

He said:

"I suppose I'd better explain again."

He did so, telling the story briefly and succinctly.

Blore said sharply:

"What's to prove it? There's nothing to corroborate your story."

The judge coughed.

"Unfortunately," he said, "we are all in that position. There is only our own word to go upon."

He leaned forward.

"You have none of you yet grasped what a very peculiar situation this is. To my mind there is only one course of procedure to adopt. Is there any one whom we can definitely eliminate from suspicion on the evidence which is in our possession?"

Dr. Armstrong said quickly:

"I am a well-known professional man. The mere idea that I can be suspected of—"

Again a gesture of the judge's hand arrested a speaker before he finished his speech. Mr. Justice Wargrave said in his small clear voice:

"I, too, am a well-known person! But, my dear sir, that proves less than nothing! Doctors have gone mad before now. Judges have gone mad. So," he added, looking at Blore, "have policemen!"

Lombard said:

"At any rate, I suppose you'll leave the women out of it."

The judge's eyebrows rose. He said in the famous "acid" tone that Counsel knew so well:

"Do I understand you to assert that women are not subject to homicidal mania?"

Lombard said irritably:

"Of course not. But all the same, it hardly seems possible—"

He stopped. Mr. Justice Wargrave still in the same thin sour voice addressed Armstrong.

"I take it, Dr. Armstrong, that a woman would have been physically capable of striking the blow that killed poor Macarthur?"

The doctor said calmly:

"Perfectly capable—given a suitable instrument, such as a rubber truncheon or cosh."

"It would require no undue exertion of force?"

"Not at all."

Mr. Justice Wargrave wriggled his tortoise-like neck. He said:

"The other two deaths have resulted from the administration of drugs. That, no one will dispute, is easily compassed by a person of the smallest physical strength."

Vera cried angrily:

"I think you're mad!"

His eyes turned slowly till they rested on her. It was the dispassionate stare of a man well used to weighing humanity in the balance. She thought:

"He's just seeing me as a—as a specimen. And"—the thought came to her with real surprise—"he doesn't like me much!"

In measured tones the judge was saying:

"My dear young lady, do try and restrain your feelings. I am not accusing you." He bowed to Miss Brent. "I hope, Miss Brent, that you are not offended by my insistence that *all* of us are equally under suspicion?"

Emily Brent was knitting. She did not look up. In a cold voice she said:

"The idea that I should be accused of taking a fellow creature's life—not to speak of the lives of *three* fellow creatures—is of course, quite absurd to any one who knows anything of my character. But I quite appreciate the fact that we are all strangers to one another and that, in those circumstances, nobody can be exonerated without the fullest proof. There is, as I have said, a devil amongst us."

The judge said:

"Then we are agreed. There can be no elimination on the ground of character or position alone."

Lombard said: "What about Rogers?"

The judge looked at him unblinkingly.

"What about him?"

Lombard said:

"Well, to my mind, Rogers seems pretty well ruled out."

Mr. Justice Wargrave said:

"Indeed, and on what grounds?"

Lombard said:

"He hasn't got the brains for one thing. And for another his wife was one of the victims."

The judge's heavy eyebrows rose once more. He said:

"In my time, young man, several people have come before me accused of the murders of their wives—*and* have been found guilty."

"Oh! I agree. Wife murder is perfectly possible—almost natural, let's say! But not this particular kind! I can believe in Rogers killing his wife because he was scared of her breaking down and giving him away, or because he'd taken a dislike to her, or because he wanted to link up with some nice little bit rather less long in the tooth. But I can't see him as the lunatic Mr. Owen dealing out crazy justice and starting on his own wife for a crime they both committed."

Mr. Justice Wargrave said:

"You are assuming hearsay to be evidence. We do not know that Rogers and his wife conspired to murder their employer. That may have been a false statement, made so that Rogers should appear to be in the same position as ourselves. Mrs. Rogers' terror last night may have been due to the fact that she realized her husband was mentally unhinged."

Lombard said:

"Well, have it your own way. U.N. Owen is one of us. No exceptions allowed. We all qualify."

Mr. Justice Wargrave said:

"My point is that there can be no exceptions allowed on the score of *character, position,* or *probability*. What we must now examine is the possibility of eliminating one or more persons on the *facts*. To put it simply, is there among us one or more persons who could not possibly have administered either cyanide to Anthony Marston, or an overdose of sleeping draught to Mrs. Rogers, and who had no opportunity of striking the blow that killed General Macarthur?"

Blore's rather heavy face lit up. He leant forward.

"Now you're talking, sir!" he said. "That's the stuff! Let's go into it. As regards young Marston I don't think there's anything to be done. It's already been suggested that some one from outside slipped something into the dregs of his glass before he refilled it for the last time. A person actually in the room could have done that even more easily. I can't remember if Rogers was in the room, but any of the rest of us could certainly have done it."

He paused, then went on.

"Now take the woman Rogers. The people who stand out there are her husband and the doctor. Either of them could have done it as easy as winking—"

Armstrong sprang to his feet. He was trembling.

"I protest—this is absolutely uncalled for! I swear that the dose I gave the woman was perfectly—"

"Dr. Armstrong."

The small sour voice was compelling. The doctor stopped with a jerk in the middle of his sentence. The small cold voice went on.

"Your indignation is very natural. Nevertheless you must admit that the facts have got to be faced. Either you or Rogers *could* have administered a fatal dose with the greatest ease. Let us now consider the position of the other people present. What chance had I, had Inspector Blore, had Miss Brent, had Miss Claythorne, had Mr. Lombard of administering poison? Can any one of us be completely and entirely eliminated?" He paused. "I think not."

Vera said angrily:

"I was nowhere near the woman! All of you can swear to that."

Mr. Justice Wargrave waited a minute, then he said:

"As far as my memory serves me the facts were these—will any one please correct me if I make a misstatement? Mrs. Rogers was lifted onto the sofa by Anthony Marston and Mr. Lombard and Dr. Armstrong went to her. He sent Rogers for brandy. There was then a question raised as to where the voice we had just heard had come from. We all went into the next room with the exception of Miss Brent who remained in this room—alone with the unconscious woman."

A spot of colour came into Emily Brent's cheeks. She stopped knitting. She said:

"This is outrageous!"

The remorseless small voice went on.

"When we returned to this room, you, Miss Brent, were bending over the woman on the sofa."

Emily Brent said:

"Is common humanity a criminal offence?"

Mr. Justice Wargrave said:

"I am only establishing facts. Rogers then entered the room with the brandy which, of course, he could quite well have doctored before entering the room. The brandy was administered to the woman and shortly afterwards her husband and Dr. Armstrong assisted her up to bed where Dr. Armstrong gave her a sedative."

Blore said:

"That's what happened. Absolutely. And that lets out the judge, Mr. Lombard, myself and Miss Claythorne."

His voice was loud and jubilant. Mr. Justice Wargrave, bringing a cold eye to bear upon him, murmured:

"Ah, but does it? We must take into account *every possible eventuality.*"

Blore stared. He said:

"I don't get you."

Mr. Justice Wargrave said:

"Upstairs in her room, Mrs. Rogers is lying in bed. The sedative that the doctor has given her begins to take effect. She is vaguely sleepy and acquiescent. Supposing that at that moment there is a tap on the door and someone enters bringing her, shall we say, a tablet, or a draught, with the message that 'The doctor says you're to take this.' Do you imagine for one minute that she would not have swallowed it obediently without thinking twice about it?"

There was a silence. Blore shifted his feet and frowned. Philip Lombard said:

"I don't believe in that story for a minute. Besides none of us left this room for hours afterwards. There was Marston's death and all the rest of it."

The judge said:

"Someone could have left his or her bedroom—later."

Lombard objected:

"But then Rogers would have been up there."

Dr. Armstrong stirred.

"No," he said. "Rogers went downstairs to clear up in the dining room and pantry. Anyone could have gone up to the woman's bedroom then without being seen."

Emily Brent said:

"Surely, doctor, the woman would have been fast asleep by then under the influence of the drug you had administered?"

"In all likelihood, yes. But it is not a certainty. Until you have prescribed for a patient more than once you cannot tell their reaction to different drugs. There is, sometimes, a considerable period before a sedative takes effect. It depends on the personal idiosyncrasy of the patient towards that particular drug."

Lombard said:

"Of course you *would* say that, doctor. Suits your book—eh?"

Again Armstrong's face darkened with anger.

But again that passionless cold little voice stopped the words on his lips.

"No good result can come from recrimination. Facts are what we have to deal with. It is established, I think, that there is a possibility of such a thing as I have outlined occurring. I agree that its probability value is not high; though there again, it depends on who that person might have been. The appearance of Miss Brent or of Miss Claythorne on such an errand would have occasioned no surprise in the patient's mind. I agree that the appearance of myself, or of Mr. Blore, or of Mr. Lombard would have been, to say the least of it, unusual, but I still think the visit would have been received without the awakening of any real suspicion."

Blore said:

"And that gets us—*where?*"

VII

Mr. Justice Wargrave, stroking his lip and looking quite passionless and inhuman, said:

"We have now dealt with the second killing, and have established the fact that no one of us can be completely exonerated from suspicion."

He paused and went on.

"We come now to the death of General Macarthur. That took place this morning. I will ask anyone who considers that he or she has an alibi to state it in so many words. I myself will state at once that I have no valid alibi. I spent the morning sitting on the terrace and meditating on the singular position in which we all find ourselves.

"I sat on that chair on the terrace for the whole morning until the gong went, but there were, I should imagine, several periods during the morning when I was quite unobserved and during which it would have been possible for me to walk down to the sea, kill the General, and return to my chair. There is only my word for the fact that I never left the terrace. In the circumstances that is not enough. There must be *proof*."

Blore said:

"I was with Mr. Lombard and Dr. Armstrong all the morning. They'll bear me out."

Dr. Armstrong said:

"You went to the house for a rope."

Blore said:

"Of course, I did. Went straight there and straight back. You know I did."

Armstrong said:

"You were a long time..."

Blore turned crimson. He said:

"What the hell do you mean by that, Dr. Armstrong?"

Armstrong repeated:

"I only said you were a long time."

"Had to find it, didn't I? Can't lay your hands on a coil of rope all in a minute."

Mr. Justice Wargrave said:

"During Inspector Blore's absence, were you two gentlemen together?"

Armstrong said hotly:

"Certainly. That is, Lombard went off for a few minutes. I remained where I was."

Lombard said with a smile:

"I wanted to test the possibilities of heliographing to the mainland. Wanted to find the best spot. I was only absent a minute or two."

Armstrong nodded. He said:

"That's right. Not long enough to do a murder, I assure you."

The judge said:

"Did either of you two glance at your watches?"

"Well, no."

Philip Lombard said:

"I wasn't wearing one."

The judge said evenly:

"A minute or two is a vague expression."

He turned his head to the upright figure with the knitting lying on her lap.

"Miss Brent?"

Emily Brent said:

"I took a walk with Miss Claythorne up to the top of the island. Afterwards I sat on the terrace in the sun."

The judge said:

"I don't think I noticed you there."

"No, I was round the corner of the house to the east. It was out of the wind there."

"And you sat there till lunchtime?"

"Yes."

"Miss Claythorne?"

Vera answered readily and clearly.

"I was with Miss Brent early this morning. After that I wandered about a bit. Then I went down and talked to General Macarthur."

Mr. Justice Wargrave interrupted. He said:

"What time was that?"

Vera for the first time was vague. She said:

"I don't know. About an hour before lunch, I think—or it might have been less."

Blore asked:

"Was it after we'd spoken to him or before?"

Vera said:

"I don't know. He—he was very queer."

She shivered.

"In what way was he queer?" the judge wanted to know.

Vera said in a low voice:

"He said we were all going to die—he said he was waiting for the end. He—he frightened me..."

The judge nodded. He said:

"What did you do next?"

"I went back to the house. Then, just before lunch, I went out again and up behind the house. I've been terribly restless all day."

Mr. Justice Wargrave stroked his chin. He said:

"There remains Rogers. Though I doubt if his evidence will add anything to our sum of knowledge."

Rogers, summoned before the court, had very little to tell. He had been busy all the morning about household duties and with the preparation of lunch. He had taken cocktails onto the terrace before lunch and had then gone up to remove his things from the attic to another room. He had not looked out of the window during the morning and had seen nothing that could have any bearing upon the death of General Macarthur. He would swear definitely that there had been eight china figures upon the dining table when he laid the table for lunch.

At the conclusion of Rogers' evidence there was a pause.

Mr. Justice Wargrave cleared his throat.

Lombard murmured to Vera Claythorne:

"The summing up will now take place!"

The judge said:

"We have inquired into the circumstances of these three deaths to the best of our ability. Whilst probability in some cases is against certain people being implicated, yet we cannot say definitely that any one person can be considered as cleared of all complicity. I reiterate my positive belief that of the seven persons assembled in this room one is a dangerous and probably insane criminal. There is no evidence before us as to who that person is. All we can do at the present juncture is to consider what measures we can take for communicating with the mainland for help, and in the event of help being delayed (as is only too possible given the state of the weather) what measures we must adopt to ensure our safety.

"I would ask you all to consider this carefully and to give me any suggestions that may occur to you. In the meantime I warn everybody to be upon his or her guard. So far the murderer has had an easy task, since his victims have been unsuspicious. From now on, it is our task to suspect each and every one amongst us. Forewarned is forearmed. Take no risks and be alert to danger. That is all."

Philip Lombard murmured beneath his breath:

"The court will now adjourn . . ."

Chapter 10

I

"Do you believe it?" Vera asked.

She and Philip Lombard sat on the windowsill of the living room. Outside the rain poured down and the wind howled in great shuddering gusts against the windowpanes.

Philip Lombard cocked his head slightly on one side before answering. Then he said:

"You mean, do I believe that old Wargrave is right when he says it's one of us?"

"Yes."

Philip Lombard said slowly:

"It's difficult to say. Logically, you know, he's right, and yet—"

Vera took the words out of his mouth.

"And yet it seems so incredible!"

Philip Lombard made a grimace.

"The whole thing's incredible! But after Macarthur's death there's no more doubt as to one thing. There's no question now of accidents or suicides. It's definitely murder. Three murders up to date."

Vera shivered. She said:

"It's like some awful dream. I keep feeling that things like this *can't* happen!"

He said with understanding:

"I know. Presently a tap will come on the door, and early morning tea will be brought in."

Vera said:

"Oh, how I wish that could happen!"

Philip Lombard said gravely:

"Yes, but it won't! We're all in the dream! And we've got to be pretty much upon our guard from now on."

Vera said, lowering her voice:

"If—if it *is* one of them—which do you think it is?"

Philip Lombard grinned suddenly. He said:

"I take it you are excepting our two selves? Well, that's all right. I know very well that I'm not the murderer, and I don't fancy that there's anything insane about you, Vera. You strike me as being one of the sanest and most level-headed girls I've come across. I'd stake my reputation on your sanity."

With a slightly wry smile, Vera said:

"Thank you."

He said: "Come now, Miss Vera Claythorne, aren't you going to return the compliment?"

Vera hesitated a minute, then she said:

"You've admitted, you know, that you don't hold human life particularly sacred, but all the same I can't see you as—

as the man who dictated that gramophone record."

Lombard said:

"Quite right. If I were to commit one or more murders it would be solely for what I could get out of them. This mass clearance isn't my line of country. Good, then we'll eliminate ourselves and concentrate on our five fellow prisoners. Which of them is U.N. Owen. Well, at a guess, and with absolutely nothing to go upon, I'd plump for Wargrave!"

"Oh!" Vera sounded surprised. She thought a minute or two and then said, "Why?"

"Hard to say exactly. But to begin with, he's an old man and he's been presiding over courts of law for years. That is to say, he's played God Almighty for a good many months every year. That must go to a man's head eventually. He gets to see himself as all powerful, as holding the power of life and death—and it's possible that his brain might snap and he might want to go one step farther and be Executioner and Judge Extraordinary."

Vera said slowly:

"Yes, I suppose that's *possible* . . ."

Lombard said:

"Who do you plump for?"

Without any hesitation Vera answered:

"Dr. Armstrong."

Lombard gave a low whistle.

"The doctor, eh? You know, I should have put him last of

all."

Vera shook her head.

"Oh no! Two of the deaths have been poison. That rather points to a doctor. And then you can't get over the fact that the only thing we are absolutely certain Mrs. Rogers had was the sleeping draught that *he* gave her."

Lombard admitted:

"Yes, that's true."

Vera persisted:

"If a doctor went mad, it would be a long time before any one suspected. And doctors overwork and have a lot of strain."

Philip Lombard said:

"Yes but I doubt if he could have killed Macarthur. He wouldn't have had time during that brief interval when I left him—not, that is, unless he fairly hared down there and back again, and I doubt if he's in good enough training to do that and show no signs of it."

Vera said:

"He didn't do it then. He had an opportunity later."

"When?"

"When he went down to call the General to lunch."

Philip whistled again very softly. He said:

"So you think he did it then? Pretty cool thing to do."

Vera said impatiently:

"What risk was there? He's the only person here with medical knowledge. He can swear the body's been dead at least an hour and who's to contradict him?"

Philip looked at her thoughtfully.

"You know," he said, "that's a clever idea of yours. I wonder—"

II

"Who is it, Mr. Blore? That's what I want to know. Who is it?"

Rogers' face was working. His hands were clenched round the polishing leather that he held in his hand.

Ex-Inspector Blore said:

"Eh, my lad, that's the question!"

"One of us, 'is lordship said. Which one? That's what I want to know. Who's the fiend in 'uman form?"

"That," said Blore, "is what we all would like to know."

Rogers said shrewdly:

"But you've got an idea, Mr. Blore. You've got an idea, 'aven't you?"

"I may have an idea," said Blore slowly. "But that's a long way from being sure. I may be wrong. All I can say is that if I'm right the person in question is a very cool customer—a very cool customer indeed."

Rogers wiped the perspiration from his forehead. He said hoarsely:

"It's like a bad dream, that's what it is."

Blore said, looking at him curiously:

"Got any ideas yourself, Rogers?"

The butler shook his head. He said hoarsely:

"I don't know. I don't know at all. And that's what's frightening the life out of me. To have no idea..."

III

Dr. Armstrong said violently:

"We must get out of here—we must—we must! At all costs!"

Mr. Justice Wargrave looked thoughtfully out of the smoking room window. He played with the cord of his eye-glasses. He said:

"I do not, of course, profess to be a weather prophet. But I should say that it is very unlikely that a boat could reach us—even if they knew of our plight—under twenty-four hours—and even then only if the wind drops."

Dr. Armstrong dropped his head in his hands and groaned.

He said:

"And in the meantime we may all be murdered in our beds?"

"I hope not," said Mr. Justice Wargrave. "I intend to take every possible precaution against such a thing happening."

It flashed across Dr. Armstrong's mind that an old man

like the judge was far more tenacious of life than a younger man would be. He had often marvelled at that fact in his professional career. Here was he, junior to the judge by perhaps twenty years, and yet with a vastly inferior sense of self-preservation.

Mr. Justice Wargrave was thinking:

"Murdered in our beds! These doctors are all the same—they think in *clichés*. A thoroughly commonplace mind."

The doctor said:

"There have been three victims already, remember."

"Certainly. But you must remember that they were unprepared for the attack. We are forewarned."

Dr. Armstrong said bitterly:

"What can we do? Sooner or later—"

"I think," said Mr. Justice Wargrave, "that there are several things we can do."

Armstrong said:

"We've no idea, even, who it can be—"

The judge stroked his chin and murmured:

"Oh, you know, I wouldn't quite say that."

Armstrong stared at him.

"Do you mean you *know*?"

Mr. Justice Wargrave said cautiously:

"As regards actual evidence, such as is necessary in court, I admit that I have none. But it appears to me, reviewing the whole business, that one particular person is sufficiently clearly indicated. Yes, I think so."

Armstrong stared at him.

He said:

"I don't understand."

IV

Miss Brent was upstairs in her bedroom.

She took up her Bible and went to sit by the window.

She opened it. Then, after a minute's hesitation, she set it aside and went over to the dressing table. From a drawer in it she took out a small black-covered notebook.

She opened it and began writing.

"A terrible thing has happened. General Macarthur is dead. (His cousin married Elsie MacPherson.) There is no doubt but that he was murdered. After luncheon the judge made us a most interesting speech. He is convinced that the murderer is one of us. That means that one of us is possessed by a devil. I had already suspected that. Which of us is it? They are all asking themselves that. I alone know ..."

She sat for some time without moving. Her eyes grew vague and filmy. The pencil straggled drunkenly in her fingers. In shaking loose capitals she wrote:

THE MURDERER'S NAME IS BEATRICE

TAYLOR...

Her eyes closed.

Suddenly, with a start, she awoke. She looked down at the notebook. With an angry exclamation she scored through the vague unevenly scrawled characters of the last sentence.

She said in a low voice:

"Did *I* write that? Did I? *I must be going mad ...*"

V

The storm increased. The wind howled against the side of the house.

Every one was in the living room. They sat listlessly huddled together. And, surreptitiously, they watched each other.

When Rogers brought in the tea tray, they all jumped. He said:

"Shall I draw the curtains? It would make it more cheerful like."

Receiving an assent to this, the curtains were drawn and the lamps turned on. The room grew more cheerful. A little of the shadow lifted. Surely, by tomorrow, the storm would be over and someone would come—a boat would arrive ...

Vera Claythorne said:

"Will you pour out tea, Miss Brent?"

The elder woman replied:

"No, you do it, dear. That teapot is so heavy. And I have lost two skeins of my grey knitting wool. So annoying."

Vera moved to the tea table. There was a cheerful rattle and clink of china. Normality returned.

Tea! Blessed ordinary everyday afternoon tea! Philip Lombard made a cheery remark. Blore responded. Dr. Armstrong told a humorous story. Mr. Justice Wargrave, who ordinarily hated tea, sipped approvingly.

Into this relaxed atmosphere came Rogers.

And Rogers was upset. He said nervously and at random:

"Excuse me, sir, but does any one know what's become of the bathroom curtain?"

Lombard's head went up with a jerk.

"The bathroom curtain? What the devil do you mean, Rogers?"

"It's gone, sir, clean vanished. I was going round drawing all the curtains and the one in the lav—bathroom wasn't there any longer."

Mr. Justice Wargrave asked:

"Was it there this morning?"

"Oh yes, sir."

Blore said:

"What kind of a curtain was it?"

"Scarlet oilsilk, sir. It went with the scarlet tiles."

Lombard said:

"And it's gone?"

"Gone, sir."

They stared at each other.

Blore said heavily:

"Well—after all—what of it? It's mad—but so's everything else. Anyway it doesn't matter. You can't kill anybody with an oilsilk curtain. Forget about it."

Rogers said:

"Yes, sir, thank you, sir."

He went out shutting the door behind him.

Inside the room, the pall of fear had fallen anew.

Again, surreptitiously, they watched each other.

VI

Dinner came, was eaten, and cleared away. A simple meal, mostly out of tins.

Afterwards, in the living room, the strain was almost too great to be borne.

At nine o'clock, Emily Brent rose to her feet.

She said:

"I'm going to bed."

Vera said:

"I'll go to bed too."

The two women went up the stairs and Lombard and Blore came with them. Standing at the top of the stairs, the two men watched the women go into their respective rooms and shut the doors. They heard the sound of two bolts being shot and the turning of two keys.

Blore said with a grin:

"No need to tell 'em to lock their doors!"

Lombard said:

"Well, *they*'re all right for the night, at any rate!"

He went down again and the other followed him.

VII

The four men went to bed an hour later. They went up together. Rogers, from the dining room where he was setting the table for breakfast, saw them go up. He heard them pause on the landing above.

Then the judge's voice spoke.

"I need hardly advise you, gentlemen, to lock your doors."

Blore said:

"And what's more, put a chair under the handle. There are ways of turning locks from the outside."

Lombard murmured:

"My dear Blore, the trouble with you is you know too much!"

The judge said gravely:

"Good night, gentlemen. May we all meet safely in the morning!"

Rogers came out of the dining room and slipped halfway up the stairs. He saw four figures pass through four doors and heard the turning of four locks and the shooting of four bolts.

He nodded his head.

"That's all right," he muttered.

He went back into the dining room. Yes, everything was ready for the morning. His eye lingered on the centre plaque of looking glass and the seven little china figures.

A sudden grin transformed his face.

He murmured:

"I'll see no one plays tricks tonight, at any rate."

Crossing the room he locked the door to the pantry. Then going through the other door to the hall he pulled the door to, locked it and slipped the key into his pocket.

Then, extinguishing the lights, he hurried up the stairs and into his new bedroom.

There was only one possible hiding place in it, the tall wardrobe, and he looked into that immediately. Then, locking and bolting the door, he prepared for bed.

He said to himself:

"No more china-soldier tricks tonight. I've seen to that ..."

Chapter 11

I

Philip Lombard had the habit of waking at daybreak. He did so on this particular morning. He raised himself on an elbow and listened. The wind had somewhat abated but was still blowing. He could hear no sound of rain . . .

At eight o'clock the wind was blowing more strongly, but Lombard did not hear it. He was asleep again.

At nine-thirty he was sitting on the edge of his bed looking at his watch. He put it to his ear. Then his lips drew back from his teeth in that curious wolf-like smile characteristic of the man.

He said very softly:

"I think the time has come to do something about this."

At twenty-five minutes to ten he was tapping on the closed door of Blore's room.

The latter opened it cautiously. His hair was tousled and his eyes were still dim with sleep.

Philip Lombard said affably:

"Sleeping the clock round? Well, shows you've got an easy conscience."

Blore said shortly:

"What's the matter?"

Lombard answered:

"Anybody called you—or brought you any tea? Do you know what time it is?"

Blore looked over his shoulder at a small travelling clock by his bedside.

He said:

"Twenty-five to ten. Wouldn't have believed I could have slept like that. Where's Rogers?"

Philip Lombard said:

"It's a case of echo answers where."

"What d'you mean?" asked the other sharply.

Lombard said:

"I mean that Rogers is missing. He isn't in his room or anywhere else. And there's no kettle on and the kitchen fire isn't even lit."

Blore swore under his breath. He said:

"Where the devil can he be? Out on the island somewhere? Wait till I get some clothes on. See if the others know anything."

Philip Lombard nodded. He moved along the line of closed doors.

He found Armstrong up and nearly dressed. Mr. Justice Wargrave, like Blore, had to be roused from sleep. Vera Claythorne was dressed. Emily Brent's room was empty.

The little party moved through the house. Rogers' room, as Philip Lombard had already ascertained, was untenanted. The bed had been slept in, and his razor and sponge and soap were wet.

Lombard said:

"He got up all right."

Vera said in a low voice which she tried to make firm and assured:

"You don't think he's—hiding somewhere—waiting for us?"

Lombard said:

"My dear girl, I'm prepared to think anything of anyone! My advice is that we keep together until we find him."

Armstrong said:

"He must be out on the island somewhere."

Blore who had joined them, dressed, but still unshaved, said:

"Where's Miss Brent got to—that's another mystery?"

But as they arrived in the hall, Emily Brent came in through the front door. She had on a mackintosh. She said:

"The sea is as high as ever. I shouldn't think any boat could put out today."

Blore said:

"Have you been wandering about the island alone, Miss Brent? Don't you realize that that's an exceedingly foolish thing to do?"

Emily Brent said:

"I assure you, Mr. Blore, that I kept an extremely sharp look out."

Blore grunted. He said:

"Seen anything of Rogers?"

Miss Brent's eyebrows rose.

"Rogers? No, I haven't seen him this morning. Why?"

Mr. Justice Wargrave, shaved, dressed and with his false teeth in position, came down the stairs. He moved to the open dining room door. He said:

"He laid the table for breakfast, I see."

Lombard said:

"He might have done that last night."

They all moved inside the room, looking at the neatly set plates and cutlery. At the row of cups on the sideboard. At the felt mats placed ready for the coffee urn.

It was Vera who saw it first. She caught the judge's arm and the grip of her athletic fingers made the old gentleman wince.

She cried out:

"The soldiers! Look!"

There were only six china figures in the middle of the table.

II

They found him shortly afterwards.

He was in the little washhouse across the yard. He had been chopping sticks in preparation for lighting the kitchen fire. The small chopper was still in his hand. A bigger chopper, a heavy affair, was leaning against the door—the metal of it stained a dull brown. It corresponded only too well with the deep wound in the back of Rogers' head ...

III

"Perfectly clear," said Armstrong. "The murderer must have crept up behind him, swung the chopper once and brought it down on his head as he was bending over."

Blore was busy on the handle of the chopper and the flour sifter from the kitchen.

Mr. Justice Wargrave asked:

"Would it have needed great force, doctor?"

Armstrong said gravely:

"A woman could have done it if that's what you mean." He gave a quick glance round. Vera Claythorne and Emily Brent had retired to the kitchen. "The girl could have done it easily—she's an athletic type. In appearance Miss Brent is fragile-looking, but that type of woman has often a lot of wiry strength. And you must remember that anyone who's mentally unhinged has a good deal of unsuspected strength."

The judge nodded thoughtfully.

Blore rose from his knees with a sigh. He said:

"No fingerprints. Handle was wiped afterwards."

A sound of laughter was heard—they turned sharply. Vera Claythorne was standing in the yard. She cried out in a high shrill voice, shaken with wild bursts of laughter:

"Do they keep bees on this island? Tell me that. Where do we go for honey? Ha! ha!"

They stared at her uncomprehendingly. It was as though the sane well-balanced girl had gone mad before their eyes. She went on in that high unnatural voice:

"Don't stare like that! As though you thought I was mad. It's sane enough what I'm asking. Bees, hives, bees! Oh, don't you understand? Haven't you read that idiotic rhyme? It's up in all your bedrooms—put there for you to study! We might have come here straightaway if we'd had sense. *Seven little soldier boys chopping up sticks.* And the next verse. I know the whole thing by heart, I tell you! *Six little soldier boys playing with a hive.* And that's why I'm asking—do they keep bees on this island?—isn't it funny?—isn't it damned funny . . . ?"

She began laughing wildly again. Dr. Armstrong strode forward. He raised his hand and struck her a flat blow on the cheek.

She gasped, hiccuped—and swallowed. She stood motionless a minute, then she said:

"Thank you . . . I'm all right now."

Her voice was once more calm and controlled—the voice of the efficient games mistress.

She turned and went across the yard into the kitchen saying: "Miss Brent and I are getting you breakfast. Can you—bring some sticks to light the fire?"

The marks of the doctor's hand stood out red on her cheek.

As she went into the kitchen Blore said:

"Well, you dealt with that all right, doctor."

Armstrong said apologetically:

"Had to! We can't cope with hysteria on the top of everything else."

Philip Lombard said:

"She's not a hysterical type."

Armstrong agreed.

"Oh no. Good healthy sensible girl. Just the sudden shock. It might happen to anybody."

Rogers had chopped a certain amount of firewood before he had been killed. They gathered it up and took it into the kitchen. Vera and Emily Brent were busy, Miss Brent was raking out the stove. Vera was cutting the rind off the bacon.

Emily Brent said:

"Thank you. We'll be as quick as we can—say half an hour to three-quarters. The kettle's got to boil."

IV

Ex-Inspector Blore said in a low hoarse voice to Philip Lombard:

"Know what I'm thinking?"

Philip Lombard said:

"As you're just about to tell me, it's not worth the trouble of guessing."

Ex-Inspector Blore was an earnest man. A light touch was incomprehensible to him. He went on heavily:

"There was a case in America. Old gentleman and his wife—both killed with an axe. Middle of the morning. Nobody in the house but the daughter and the maid. Maid, it was proved, couldn't have done it. Daughter was a respectable middle-aged spinster. Seemed incredible. So incredible that they acquitted her. But they never found any other explanation." He paused. "I thought of that when I saw the axe—and then when I went into the kitchen and saw her there so neat and calm. Hadn't turned a hair! That girl, coming all over hysterical—well, that's natural—the sort of thing you'd expect—don't you think so?"

Philip Lombard said laconically:

"It might be."

Blore went on.

"But the other! So neat and prim—wrapped up in that apron—Mrs. Rogers' apron, I suppose—saying: 'Breakfast will be ready in half an hour or so.' If you ask me that woman's as mad as a hatter! Lots of elderly spinsters go that way—I don't mean go in for homicide on the grand scale, but go queer in their heads. Unfortunately it's taken her this way. Religious mania—thinks she's God's instrument, something of that kind! She sits in her room, you know, reading her Bible."

Philip Lombard sighed and said:

"That's hardly proof positive of an unbalanced mentality, Blore."

But Blore went on, ploddingly, perseveringly:

"And then she was out—in her mackintosh, said she'd been down to look at the sea."

The other shook his head.

He said:

"Rogers was killed as he was chopping firewood—that is to say first thing when he got up. The Brent woman wouldn't have needed to wander about outside for hours afterwards. If you ask me, the murderer of Rogers would take jolly good care to be rolled up in bed snoring."

Blore said:

"You're missing the point, Mr. Lombard. If the woman was innocent she'd be too dead scared to go wandering about by herself. She'd only do that *if she knew that she had nothing to fear.* That's to say *if she herself is the criminal.*"

Philip Lombard said:

"That's a good point . . . Yes, I hadn't thought of that."

He added with a faint grin:

"Glad you don't still suspect me."

Blore said rather shamefacedly:

"I did start by thinking of you—that revolver—and the queer story you told—or didn't tell. But I've realized now that that was really a bit too obvious." He paused and said: "Hope you feel the same about me."

Philip said thoughtfully:

"I may be wrong, of course, but I can't feel that you've got enough imagination for this job. All I can say is, if you're the criminal, you're a damned fine actor and I take my hat off to you." He lowered his voice. "Just between ourselves, Blore, and taking into account that we'll probably both be a couple of stiffs before another day is out, you did indulge in that spot of perjury, I suppose?"

Blore shifted uneasily from one foot to the other. He said at last:

"Doesn't seem to make much odds now. Oh well, here goes, Landor was innocent right enough. The gang had got me squared and between us we got him put away for a stretch. Mind you, I wouldn't admit this—"

"If there were any witnesses," finished Lombard with a grin. "It's just between you and me. Well, I hope you made a tidy bit out of it."

"Didn't make what I should have done. Mean crowd, the Purcell gang. I got my promotion, though."

"And Landor got penal servitude and died in prison."

"I couldn't know he was going to die, could I?" demanded Blore.

"No, that was your bad luck."

"Mine? His, you mean."

"Yours, too. Because, as a result of it, it looks as though your own life is going to be cut unpleasantly short."

"Me?" Blore stared at him. "Do you think I'm going to go the way of Rogers and the rest of them? Not me! I'm watching out for myself pretty carefully, I can tell you."

Lombard said:

"Oh, well—I'm not a betting man. And anyway if you were dead I wouldn't get paid."

"Look here, Mr. Lombard, what do you mean?"

Philip Lombard showed his teeth. He said:

"I mean, my dear Blore, that in my opinion you haven't got a chance!"

"What?"

"Your lack of imagination is going to make you absolutely a sitting target. A criminal of the imagination of U.N. Owen can make rings round you any time he—or she—wants to."

Blore's face went crimson. He demanded angrily:

"And what about you?"

Philip Lombard's face went hard and dangerous.

He said:

"I've a pretty good imagination of my own. I've been in tight places before now and got out of them! I think—I won't say more than that but I *think* I'll get out of this one."

V

The eggs were in the frying pan. Vera, toasting bread, thought to herself:

"Why did I make a hysterical fool of myself? That was a mistake. Keep calm, my girl, keep calm."

After all, she'd always prided herself on her levelheadedness!

"*Miss Claythorne was wonderful—kept her head—started off swimming after Cyril at once.*"

Why think of that now? All that was over—over . . . Cyril had disappeared long before she got near the rock. She had felt the current take her, sweeping her out to sea. She had let herself go with it—swimming quietly, floating—till the boat arrived at last . . .

They had praised her courage and her *sang-froid* . . .

But not Hugo. Hugo had just—looked at her . . .

God, how it hurt, even now, to think of Hugo . . .

Where was he? What was he doing? Was he engaged—married?

Emily Brent said sharply:

"Vera, that toast is burning."

"Oh sorry, Miss Brent, so it is. How stupid of me."

Emily Brent lifted out the last egg from the sizzling fat.

Vera, putting a fresh piece of toast on the toasting-fork, said curiously:

"You're wonderfully calm, Miss Brent."

Emily Brent said, pressing her lips together:

"I was brought up to keep my head and never to make a fuss."

Vera thought mechanically:

"Repressed as a child... That accounts for a lot..."

She said:

"Aren't you afraid?"

She paused and then added:

"Or don't you mind dying?"

Dying! It was as though a sharp little gimlet had run into the solid congealed mass of Emily Brent's brain. Dying? But *she* wasn't going to die! The others would die—yes—but not she, Emily Brent. This girl didn't understand! Emily wasn't afraid, naturally—none of the Brents were afraid. All her people were Service people. They faced death unflinchingly. They led upright lives just as she, Emily Brent, had led an upright life... She had never done anything to be ashamed of... And so, naturally, *she* wasn't going to die...

"The Lord is mindful of his own." "Thou shalt not be afraid for the terror by night; nor for the arrow that flieth by day..." It was daylight now—there was no terror. *"We shall none of us leave this island."* Who had said that? General Macarthur, of course, whose cousin had married Elsie MacPherson. He hadn't seemed to *care*. He had seemed—actually—to *welcome* the idea! Wicked! Almost impious to feel that way. Some people thought so little of

death that they actually took their own lives. *Beatrice Taylor* ... Last night she had dreamed of Beatrice—dreamt that she was outside pressing her face against the window and moaning, asking to be let in. But Emily Brent hadn't wanted to let her in. Because, if she did, something terrible would happen ...

Emily came to herself with a start. That girl was looking at her very strangely. She said in a brisk voice:

"Everything's ready, isn't it? We'll take the breakfast in."

VI

Breakfast was a curious meal. Every one was very polite.

"May I get you some more coffee, Miss Brent?"

"Miss Claythorne, a slice of ham?"

"Another piece of toast?"

Six people, all outwardly self-possessed and normal.

And within? Thoughts that ran round in a circle like squirrels in a cage ...

"*What next? What next? Who? Which?*"

"*Would it work? I wonder. It's worth trying. If there's time. My God, if there's time ...*"

"*Religious mania, that's the ticket ... Looking at her, though, you can hardly believe it ... Suppose I'm wrong ...*"

"*It's crazy—everything's crazy. I'm going crazy. Wool disappearing—red silk curtains—it doesn't make sense. I can't get the hang of it...*"

"*The damned fool, he believed every word I said to him. It was easy... I must be careful, though, very careful...*"

"*Six of those little china figures... only six—how many will there be by tonight?...*"

"Who'll have the last egg?"

"Marmalade?"

"Thanks, can I cut you some bread?"

Six people, behaving normally at breakfast...

Chapter 12

I

The meal was over.

Mr. Justice Wargrave cleared his throat. He said in a small authoritative voice:

"It would be advisable, I think, if we met to discuss the situation. Shall we say in half an hour's time in the drawing room?"

Every one made a sound suggestive of agreement.

Vera began to pile plates together.

She said:

"I'll clear away and wash up."

Philip Lombard said:

"We'll bring the stuff out to the pantry for you."

"Thanks."

Emily Brent, rising to her feet sat down again. She said:

"Oh dear."

The judge said:

"Anything the matter, Miss Brent?"

Emily said apologetically:

"I'm sorry. I'd like to help Miss Claythorne, but I don't know how it is. I feel just a little giddy."

"Giddy, eh?" Dr. Armstrong came towards her. "Quite natural. Delayed shock. I can give you something to—"

"No!"

The word burst from her lips like an exploding shell.

It took every one aback. Dr. Armstrong flushed a deep red.

There was no mistaking the fear and suspicion in her face. He said stiffly:

"Just as you please, Miss Brent."

She said:

"I don't wish to take anything—anything at all. I will just sit here quietly till the giddiness passes off."

They finished clearing away the breakfast things.

Blore said:

"I'm a domestic sort of man. I'll give you a hand, Miss Claythorne."

Vera said: "Thank you."

Emily Brent was left alone sitting in the dining room.

For a while she heard a faint murmur of voices from the pantry.

The giddiness was passing. She felt drowsy now, as though she could easily go to sleep.

There was a buzzing in her ears—or was it a real buzzing in the room?

She thought:

"It's like a bee—a bumble bee."

Presently she saw the bee. It was crawling up the window pane.

Vera Claythorne had talked about bees this morning.

Bees and honey...

She liked honey. Honey in the comb, and strain it yourself through a muslin bag. Drip, drip, drip...

There was somebody in the room... somebody all wet and dripping... *Beatrice Taylor came from the river...*

She had only to turn her head and she would see her.

But she couldn't turn her head...

If she were to call out...

But she couldn't call out...

There was no one else in the house. She was all alone...

She heard footsteps—soft dragging footsteps coming up behind her. The stumbling footsteps of the drowned girl...

There was a wet dank smell in her nostrils...

On the windowpane the bee was buzzing—buzzing...

And then she felt the prick.

The bee sting on the side of her neck...

II

In the drawing room they were waiting for Emily Brent.

Vera Claythorne said:

"Shall I go and fetch her?"

Blore said quickly:

"Just a minute."

Vera sat down again. Every one looked inquiringly at

Blore. He said:

"Look here, everybody, my opinion's this: we needn't look farther for the author of these deaths than the dining room at this minute. I'd take my oath that woman's the one we're after!"

Armstrong said:

"And the motive?"

"Religious mania. What do you say, doctor?"

Armstrong said:

"It's perfectly possible. I've nothing to say against it. But of course we've no proof."

Vera said:

"She was very odd in the kitchen when we were getting breakfast. Her eyes—" She shivered.

Lombard said:

"You can't judge her by that. We're all a bit off our heads by now!"

Blore said:

"There's another thing. She's the only one who wouldn't give an explanation after that gramophone record. Why? Because she hadn't any to give."

Vera stirred in her chair. She said:

"That's not quite true. She told me—afterwards."

Wargrave said:

"What did she tell you, Miss Claythorne?"

Vera repeated the story of Beatrice Taylor.

Mr. Justice Wargrave observed:

"A perfectly straightforward story. I personally should have no difficulty in accepting it. Tell me, Miss Claythorne, did she appear to be troubled by a sense of guilt or a feeling of remorse for her attitude in the matter?"

"None whatever," said Vera. "She was completely unmoved."

Blore said:

"Hearts as hard as flints, these righteous spinsters! Envy, mostly!"

Mr. Justice Wargrave said:

"It is now five minutes to eleven. I think we should summon Miss Brent to join our conclave."

Blore said:

"Aren't you going to take any action?"

The judge said:

"I fail to see what action we can take. Our suspicions are, at the moment, only suspicions. I will, however, ask Dr. Armstrong to observe Miss Brent's demeanour very carefully. Let us now go into the dining room."

They found Emily Brent sitting in the chair in which they had left her. From behind they saw nothing amiss, except that she did not seem to hear their entrance into the room.

And then they saw her face—suffused with blood, with blue lips and staring eyes.

Blore said:

"My God, she's dead!"

III

The small quiet voice of Mr. Justice Wargrave said:

"One more of us acquitted—too late!"

Armstrong was bent over the dead woman. He sniffed the lips, shook his head, peered into the eyelids.

Lombard said impatiently:

"How did she die, doctor? She was all right when we left her here!"

Armstrong's attention was riveted on a mark on the right side of the neck.

He said:

"That's the mark of a hypodermic syringe."

There was a buzzing sound from the window. Vera cried:

"Look—a bee—*a bumble bee*. Remember what I said this morning!"

Armstrong said grimly:

"It wasn't that bee that stung her! A human hand held the syringe."

The judge asked:

"What poison was injected?"

Armstrong answered:

"At a guess, one of the cyanides. Probably potassium cyanide, same as Anthony Marston. She must have died almost immediately by asphyxiation."

Vera cried:

"But that *bee*? It can't be *coincidence*?"

Lombard said grimly:

"Oh no, it isn't coincidence! It's our murderer's touch of local colour! He's a playful beast. Likes to stick to his damnable nursery jingle as closely as possible!"

For the first time his voice was uneven, almost shrill. It was as though even his nerves, seasoned by a long career of hazards and dangerous undertakings, had given out at last.

He said violently:

"It's mad!—absolutely mad—we're all mad!"

The judge said calmly:

"We have still, I hope, our reasoning powers. *Did any one bring a hypodermic syringe to this house?*"

Dr. Armstrong, straightening himself, said in a voice that was not too well assured:

"Yes, I did."

Four pairs of eyes fastened on him. He braced himself against the deep hostile suspicion of those eyes. He said:

"Always travel with one. Most doctors do."

Mr. Justice Wargrave said calmly:

"Quite so. Will you tell us, doctor, where that syringe is now?"

"In the suitcase in my room."

Wargrave said:

"We might, perhaps, verify that fact."

The five of them went upstairs, a silent procession.

The contents of the suitcase were turned out on the floor.

The hypodermic syringe was not there.

IV

Armstrong said violently:

"Somebody must have taken it!"

There was silence in the room.

Armstrong stood with his back to the window. Four pairs of eyes were on him, black with suspicion and accusation. He looked from Wargrave to Vera and repeated helplessly—weakly:

"I tell you someone must have taken it."

Blore was looking at Lombard who returned his gaze.

The judge said:

"There are five of us here in this room. *One of us is a murderer.* The position is fraught with grave danger. Everything must be done in order to safeguard the four of us who are innocent. I will now ask you, Dr. Armstrong, what drugs you have in your possession."

Armstrong replied:

"I have a small medicine case here. You can examine it. You will find some sleeping stuff—trional and sulphonal tablets—a packet of bromide, bicarbonate of soda, aspirin. Nothing else. I have no cyanide in my possession."

The judge said:

"I have, myself, some sleeping tablets—sulphonal, I think they are. I presume they would be lethal if a sufficiently large dose were given. You, Mr. Lombard, have in your possession a revolver."

Philip Lombard said sharply:

"What if I have?"

"Only this. I propose that the doctor's supply of drugs, my own sulphonal tablets, your revolver and anything else of the nature of drugs or firearms should be collected together and placed in a safe place. That after this is done, we should each of us submit to a search—both of our persons and of our effects."

Lombard said:

"I'm damned if I'll give up my revolver!"

Wargrave said sharply:

"Mr. Lombard, you are a very strongly built and powerful young man, but ex-Inspector Blore is also a man of powerful physique. I do not know what the outcome of a struggle between you would be but I can tell you this. On Blore's side, assisting him to the best of our ability will be myself, Dr. Armstrong and Miss Claythorne. You will appreciate therefore, that the odds against you if you choose to resist will be somewhat heavy."

Lombard threw his head back. His teeth showed in what was almost a snarl.

"Oh, very well, then. Since you've got it all taped out."

Mr. Justice Wargrave nodded his head.

"You are a sensible young man. Where is this revolver of yours?"

"In the drawer of the table by my bed."

"Good."

"I'll fetch it."

"I think it would be desirable if we went with you."

Philip said with a smile that was still nearer a snarl:

"Suspicious devil, aren't you?"

They went along the corridor to Lombard's room.

Philip strode across to the bed table and jerked open the drawer.

Then he recoiled with an oath.

The drawer of the bed table was empty.

V

"Satisfied?" asked Lombard.

He had stripped to the skin and he and his room had been meticulously searched by the other three men. Vera Claythorne was outside in the corridor.

The search proceeded methodically. In turn, Armstrong, the judge, and Blore submitted to the same test.

The four men emerged from Blore's room and approached Vera. It was the judge who spoke.

"I hope you will understand, Miss Claythorne, that we can make no exceptions. That revolver must be found. You have, I presume, a bathing dress with you?"

Vera nodded.

"Then I will ask you to go into your room and put it on and then come out to us here."

Vera went into her room and shut the door. She reappeared in under a minute dressed in a tight-fitting silk rucked bathing dress.

Wargrave nodded approval.

"Thank you, Miss Claythorne. Now if you will remain here, we will search your room."

Vera waited patiently in the corridor until they emerged. Then she went in, dressed, and came out to where they were waiting.

The judge said:

"We are now assured of one thing. There are no lethal weapons or drugs in the possession of any of us five. That is one point to the good. We will now place the drugs in a safe place. There is, I think, a silver chest, is there not, in the pantry?"

Blore said:

"That's all very well, but who's to have the key? You, I suppose."

Mr. Justice Wargrave made no reply.

He went down to the pantry and the others followed him. There was a small case there designed for the purpose of holding silver and plate. By the judge's directions, the various drugs were placed in this and it was locked. Then, still on Wargrave's instructions, the chest was lifted into the plate cupboard and this in turn was locked. The judge then gave the key of the chest to Philip Lombard and the key of the cupboard to Blore.

He said:

"You two are the strongest physically. It would be difficult for either of you to get the key from the other. It would be impossible for any of us three to do so. To break open the cupboard—or the plate chest—would be a noisy and cumbersome proceeding and one which could hardly be carried out without attention being attracted to what was going on."

He paused, then went on:

"We are still faced by one very grave problem. *What has become of Mr. Lombard's revolver?*"

Blore said:

"Seems to me its owner is the most likely person to know that."

A white dint showed in Philip Lombard's nostrils. He said:

"You damned pig-headed fool! I tell you it's been stolen from me!"

Wargrave asked:

"When did you see it last?"

"Last night. It was in the drawer when I went to bed—ready in case anything happened."

The judge nodded.

He said:

"It must have been taken this morning during the confusion of searching for Rogers or after his dead body was discovered."

Vera said:

"It must be hidden somewhere about the house. We must look for it."

Mr. Justice Wargrave's finger was stroking his chin. He said:

"I doubt if our search will result in anything. Our murderer has had plenty of time to devise a hiding place. I do not fancy we shall find that revolver easily."

Blore said forcefully:

"I don't know where the revolver is, but I'll bet I know where something else is—that hypodermic syringe. Follow me."

He opened the front door and led the way round the house.

A little distance away from the dining room window he found the syringe. Beside it was a smashed china figure—a sixth broken soldier boy.

Blore said in a satisfied voice:

"Only place it could be. After he'd killed her, he opened the window and threw out the syringe and picked up the china figure from the table and followed on with that."

There were no prints on the syringe. It had been carefully wiped.

Vera said in a determined voice:

"Now let us look for the revolver."

Mr. Justice Wargrave said:

"By all means. But in doing so let us be careful to keep

together. Remember, if we separate, the murderer gets his chance."

They searched the house carefully from attic to cellars, but without result. The revolver was still missing.

Chapter 13

I

"One of us... One of us... One of us..."

Three words, endlessly repeated, dinning themselves hour after hour into receptive brains.

Five people—five frightened people. Five people who watched each other, who now hardly troubled to hide their state of nervous tension.

There was little pretence now—no formal veneer of conversation. They were five enemies linked together by a mutual instinct of self-preservation.

And all of them, suddenly, looked less like human beings. They were reverted to more bestial types. Like a wary old tortoise, Mr. Justice Wargrave sat hunched up, his body motionless, his eyes keen and alert. Ex-Inspector Blore looked coarser and clumsier in build. His walk was that of a slow padding animal. His eyes were bloodshot. There was a look of mingled ferocity and stupidity about him. He was like a beast at bay ready to charge its pursuers. Philip Lombard's senses seemed heightened, rather than diminished. His ears reacted to the slightest sound. His step was lighter and quicker, his body was lithe and graceful. And he smiled often, his lips curling back from his long white teeth.

Vera Claythorne was very quiet. She sat most of the time huddled in a chair. Her eyes stared ahead of her into space. She looked dazed. She was like a bird that has dashed its head against glass and that has been picked up by a human hand. It crouches there, terrified, unable to move, hoping to save itself by its immobility.

Armstrong was in a pitiable condition of nerves. He twitched and his hands shook. He lighted cigarette after cigarette and stubbed them out almost immediately. The forced inaction of their position seemed to gall him more than the others. Every now and then he broke out into a torrent of nervous speech.

"We—we shouldn't just sit here doing nothing! There must be *something*—surely, surely, there is *something* that we can do? If we lit a bonfire—"

Blore said heavily:

"In this weather?"

The rain was pouring down again. The wind came in fitful gusts. The depressing sound of the pattering rain nearly drove them mad.

By tacit consent, they had adopted a plan of campaign. They all sat in the big drawing room. Only one person left the room at a time. The other four waited till the fifth returned.

Lombard said:

"It's only a question of time. The weather will clear. Then we can do something —signal—light fires—make a raft—something!"

Armstrong said with a sudden cackle of laughter:

"A question of time—*time*? We can't afford time! We shall all be dead ..."

Mr. Justice Wargrave said and his small clear voice was heavy with passionate determination:

"Not if we are careful. *We must be very careful...*"

The midday meal had been duly eaten—but there had been no conventional formality about it. All five of them had gone to the kitchen. In the larder they had found a great store of tinned foods. They had opened a tin of tongue and two tins of fruit. They had eaten standing round the kitchen table. Then, herding close together, they had returned to the drawing room—to sit there—sit, watching each other.

And by now the thoughts that ran through their brains were abnormal, feverish, diseased ...

"It's Armstrong ... I saw him looking at me sideways just then ... his eyes are mad ... quite mad ... Perhaps he isn't a doctor at all ... That's it, of course! ... He's a lunatic, escaped from some doctor's house—pretending to be a doctor ... It's true ... shall I tell them? ... Shall I scream out? ... No, it won't do to put him on his guard ... Besides he can seem so sane ... What time is it? ... Only a quarter past three! ... Oh, God, I shall go mad myself ... *Yes, it's*

Armstrong... He's watching me now..."

"They won't get *me*! I can take care of myself... I've been in tight places before... Where the hell is that revolver?... Who took it?... Who's got it?... Nobody's got it—we know that. We were all searched... Nobody *can* have it... *But someone knows where it is...*"

"They're going mad... they'll all go mad... Afraid of death... we're all afraid of death... *I'm* afraid of death... Yes, but that doesn't stop death coming... '*The hearse is at the door, sir.*' Where did I read that? The girl... I'll watch the girl. Yes, I'll watch the girl..."

"Twenty to four... only twenty to four... perhaps the clock has stopped... I don't understand—no, I don't understand... This sort of thing can't happen... *it is happening*... Why don't we wake up? Wake up—Judgment Day—no, not that! If I only could think... My head—something's happening in my head—it's going to burst—it's going to split... This sort of thing can't happen... What's the time? Oh, God, it's only a quarter to four."

"I must keep my head... I must keep my head... If only I keep my head... It's all perfectly clear—all worked out. But nobody must suspect. It may do the trick. It must! Which one? That's the question—which one? I think—yes, I rather think—yes—*him.*"

When the clock struck five they all jumped.

Vera said:

"Does anyone—want tea?"

There was a moment's silence. Blore said:

"I'd like a cup."

Vera rose. She said:

"I'll go and make it. You can all stay here."

Mr. Justice Wargrave said gently:

"I think, my dear young lady, we would all prefer to come and watch you make it."

Vera stared, then gave a short rather hysterical laugh. She said:

"Of course! You would!"

Five people went into the kitchen. Tea was made and drunk by Vera and Blore. The other three had whisky—opening a fresh bottle and using a siphon from a nailed up case.

The judge murmured with a reptilian smile:

"We must be very careful . . ."

They went back again to the drawing room. Although it was summer the room was dark. Lombard switched on the lights but they did not come on. He said:

"Of course! The engine's not been run today since Rogers hasn't been there to see to it."

He hesitated and said:

"We could go out and get it going, I suppose."

Mr. Justice Wargrave said:

"There are packets of candles in the larder, I saw them, better use those."

Lombard went out. The other four sat watching each other.

He came back with a box of candles and a pile of saucers. Five candles were lit and placed about the room.

The time was a quarter to six.

I I

At twenty past six, Vera felt that to sit there longer was unbearable. She would go to her room and bathe her aching head and temples in cold water.

She got up and went towards the door. Then she remembered and came back and got a candle out of the box. She lighted it, let a little wax pour into a saucer and stuck the candle firmly to it. Then she went out of the room, shutting the door behind her and leaving the four men inside. She went up the stairs and along the passage to her room.

As she opened her door, she suddenly halted and stood stock still.

Her nostrils quivered.

The sea ... The smell of the sea at St. Tredennick.

That was it. She could not be mistaken. Of course, one smelt the sea on an island anyway, but this was different. It was the smell there had been on the beach that day—with the tide out and the rocks covered with seaweed drying in the sun.

"Can I swim out to the island, Miss Claythorne?"

"Why can't I swim out to the island? . . ."

Horrid whiney spoilt little brat! If it weren't for him, Hugo would be rich . . . able to marry the girl he loved . . .

Hugo . . .

Surely—surely—Hugo was beside her? No, waiting for her in the room . . .

She made a step forward. The draught from the window caught the flame of the candle. It flickered and went out . . .

In the dark she was suddenly afraid . . .

"Don't be a fool," Vera Claythorne urged herself. "It's all right. The others are downstairs. All four of them. There's no one in the room. There can't be. You're imagining things, my girl."

But that smell—that smell of the beach at St. Tredennick . . . That wasn't imagined. *It was true . . .*

And there *was* someone in the room . . . She had heard something—surely she had heard something . . .

And then, as she stood there, listening—a cold, clammy hand touched her throat—a wet hand, smelling of the sea . . .

III

Vera screamed. She screamed and screamed—screams of the utmost terror—wild desperate cries for help.

She did not hear the sounds from below, of a chair being overturned, of a door opening, of men's feet running up the stairs. She was conscious only of supreme terror.

Then, restoring her sanity, lights flickered in the doorway—candles—men hurrying into the room.

"What the devil?" "What's happened?" "Good God, what is it?"

She shuddered, took a step forward, collapsed on the floor.

She was only half aware of someone bending over her, of someone forcing her head down between her knees.

Then at a sudden exclamation, a quick "My God, look at that!" her senses returned. She opened her eyes and raised her head. She saw what it was the men with the candles were looking at.

A broad ribbon of wet seaweed was hanging down from the ceiling. It was that which in the darkness had swayed against her throat. It was that which she had taken for a clammy hand, a drowned hand come back from the dead to squeeze the life out of her!

She began to laugh hysterically. She said:

"It was seaweed—only seaweed—and that's what the smell was . . ."

And then the faintness came over her once more—waves upon waves of sickness. Again someone took her head and forced it between her knees.

Aeons of time seemed to pass. They were offering her something to drink—pressing the glass against her lips. She smelt brandy.

She was just about to gulp the spirit gratefully down when, suddenly, a warning note—like an alarm bell—sounded in her brain. She sat up, pushing the glass away.

She said sharply: "Where did this come from?"

Blore's voice answered. He stared a minute before speaking. He said:

"I got it from downstairs."

Vera cried:

"I won't drink it..."

There was a moment's silence, then Lombard laughed.

He said with appreciation:

"Good for you, Vera. You've got your wits about you—even if you have been scared half out of your life. I'll get a fresh bottle that hasn't been opened."

He went swiftly out.

Vera said uncertainly:

"I'm all right now. I'll have some water."

Armstrong supported her as she struggled to her feet. She went over to the basin, swaying and clutching at him for support. She let the cold tap run and then filled the glass.

Blore said resentfully:

"That brandy's all right."

Armstrong said:

"How do you know?"

Blore said angrily:

"I didn't put anything in it. That's what you're getting at,

I suppose."

Armstrong said:

"I'm not saying you did. You might have done, or someone might have tampered with the bottle for just this emergency."

Lombard came swiftly back into the room.

He had a new bottle of brandy in his hands and a corkscrew.

He thrust the sealed bottle under Vera's nose.

"There you are, my girl. Absolutely no deception." He peeled off the tin foil and drew the cork. "Lucky there's a good supply of spirits in the house. Thoughtful of U.N. Owen."

Vera shuddered violently.

Armstrong held the glass while Philip poured the brandy into it. He said:

"You'd better drink this, Miss Claythorne. You've had a nasty shock."

Vera drank a little of the spirit. The colour came back to her face.

Philip Lombard said with a laugh:

"Well, here's one murder that hasn't gone according to plan!"

Vera said almost in a whisper:

"You think—that was what was meant?"

Lombard nodded.

"Expected you to pass out through fright! Some people

would have, wouldn't they, doctor?"

Armstrong did not commit himself. He said doubtfully:

"H'm, impossible to say. Young healthy subject—no cardiac weakness. Unlikely. On the other hand—"

He picked up the glass of brandy that Blore had brought. He dipped a finger in it, tasted it gingerly. His expression did not alter. He said dubiously: "H'm, tastes all right."

Blore stepped forward angrily. He said:

"If you're saying that I tampered with that, I'll knock your ruddy block off."

Vera, her wits revived by the brandy, made a diversion by saying:

"Where's the judge?"

The three men looked at each other.

"*That's odd* . . . Thought he came up with us."

Blore said:

"*So did I* . . . What about it, doctor, you came up the stairs behind me?"

Armstrong said:

"I thought he was following me . . . Of course, he'd be bound to go slower than we did. He's an old man."

They looked at each other again.

Lombard said:

"It's damned odd . . ."

Blore cried:

"We must look for him."

He started for the door. The others followed him, Vera

last.

As they went down the stairs Armstrong said over his shoulder:

"Of course he *may* have stayed in the living room."

They crossed the hall. Armstrong called out loudly:

"Wargrave, Wargrave, where are you?"

There was no answer. A deadly silence filled the house apart from the gentle patter of the rain.

Then, in the entrance to the drawing room door, Armstrong stopped dead. The others crowded up and looked over his shoulder.

Somebody cried out.

Mr. Justice Wargrave was sitting in his high-backed chair at the end of the room. Two candles burnt on either side of him. But what shocked and startled the onlookers was the fact that he sat there robed in scarlet with a judge's wig upon his head ...

Dr. Armstrong motioned to the others to keep back. He himself walked across to the silent staring figure, reeling a little as he walked like a drunken man.

He bent forward, peering into the still face. Then, with a swift movement, he raised the wig. It fell to the floor revealing the high bald forehead with, in the very middle, a round stained mark from which something had trickled.

Dr. Armstrong lifted the lifeless hand and felt for the pulse. Then he turned to the others.

He said—and his voice was expressionless, dead, far

away...

"*He's been shot...*"

Blore said:

"God—*the revolver!*"

The doctor said, still in the same lifeless voice:

"Got him through the head. Instantaneous."

Vera stooped to the wig. She said, and her voice shook with terror:

"*Miss Brent's missing grey wool...*"

Blore said:

"And the scarlet curtain that was missing from the bathroom..."

Vera whispered:

"So this is what they wanted them for..."

Suddenly Philip Lombard laughed—a high unnatural laugh.

"*Five little soldier boys going in for law; one got in Chancery and then there were Four.* That's the end of Mr. Bloody Justice Wargrave. No more pronouncing sentence for him! No more putting on of the black cap! Here's the last time *he*'ll ever sit in court! No more summing up and sending innocent men to death. How Edward Seton would laugh if he were here! God, how he'd laugh!"

His outburst shocked and startled the others.

Vera cried:

"Only this morning you said *he* was the one!"

Philip Lombard's face changed—sobered.

He said in a low voice:

"I know I did... Well, I was wrong. Here's one more of us who's been proved innocent—*too late*!"

Chapter 14

I

They had carried Mr. Justice Wargrave up to his room and laid him on the bed.

Then they had come down again and had stood in the hall looking at each other.

Blore said heavily:

"What do we do now?"

Lombard said briskly:

"Have something to eat. We've got to eat, you know."

Once again they went into the kitchen. Again they opened a tin of tongue. They ate mechanically, almost without tasting.

Vera said:

"I shall never eat tongue again."

They finished the meal. They sat round the kitchen table staring at each other.

Blore said:

"Only four of us now ... *Who'll be the next?*"

Armstrong stared. He said, almost mechanically:

"We must be very careful—" and stopped.

Blore nodded.

"That's what *he* said... And now he's dead!"

Armstrong said:

"How did it happen, I wonder?"

Lombard swore. He said:

"A damned clever doublecross! That stuff was planted in Miss Claythorne's room and it worked just as it was intended to. Everyone dashes up there thinking *she's* being murdered. And so—in the confusion—someone—caught the old boy off his guard."

Blore said:

"Why didn't anyone hear the shot?"

Lombard shook his head.

"Miss Claythorne was screaming, the wind was howling, we were running about and calling out. No, it wouldn't be heard." He paused. "But that trick's not going to work again. He'll have to try something else next."

Blore said:

"He probably will."

There was an unpleasant tone in his voice. The two men eyed each other.

Armstrong said:

"Four of us, and we don't know which..."

Blore said:

"*I* know..."

Vera said:

"I haven't the least doubt..."

Armstrong said slowly:

"I suppose I do know really ..."

Philip Lombard said:

"I think I've got a pretty good idea now ..."

Again they all looked at each other ...

Vera staggered to her feet. She said:

"I feel awful. I must go to bed ... I'm dead beat."

Lombard said:

"Might as well. No good sitting watching each other."

Blore said:

"*I've* no objection ..."

The doctor murmured:

"The best thing to do—although I doubt if any of us will sleep."

They moved to the door. Blore said:

"*I wonder where that revolver is now? ...*"

I I

They went up the stairs.

The next move was a little like a scene in a farce.

Each one of the four stood with a hand on his or her bedroom door handle. Then, as though at a signal, each one stepped into the room and pulled the door shut. There were sounds of bolts and locks, of the moving of furniture.

Four frightened people were barricaded in until morning.

III

Philip Lombard drew a breath of relief as he turned from adjusting a chair under the door handle.

He strolled across to the dressing table.

By the light of the flickering candle he studied his face curiously.

He said softly to himself:

"Yes, this business has got you rattled all right."

His sudden wolf-like smile flashed out.

He undressed quickly.

He went over to the bed, placing his wristwatch on the table by the bed.

Then he opened the drawer of the table.

He stood there, staring down at the revolver that was inside it ...

IV

Vera Claythorne lay in bed.

The candle still burned beside her.

As yet she could not summon the courage to put it out.

She was afraid of the dark ...

She told herself again and again: "*You're all right until morning. Nothing happened last night. Nothing will happen tonight. Nothing can happen. You're locked and bolted in. No one can come near you...*"

And she thought suddenly:

"Of course! I can stay here! Stay here locked in! Food doesn't really matter! I can stay here—safely—till help comes! Even if it's a day—or two days..."

Stay here. Yes, but could she stay here? Hour after hour—with no one to speak to, with nothing to do but *think*...

She'd begin to think of Cornwall—of Hugo—of—of what she'd said to Cyril.

Horrid whiney little boy, always pestering her...

"*Miss Claythorne, why can't I swim out to the rock? I can. I know I can.*"

Was it her voice that had answered?

"*Of course you can, Cyril, really. I know that.*"

"Can I go then, Miss Claythorne?"

"Well, you see, Cyril, your mother gets so nervous about you. I'll tell you what. Tomorrow you can swim out to the rock. I'll talk to your mother on the beach and distract her attention. And then, when she looks for you, there you'll be standing on the rock waving to her! It *will* be a surprise!"

"Oh, good egg, Miss Claythorne! That will be a lark!"

She'd said it now. Tomorrow! Hugo was going to Newquay. When he came back—it would be all over.

Yes, but supposing it wasn't? Supposing it went wrong? Cyril might be rescued in time. And then—then he'd say, "*Miss Claythorne said I could.*" Well, what of it? One must take *some* risk! If the worst happened she'd brazen it out. *"How can you tell such a wicked lie, Cyril? Of course I never said any such thing!"* They'd believe her all right. Cyril often told stories. He was an untruthful child. Cyril would know, of course. But that didn't matter ... and anyway nothing *would* go wrong. She'd pretend to swim out after him. But she'd arrive too late ... Nobody would ever suspect ...

Had Hugo suspected? Was that why he had looked at her in that queer far-off way? ... Had Hugo *known?*

Was that why he had gone off after the inquest so hurriedly?

He hadn't answered the one letter she had written to him ...

Hugo...

Vera turned restlessly in bed. No, no, she mustn't think of Hugo. It hurt too much! That was all over, over and done with ... Hugo must be forgotten ...

Why, this evening, had she suddenly felt that Hugo was in the room with her?

She stared up at the ceiling, stared at the big black hook in the middle of the room.

She'd never noticed that hook before.

The seaweed had hung from that.

She shivered as she remembered that cold clammy touch on her neck.

She didn't like that hook on the ceiling. It drew your eyes, fascinated you ... a big black hook ...

V

Ex-Inspector Blore sat on the side of his bed.

His small eyes, red-rimmed and bloodshot, were alert in the solid mass of his face. He was like a wild boar waiting to charge.

He felt no inclination to sleep.

The menace was coming very near now ... Six out of ten!

For all his sagacity, for all his caution and astuteness, the old judge had gone the way of the rest.

Blore snorted with a kind of savage satisfaction.

What was it the old geezer had said?

"We must be very careful ..."

Self-righteous smug old hypocrite. Sitting up in court feeling like God Almighty. He'd got his all right ... No more being careful for him.

And now there were four of them. The girl, Lombard, Armstrong and himself.

Very soon another of them would go ... But it wouldn't be William Henry Blore. He'd see to that all right.

(But the revolver ... What about the revolver? That was the disturbing factor—the revolver!)

Blore sat on his bed, his brow furrowed, his little eyes creased and puckered while he pondered the problem of the revolver ...

In the silence he could hear the clocks strike downstairs.

Midnight.

He relaxed a little now—even went so far as to lie down on his bed. But he did not undress.

He lay there thinking. Going over the whole business from the beginning, methodically, painstakingly, as he had been wont to do in his police officer days. It was thoroughness that paid in the end.

The candle was burning down. Looking to see if the matches were within easy reach of his hand, he blew it out.

Strangely enough, he found the darkness disquieting. It was as though a thousand age-old fears awoke and struggled for supremacy in his brain. Faces floated in the air—the judge's face crowned with that mockery of grey wool—the cold dead face of Mrs. Rogers—the convulsed purple face of Anthony Marston.

Another face—pale, spectacled, with a small straw-coloured moustache...

A face he had seen sometime or other—but when? Not on the island. No, much longer ago than that.

Funny that he couldn't put a name to it... Silly sort of face really—fellow looked a bit of a mug.

Of course!

It came to him with a real shock.

Landor!

Odd to think he'd completely forgotten what Landor looked like. Only yesterday he'd been trying to recall the fellow's face, and hadn't been able to.

And now here it was, every feature clear and distinct, as

though he had seen it only yesterday.

Landor had had a wife—a thin slip of a woman with a worried face. There'd been a kid too, a girl about fourteen. For the first time, he wondered what had become of them.

(The revolver. What had become of the revolver? That was much more important.)

The more he thought about it the more puzzled he was... He didn't understand this revolver business...

Somebody in the house had got that revolver...

Downstairs a clock struck one.

Blore's thoughts were cut short. He sat up on the bed, suddenly alert. For he had heard a sound—a very faint sound—somewhere outside his bedroom door.

There was someone moving about in the darkened house.

The perspiration broke out on his forehead. Who was it, moving secretly and silently along the corridors? Someone who was up to no good, he'd bet that!

Noiselessly, in spite of his heavy build, he dropped off the bed and with two strides was standing by the door listening.

But the sound did not come again. Nevertheless Blore was convinced that he was not mistaken. He had heard a footfall just outside his door. The hair rose slightly on his scalp. He knew fear again...

Someone creeping about stealthily in the night.

He listened—but the sound was not repeated.

And now a new temptation assailed him. He wanted,

desperately, to go out and investigate. If he could only see who it was prowling about in the darkness.

But to open his door would be the action of a fool. Very likely that was exactly what the other was waiting for. He might even have meant Blore to hear what he had heard, counting on him coming out to investigate.

Blore stood rigid—listening. He could hear sounds everywhere now, cracks, rustles, mysterious whispers—but his dogged realistic brain knew them for what they were—the creations of his own heated imagination.

And then suddenly he heard something that was *not* imagination. Footsteps, very soft, very cautious, but plainly audible to a man listening with all his ears as Blore was listening.

They came softly along the corridor (both Lombard's and Armstrong's rooms were farther from the stairhead than his). They passed his door without hesitating or faltering.

And as they did so, Blore made up his mind.

He meant to see who it was! The footsteps had definitely passed his door going to the stairs. Where was the man going?

When Blore acted, he acted quickly, surprisingly so for a man who looked so heavy and slow. He tiptoed back to the bed, slipped matches into his pocket, detached the plug of the electric lamp by his bed and picked it up, winding the flex round it. It was a chromium affair with a heavy ebonite base—a useful weapon.

He sprinted noiselessly across the room, removed the chair from under the door handle and with precaution unlocked and unbolted the door. He stepped out into the corridor. There was a faint sound in the hall below. Blore ran noiselessly in his stockinged feet to the head of the stairs.

At that moment he realized why it was he had heard all these sounds so clearly. The wind had died down completely and the sky must have cleared. There was faint moonlight coming in through the landing window and it illuminated the hall below.

Blore had an instantaneous glimpse of a figure just passing out through the front door.

In the act of running down the stairs in pursuit, he paused.

Once again, he had nearly made a fool of himself! This was a trap, perhaps, to lure him out of the house!

But what the other man didn't realize was that he had made a mistake, had delivered himself neatly into Blore's hands.

For, of the three tenanted rooms upstairs, *one must now be empty.* All that had to be done was to ascertain *which!*

Blore went swiftly back along the corridor.

He paused first at Dr. Armstrong's door and tapped. There was no answer.

He waited a minute, then went on to Philip Lombard's

room.

Here the answer came at once.

"Who's there?"

"It's Blore. I don't think Armstrong is in his room. Wait a minute."

He went on to the door at the end of the corridor. Here he tapped again.

"Miss Claythorne. Miss Claythorne."

Vera's voice, startled, answered him.

"Who is it? What's the matter?"

"It's all right, Miss Claythorne. Wait a minute. I'll come back."

He raced back to Lombard's room. The door opened as he did so. Lombard stood there. He held a candle in his left hand. He had pulled on his trousers over his pyjamas. His right hand rested in the pocket of his pyjama jacket. He said sharply:

"What the hell's all this?"

Blore explained rapidly. Lombard's eyes lit up.

"*Armstrong—eh?* So *he's* our pigeon!" He moved along to Armstrong's door. "Sorry, Blore, but I don't take anything on trust."

He rapped sharply on the panel.

"Armstrong—Armstrong."

There was no answer.

Lombard dropped to his knees and peered through the keyhole. He inserted his little finger gingerly into the lock.

He said:

"Key's not in the door on the inside."

Blore said:

"That means he locked it on the outside and took it with him."

Philip nodded:

"Ordinary precaution to take. *We'll get him, Blore* ... This time, *we'll get him*! Half a second."

He raced along to Vera's room.

"Vera."

"Yes."

"We're hunting Armstrong. He's out of his room. Whatever you do, *don't open your door*. Understand?"

"Yes, I understand."

"If Armstrong comes along and says that I've been killed, or Blore's been killed, *pay no attention*. See? Only open your door *if both Blore and I speak to you*. Got that?"

Vera said:

"Yes. I'm not a complete fool."

Lombard said:

"Good."

He joined Blore. He said:

"And now—after him! The hunt's up!"

Blore said:

"We'd better be careful. He's got a revolver, remember."

Philip Lombard racing down the stairs chuckled.

He said:

"That's where you're wrong." He undid the front door, remarking, "Latch pushed back—so he could get in again easily."

He went on:

"I've got that revolver!" He took it half out of his pocket as he spoke. "Found it put back in my drawer tonight."

Blore stopped dead on the doorstep. His face changed. Philip Lombard saw it.

He said impatiently:

"Don't be a damned fool, Blore! I'm not going to shoot you! Go back and barricade yourself in if you like! I'm off after Armstrong."

He started off into the moonlight. Blore, after a minute's hesitation, followed him.

He thought to himself:

"I suppose I'm asking for it. After all—"

After all he had tackled criminals armed with revolvers before now. Whatever else he lacked, Blore did not lack courage. Show him the danger and he would tackle it pluckily. He was not afraid of danger in the open, only of danger undefined and tinged with the supernatural.

VI

Vera, left to wait results, got up and dressed.

She glanced over once or twice at the door. It was a good solid door. It was both bolted and locked and had an oak chair wedged under the handle.

It could not be broken open by force. Certainly not by Dr. Armstrong. He was not a physically powerful man.

If she were Armstrong intent on murder, it was cunning that she would employ, not force.

She amused herself by reflecting on the means he might employ.

He might, as Philip had suggested, announce that one of the other two men was dead. Or he might possibly pretend to be mortally wounded himself, might drag himself groaning to her door.

There were other possibilities. He might inform her that the house was on fire. More, he might actually set the house on fire ... Yes, that would be a possibility. Lure the other two men out of the house, then, having previously laid a trail of petrol, he might set light to it. And she, like an idiot, would remain barricaded in her room until it was too late.

She crossed over to the window. Not too bad. At a pinch one could escape that way. It would mean a drop—but there was a handy flower bed.

She sat down and picking up her diary began to write in

it in a clear flowing hand.

One must pass the time.

Suddenly she stiffened to attention. She had heard a sound. It was, she thought, a sound like breaking glass. And it came from somewhere downstairs.

She listened hard, but the sound was not repeated.

She heard, or thought she heard, stealthy sounds of footsteps, the creak of stairs, the rustle of garments—but there was nothing definite and she concluded, as Blore had done earlier, that such sounds had their origin in her own imagination.

But presently she heard sounds of a more concrete nature. People moving about downstairs—the murmur of voices. Then the very decided sound of someone mounting the stairs—doors opening and shutting—feet going up to the attics overhead. More noises from there.

Finally the steps came along the passage. Lombard's voice said:

"Vera. You all right?"

"Yes. What happened?"

Blore's voice said:

"Will you let us in?"

Vera went to the door. She removed the chair, unlocked the door and slid back the bolt. She opened the door. The two men were breathing hard, their feet and the bottom of their trousers were soaking wet.

She said again:

"What's happened?"

Lombard said:

"*Armstrong's disappeared...*"

VII

Vera cried:

"What?"

Lombard said:

"Vanished clean off the island."

Blore concurred:

"Vanished—that's the word! Like some damned conjuring trick."

Vera said impatiently:

"Nonsense! He's hiding somewhere!"

Blore said:

"No, he isn't! I tell you, there's nowhere to hide on this island. It's as bare as your hand! There's moonlight outside. As clear as day it is. *And he's not to be found.*"

Vera said:

"He doubled back to the house."

Blore said:

"We thought of that. We've searched the house, too. You must have heard us. *He's not here,* I tell you. He's gone—clean vanished, vamoosed..."

Vera said incredulously:

"I don't believe it."

Lombard said:

"It's true, my dear."

He paused and then said:

"There's one other little fact. A pane in the dining room window has been smashed—*and there are only three little soldier boys on the table.*"

Chapter 15

I

Three people sat eating breakfast in the kitchen.

Outside, the sun shone. It was a lovely day. The storm was a thing of the past.

And with the change in the weather, a change had come in the mood of the prisoners on the island.

They felt now like people just awakening from a nightmare.

There was danger, yet, but it was danger in daylight. That paralysing atmosphere of fear that had wrapped them round like a blanket yesterday while the wind howled outside was gone.

Lombard said:

"We'll try heliographing today with a mirror from the highest point of the island. Some bright lad wandering on the cliff will recognize SOS when he sees it, I hope. In the evening we could try a bonfire—only there isn't much wood—and anyway they might just think it was song and dance and merriment."

Vera said:

"Surely someone can read Morse. And then they'll come

to take us off. Long before this evening."

Lombard said:

"The weather's cleared all right, but the sea hasn't gone down yet. Terrific swell on! They won't be able to get a boat near the island before tomorrow."

Vera cried:

"Another night in this place!"

Lombard shrugged his shoulders.

"May as well face it! Twenty-four hours will do it, I think. If we can last out that, we'll be all right."

Blore cleared his throat. He said:

"We'd better come to a clear understanding. *What's happened to Armstrong?*"

Lombard said:

"Well, we've got one piece of evidence. Only three little soldier boys left on the dinner table. It looks as though Armstrong had got his quietus."

Vera said:

"Then why haven't you found his dead body?"

Blore said:

"Exactly."

Lombard shook his head. He said:

"It's damned odd—no getting over it."

Blore said doubtfully:

"It might have been thrown into the sea."

Lombard said sharply:

"By whom? You? Me? You saw him go out of the front

door. You come along and find me in my room. We go out and search together. When the devil had I time to kill him and carry his body round the island?"

Blore said:

"I don't know. But I do know one thing."

Lombard said:

"What's that?"

Blore said:

"The revolver. It was your revolver. It's in your possession now. There's nothing to show that it hasn't been in your possession all along."

"Come now, Blore, we were all searched."

"Yes, you'd hidden it away before that happened. Afterwards you just took it back again."

"My good blockhead, I swear to you that it was put back in my drawer. Greatest surprise I ever had in my life when I found it there."

Blore said:

"You ask us to believe a thing like that! Why the devil should Armstrong, or anyone else for that matter, put it back?"

Lombard raised his shoulders hopelessly.

"I haven't the least idea. It's just crazy. The last thing one would expect. There seems no point in it."

Blore agreed.

"No, there isn't. You might have thought of a better story."

"Rather proof that I'm telling the truth, isn't it?"

"I don't look at it that way."

Philip said:

"You wouldn't."

Blore said:

"Look here, Mr. Lombard, if you're an honest man, as you pretend—"

Philip murmured:

"When did I lay claims to being an honest man? No, indeed, I never said that."

Blore went on stolidly:

"If you're speaking the truth—there's only one thing to be done. As long as you have that revolver, Miss Claythorne and I are at your mercy. The only fair thing is to put that revolver with the other things that are locked up—and you and I will hold the two keys still."

Philip Lombard lit a cigarette.

As he puffed smoke, he said:

"Don't be an ass."

"You won't agree to that?"

"No, I won't. That revolver's mine. I need it to defend myself—and I'm going to keep it."

Blore said:

"In that case we're bound to come to one conclusion."

"That I'm U.N. Owen? Think what you damned well please. But I'll ask you, if that's so, why I didn't pot you with the revolver last night? I could have, about twenty times over."

Blore shook his head.

He said:

"I don't know—and that's a fact. You must have had some reason."

Vera had taken no part in the discussion. She stirred now and said:

"I think you're both behaving like a pair of idiots."

Lombard looked at her.

"What's this?"

Vera said:

"You've forgotten the nursery rhyme. Don't you see there's a clue there?"

She recited in a meaning voice:

"Four little soldier boys going out to sea;
A red herring swallowed one and then there were Three."

She went on:

"*A red herring*—that's the vital clue. *Armstrong's not dead* ... He took away the china soldier to make you think he was. You may say what you like—Armstrong's on the island still. His disappearance is just a red herring across the track ..."

Lombard sat down again.

He said:

"You know, you may be right."

Blore said:

"Yes, but if so, where is he? We've searched the place.

Outside and inside."

Vera said scornfully:

"We all searched for the revolver, didn't we, and couldn't find it? But it was somewhere all the time!"

Lombard murmured:

"There's a slight difference in size, my dear, between a man and a revolver."

Vera said:

"I don't care—I'm sure I'm right."

Blore murmured:

"Rather giving himself away, wasn't it? Actually mentioning a red herring in the verse. He could have written it up a bit different."

Vera cried:

"But don't you *see*, he's *mad*? It's all mad! The whole thing of going by the rhyme is mad! Dressing up the judge, killing Rogers when he was chopping sticks—drugging Mrs. Rogers so that she overslept herself—arranging for a bumble bee when Miss Brent died! It's like some horrible child playing a game. It's all got to fit in."

Blore said:

"Yes, you're right." He thought a minute. "At any rate there's no zoo on the island. He'll have a bit of trouble getting over that."

Vera cried:

"Don't you see? *We're the Zoo* . . . Last night, we were hardly human anymore. *We're the Zoo* . . ."

11

They spent the morning on the cliffs, taking it in turns to flash a mirror at the mainland.

There were no signs that any one saw them. No answering signals. The day was fine, with a slight haze. Below, the sea weaved in a gigantic swell. There were no boats out.

They had made another abortive search of the island. There was no trace of the missing physician.

Vera looked up at the house from where they were standing.

She said, her breath coming with a slight catch in it:

"One feels safer here, out in the open ... Don't let's go back into the house again."

Lombard said:

"Not a bad idea. We're pretty safe here, no one can get at us without our seeing him a long time beforehand."

Vera said:

"We'll stay here."

Blore said:

"Have to pass the night somewhere. We'll have to go back to the house then."

Vera shuddered.

"I can't bear it. I *can't* go through another night!"

Philip said:

"You'll be safe enough—locked in your room."

Vera murmured: "I suppose so."

She stretched out her hands, murmuring:

"It's lovely—to feel the sun again..."

She thought:

"How odd... I'm almost happy. And yet I suppose I'm actually in danger... Somehow—now—nothing seems to matter... not in daylight... I feel full of power—I feel that I can't die..."

Blore was looking at his wristwatch. He said:

"It's two o'clock. What about lunch?"

Vera said obstinately:

"I'm not going back to the house. I'm going to stay here—in the open."

"Oh come now, Miss Claythorne. Got to keep your strength up, you know."

Vera said:

"If I even see a tinned tongue, I shall be sick! I don't want any food. People go days on end with nothing sometimes when they're on a diet."

Blore said:

"Well, I need my meals regular. What about you, Mr. Lombard?"

Philip said:

"You know, I don't relish the idea of tinned tongue particularly. I'll stay here with Miss Claythorne."

Blore hesitated. Vera said:

"I shall be quite all right. I don't think he'll shoot me as soon as your back is turned if that's what you're afraid of."

Blore said:

"It's all right if you say so. But we agreed we ought not to separate."

Philip said:

"You're the one who wants to go into the lion's den. I'll come with you if you like."

"No, you won't," said Blore. "You'll stay here."

Philip laughed.

"So you're still afraid of me? Why, I could shoot you both this very minute if I liked."

Blore said:

"Yes, but that wouldn't be according to plan. It's one at a time, and it's got to be done in a certain way."

"Well," said Philip, "you seem to know all about it."

"Of course," said Blore, "it's a bit jumpy going up to the house alone—"

Philip said softly:

"And therefore, *will I lend you my revolver?* Answer, no, I will *not*! Not quite so simple as that, thank you."

Blore shrugged his shoulders and began to make his way up the steep slope to the house.

Lombard said softly:

"Feeding time at the Zoo! The animals are very regular in their habits!"

Vera said anxiously:

"Isn't it very risky, what he's doing?"

"In a sense you mean—no, I don't think it is! Armstrong's

not armed, you know, and anyway Blore is twice a match for him in physique and he's very much on his guard. And anyway it's a sheer impossibility that Armstrong can be in the house. I *know* he's not there."

"But—what other solution is there?"

Philip said softly:

"There's Blore."

"Oh—do you really think—?"

"Listen, my girl. You heard Blore's story. You've got to admit that if it's true, *I can't possibly have had anything to do with Armstrong's disappearance.* His story clears me. *But it doesn't clear him.* We've only *his* word for it that he heard footsteps and saw a man going downstairs and out at the front door. The whole thing may be a lie. He may have got rid of Armstrong a couple of hours before that."

"How?"

Lombard shrugged his shoulders.

"That we don't know. But if you ask me, we've only one danger to fear—and that danger is Blore! What do we know about the man? Less than nothing! All this ex-policeman story may be bunkum! He may be anybody—a mad millionaire—a crazy business man—an escaped inmate of Broadmoor. One thing's certain. He *could* have done every one of these crimes."

Vera had gone rather white. She said in a slightly breathless voice:

"And supposing he gets—us?"

Lombard said softly, patting the revolver in his pocket:

"I'm going to take very good care he doesn't."

Then he looked at her curiously.

"Touching faith in me, haven't you, Vera? Quite sure I wouldn't shoot you?"

Vera said:

"One has got to trust some one ... As a matter of fact I think you're wrong about Blore. I still think it's Armstrong."

She turned to him suddenly.

"Don't you feel—all the time—that there's someone. Someone watching and waiting?"

Lombard said slowly:

"That's just nerves."

Vera said eagerly:

"Then you *have* felt it?"

She shivered. She bent a little closer.

"Tell me—you don't think—" She broke off, went on: "I read a story once—about two judges that came to a small American town—from the Supreme Court. They administered justice—Absolute Justice. *Because—they didn't come from this world at all ...*"

Lombard raised his eyebrows.

He said:

"Heavenly visitants, eh? No, I don't believe in the supernatural. This business is human enough."

Vera said in a low voice:

"Sometimes—I'm not sure ..."

Lombard looked at her. He said:

"That's conscience..." After a moment's silence he said very quietly: "So you *did* drown that kid after all?"

Vera said vehemently:

"I didn't! I didn't! You've no right to say that!"

He laughed easily.

"Oh, yes, you did, my good girl! I don't know why. Can't imagine. There was a man in it probably. Was that it?"

A sudden feeling of lassitude, of intense weariness, spread over Vera's limbs. She said in a dull voice:

"Yes—there was a man in it..."

Lombard said softly:

"Thanks. That's what I wanted to know..."

Vera sat up suddenly. She exclaimed:

"What was that? It wasn't an earthquake?"

Lombard said:

"No, no. Queer, though—a thud shook the ground. And I thought—did you hear a sort of cry? I did."

They stared up at the house.

Lombard said:

"It came from there. We'd better go up and see."

"No, no, I'm not going."

"Please yourself. I am."

Vera said desperately:

"All right. I'll come with you."

They walked up the slope to the house. The terrace was peaceful and innocuous-looking in the sunshine. They hesitated there a minute, then instead of entering by the front door, they made a cautious circuit of the house.

They found Blore. He was spreadeagled on the stone terrace on the east side, his head crushed and mangled by a great block of white marble.

Philip looked up. He said:

"Whose is that window just above?"

Vera said in a low shuddering voice:

"It's mine—and *that's the clock from my mantelpiece* ... I remember now. It was—shaped like a bear."

She repeated and her voice shook and quavered:

"It was shaped like a bear ..."

III

Philip grasped her shoulder.

He said, and his voice was urgent and grim:

"This settles it. Armstrong is in hiding somewhere in that house. I'm going to get him."

But Vera clung to him. She cried:

"Don't be a fool. It's *us* now! We're next! He *wants* us to look for him! He's *counting* on it!"

Philip stopped. He said thoughtfully:

"There's something in that."

Vera cried:

"At any rate you do admit now I was right."

He nodded.

"Yes—you win! It's Armstrong all right. But where the devil did he hide himself? We went over the place with a fine-tooth comb."

Vera said urgently:

"If you didn't find him last night, you *won't find him now* ... That's common sense."

Lombard said reluctantly:

"Yes, but—"

"He must have prepared a secret place beforehand—naturally—of course it's just what he would do. You know, like a Priest's Hole in old manor houses."

"This isn't an old house of that kind."

"He could have had one made."

Philip Lombard shook his head. He said:

"We measured the place—that first morning. I'll swear there's no space unaccounted for."

Vera said:

"There must be ..."

Lombard said:

"I'd like to see—"

Vera cried:

"Yes, you'd like to see! And he knows that! He's in there—waiting for you."

Lombard said, half bringing out the revolver from his pocket:

"I've got this, you know."

"You said Blore was all right—that he was more than a match for Armstrong. So he was physically, and he was on the lookout too. But what you don't seem to realize is that Armstrong is *mad*! And a madman has all the advantages on his side. He's twice as cunning as any one sane can be."

Lombard put back the revolver in his pocket. He said:

"Come on, then."

IV

Lombard said at last:

"What are we going to do when night comes?"

Vera didn't answer. He went on accusingly:

"You haven't thought of that?"

She said helplessly:

"What *can* we do? Oh, my God, I'm *frightened* . . ."

Philip Lombard said thoughtfully:

"It's fine weather. There will be a moon. We must find a place—up by the top cliffs perhaps. We can sit there and wait for morning. *We mustn't go to sleep* . . . We must watch the whole time. And if any one comes up toward us, I shall shoot!"

He paused:

"You'll be cold, perhaps, in that thin dress?"

Vera said with a raucous laugh:

"Cold? I should be colder if I were dead!"

Philip Lombard said quietly:

"Yes, that's true . . ."

Vera moved restlessly.

She said:

"I shall go mad if I sit here any longer. Let's move about."

"All right."

They paced slowly up and down, along the line of the rocks overlooking the sea. The sun was dropping towards the west. The light was golden and mellow. It enveloped them in a golden glow.

Vera said, with a sudden nervous little giggle:

"Pity we can't have a bathe . . ."

Philip was looking down towards the sea. He said abruptly:

"What's that, there? You see—by that big rock? No—a little further to the right."

Vera stared. She said:

"It looks like somebody's clothes!"

"A bather, eh?" Lombard laughed. "Queer. I suppose it's only seaweed."

Vera said:

"Let's go and look."

"It is clothes," said Lombard as they drew nearer. "A bundle of them. That's a boot. Come on, let's scramble along here."

They scrambled over the rocks.

Vera stopped suddenly. She said:

"It's not clothes—it's a man . . ."

The man was wedged between two rocks, flung there by the tide earlier in the day.

Lombard and Vera reached it in a last scramble. They bent down.

A purple discoloured face—a hideous drowned face . . .

Lombard said:

"My God! It's *Armstrong* . . ."

Chapter 16

I

Aeons passed ... worlds spun and whirled ... Time was motionless ... It stood still—it passed through a thousand ages ...

No, it was only a minute or so ...

Two people were standing looking down on a dead man ...

Slowly, very slowly, Vera Claythorne and Philip Lombard lifted their heads and looked into each other's eyes ...

II

Lombard laughed.

He said:

"So that's it, is it, Vera?"

Vera said:

"There's no one on the island—no one at all—*except* us two ..."

Her voice was a whisper—nothing more.

Lombard said:

"Precisely. So we know where we are, don't we?"

Vera said:

"How was it worked—that trick with the marble bear?"

He shrugged his shoulders.

"A conjuring trick, my dear—a very good one..."

Their eyes met again.

Vera thought:

"Why did I never see his face properly before. A wolf—that's what it is—a wolf's face... Those horrible teeth..."

Lombard said, and his voice was a snarl—dangerous—menacing:

"This is the end, you understand. We've come to the truth now. *And it's the end...*"

Vera said quietly:

"I understand..."

She stared out to sea. General Macarthur had stared out to sea—when—only yesterday? Or was it the day before? He too had said, "*This is the end...*"

He had said it with acceptance—almost with welcome.

But to Vera the words—the thought—brought rebellion.

No, it should not be the end.

She looked down at the dead man. She said:

"Poor Dr. Armstrong..."

Lombard sneered.

He said:

"What's this? Womanly pity?"

Vera said:

"Why not? Haven't *you* any pity?"

He said:

"I've no pity for you. Don't expect it!"

Vera looked down again at the body. She said:

"We must move him. Carry him up to the house."

"To join the other victims, I suppose? All neat and tidy. As far as I'm concerned he can stay where he is."

Vera said:

"At any rate, let's get him out of the reach of the sea."

Lombard laughed. He said:

"If you like."

He bent—tugging at the body. Vera leaned against him, helping him. She pulled and tugged with all her might.

Lombard panted:

"Not such an easy job."

They managed it, however, drawing the body clear of the high water mark.

Lombard said as he straightened up:

"Satisfied?"

Vera said:

"Quite."

Her tone warned him. He spun around. Even as he clapped his hand to his pocket he knew that he would find it empty.

She had moved a yard or two away and was facing him, revolver in hand.

Lombard said:

"So that's the reason for your womanly solicitude! You

wanted to pick my pocket."

She nodded.

She held it steadily and unwaveringly.

Death was very near to Philip Lombard now. It had never, he knew, been nearer.

Nevertheless he was not beaten yet.

He said authoritatively:

"Give that revolver to me."

Vera laughed.

Lombard said:

"Come on, hand it over."

His quick brain was working. Which way—which method—talk her over—lull her into security—or a swift dash—

All his life Lombard had taken the risky way. He took it now.

He spoke slowly, argumentatively:

"Now look here, my dear girl, you just listen—"

And then he sprang. Quick as a panther—as any other feline creature . . .

Automatically Vera pressed the trigger . . .

Lombard's leaping body stayed poised in mid-spring, then crashed heavily to the ground.

Vera came warily forward, the revolver ready in her hand.

But there was no need of caution.

Philip Lombard was dead—shot through the heart . . .

III

Relief possessed Vera—enormous exquisite relief.

At last it was over.

There was no more fear—no more steeling of her nerves...

She was alone on the island...

Alone with nine dead bodies...

But what did that matter? *She* was alive...

She sat there—exquisitely happy—exquisitely at peace...

No more fear...

IV

The sun was setting when Vera moved at last. Sheer reaction had kept her immobile. There had been no room in her for anything but the glorious sense of safety.

She realized now that she was hungry and sleepy. Principally sleepy. She wanted to throw herself on her bed and sleep and sleep and sleep...

Tomorrow, perhaps, they would come and rescue her—but she didn't really mind. She didn't mind staying here. Not now that she was alone...

Oh! blessed, blessed peace...

She got to her feet and glanced up at the house.

Nothing to be afraid of any longer! No terrors waiting for her! Just an ordinary well-built modern house. And yet, a little earlier in the day, she had not been able to look at it without shivering ...

Fear—what a strange thing fear was ...

Well, it was over now. She had conquered—had triumphed over the most deadly peril. By her own quick-wittedness and adroitness she had turned the tables on her would-be destroyer.

She began to walk up towards the house.

The sun was setting, the sky to the west was streaked with red and orange. It was beautiful and peaceful ...

Vera thought:

"The whole thing might be a dream ..."

How tired she was—terribly tired. Her limbs ached, her eyelids were drooping. Not to be afraid any more ... To sleep. Sleep ... sleep ... sleep ...

To sleep safely since she was alone on the island. One little soldier boy left all alone.

She smiled to herself.

She went in at the front door. The house, too, felt strangely peaceful.

Vera thought:

"Ordinarily one wouldn't care to sleep where there's a dead body in practically every bedroom!"

Should she go to the kitchen and get herself something to eat?

She hesitated a moment, then decided against it. She was really too tired ...

She paused by the dining room door. There were still three little china figures in the middle of the table.

Vera laughed.

She said:

"You're behind the times, my dears."

She picked up two of them and tossed them out through the window. She heard them crash on the stone of the terrace.

The third little figure she picked up and held in her hand. She said:

"You can come with me. We've won, my dear! We've won!"

The hall was dim in the dying light.

Vera, the little soldier clasped in her hand, began to mount the stairs. Slowly, because her legs were suddenly very tired.

"One little soldier boy left all alone." How did it end? Oh, yes! *"He got married and then there were none."*

Married . . . Funny, how she suddenly got the feeling again that Hugo was in the house . . .

Very strong. Yes, Hugo was upstairs waiting for her.

Vera said to herself:

"Don't be a fool. You're so tired that you're imagining the most fantastic things . . ."

Slowly up the stairs . . .

At the top of them something fell from her hand, making hardly any noise on the soft pile carpet. She did not notice that she had dropped the revolver. She was only conscious of clasping a little china figure.

How very quiet the house was. And yet—it didn't seem like an empty house...

Hugo, upstairs, waiting for her...

"*One little soldier boy left all alone...*" What was the last line again? Something about being married—or was it something else?

She had come now to the door of her room. Hugo was waiting for her inside—she was quite sure of it.

She opened the door...

She gave a gasp...

What was that—hanging from the hook in the ceiling? *A rope with a noose all ready? And a chair to stand upon—a chair that could be kicked away...*

That was what Hugo wanted...

And of course that was the last line of the rhyme.

"*He went and hanged himself and then there were None...*"

The little china figure fell from her hand. It rolled unheeded and broke against the fender.

Like an automaton Vera moved forward. This was the end—here where the cold wet hand (Cyril's hand, of course) had touched her throat...

"*You can go to the rock, Cyril...*"

That was what murder was—as easy as that!

But afterwards you went on remembering...

She climbed up on the chair, her eyes staring in front of

her like a sleepwalker's . . . She adjusted the noose round her neck.

Hugo was there to see she did what she had to do.

She kicked away the chair . . .

Epilogue

Sir Thomas Legge, Assistant Commissioner at Scotland Yard, said irritably:

"But the whole thing's incredible!"

Inspector Maine said respectfully:

"I know, sir."

The AC went on:

"Ten people dead on an island and not a living soul on it. It doesn't make sense!"

Inspector Maine said stolidly:

"Nevertheless, it *happened*, sir."

Sir Thomas Legge said:

"Dam' it all, Maine, somebody must have killed 'em."

"That's just our problem, sir."

"Nothing helpful in the doctor's report?"

"No, sir. Wargrave and Lombard were shot, the first through the head, the second through the heart. Miss Brent and Marston died of cyanide poisoning. Mrs. Rogers died of an overdose of chloral. Rogers' head was split open. Blore's head was crushed in. Armstrong died of drowning. Macarthur's skull was fractured by a blow on the back of the head and Vera Claythorne was hanged."

The AC winced. He said:

"Nasty business—all of it."

He considered for a minute or two. He said irritably:

"Do you mean to say that you haven't been able to get anything helpful out of the Sticklehaven people? Dash it, they must know something."

Inspector Maine shrugged his shoulders.

"They're ordinary decent seafaring folk. They know that the island was bought by a man called Owen—and that's about all they do know."

"Who provisioned the island and made all the necessary arrangements?"

"Man called Morris. Isaac Morris."

"And what does he say about it all?"

"He can't say anything, sir, he's dead."

The AC frowned.

"Do we know anything about this Morris?"

"Oh, yes, sir, we know about him. He wasn't a very savoury gentleman, Mr. Morris. He was implicated in that share-pushing fraud of Bennito's three years ago—we're sure of that though we can't prove it. And he was mixed up in the dope business. And again we can't prove it. He was a very careful man, Morris."

"And he was behind this island business?"

"Yes, sir, he put through the sale—though he made it clear that he was buying Soldier Island for a third party, unnamed."

"Surely there's something to be found out on the financial angle, there?"

Inspector Maine smiled.

"Not if you knew Morris! He can wangle figures until the best chartered accountant in the country wouldn't know if he was on his head or his heels! We've had a taste of that in the Bennito business. No, he covered his employer's tracks all right."

The other man sighed. Inspector Maine went on:

"It was Morris who made all the arrangements down at Sticklehaven. Represented himself as acting for 'Mr. Owen.' And it was he who explained to the people down there that there was some experiment on—some bet about living on a 'desert island' for a week—and that no notice was to be taken of any appeal for help from out there."

Sir Thomas Legge stirred uneasily. He said:

"And you're telling me that those people didn't smell a rat? Not even then?"

Maine shrugged his shoulders. He said:

"You're forgetting, sir, that Soldier Island previously belonged to young Elmer Robson, the American. He had the most extraordinary parties down there. I've no doubt the local people's eyes fairly popped out over them. But they got used to it and they'd begun to feel that anything to do with Soldier Island would necessarily be incredible. It's natural, that, sir, when you come to think of it."

The Assistant Commissioner admitted gloomily that he

supposed it was.

Maine said:

"Fred Narracott—that's the man who took the party out there—did say one thing that was illuminating. He said he was surprised to see what sort of people these were. 'Not at all like Mr. Robson's parties.' I think it was the fact that they were all so normal and so quiet that made him override Morris's orders and take out a boat to the island after he'd heard about the SOS signals."

"When did he and the other men go?"

"The signals were seen by a party of boy scouts on the morning of the 11th. There was no possibility of getting out there that day. The men got there on the afternoon of the 12th at the first moment possible to run a boat ashore there. They're all quite positive that nobody could have left the island before they got there. There was a big sea on after the storm."

"Couldn't someone have swum ashore?"

"It's over a mile to the coast and there were heavy seas and big breakers inshore. And there were a lot of people, boy scouts and others on the cliffs looking out towards the island and watching."

The AC sighed. He said:

"What about the gramophone record you found in the house? Couldn't you get hold of anything there that might help?"

Inspector Maine said:

"I've been into that. It was supplied by a firm that do a lot of theatrical stuff and film effects. It was sent to U. N. Owen, Esq., c/o Isaac Morris, and was understood to be required for the amateur performance of a hitherto unacted play. The typescript of it was returned with the record."

Legge said:

"And what about the subject matter, eh?"

Inspector Maine said gravely:

"I'm coming to that, sir."

He cleared his throat.

"I've investigated those accusations as thoroughly as I can.

"Starting with the Rogerses who were the first to arrive on the island. They were in service with a Miss Brady who died suddenly. Can't get anything definite out of the doctor who attended her. He says they certainly didn't poison her, or anything like that, but his personal belief is that there *was* some funny business—that she died as the result of neglect on their part. Says it's the sort of thing that's quite impossible to prove.

"Then there is Mr. Justice Wargrave. That's O.K. He was the judge who sentenced Seton.

"By the way, Seton was guilty—unmistakably guilty. Evidence turned up later, after he was hanged, which proved that beyond any shadow of doubt. But there was a good deal of comment at the time—nine people out of ten thought Seton was innocent and that the judge's summing up had been vindictive.

"The Claythorne girl, I find, was governess in a family where a death occurred by drowning. However, she doesn't seem to have had anything to do with it, and as a matter of fact she behaved very well, swam out to the rescue and was actually carried out to sea and only just rescued in time."

"Go on," said the AC with a sigh.

Maine took a deep breath.

"Dr. Armstrong now. Well-known man. Had a consulting-room in Harley Street. Absolutely straight and aboveboard in his profession. Haven't been able to trace any record of an illegal operation or anything of that kind. It's true that there *was* a woman called Clees who was operated on by him way back in 1925 at Leithmore, when he was attached to the hospital there. Peritonitis and she died on the operating table. Maybe he wasn't very skillful over the op—after all he hadn't much experience—but after all clumsiness isn't a criminal offence. There was certainly no motive.

"Then there's Miss Emily Brent. Girl, Beatrice Taylor, was in service with her. Got pregnant, was turned out by her mistress and went and drowned herself. Not a nice business—but again not criminal."

"That," said the AC, "seems to be the point. U. N. Owen dealt with cases that the law couldn't touch."

Maine went stolidly on with his list.

"Young Marston was a fairly reckless car driver—had his

license endorsed twice and he ought to have been prohibited from driving in my opinion. That's all there is to him. The two names John and Lucy Combes were those of two kids he knocked down and killed near Cambridge. Some friends of his gave evidence for him and he was let off with a fine.

"Can't find anything definite about General Macarthur. Fine record—war service—all the rest of it. Arthur Richmond was serving under him in France and was killed in action. No friction of any kind between him and the General. They were close friends as a matter of fact. There were some blunders made about that time—commanding officers sacrificed men unnecessarily—possibly this was a blunder of that kind."

"Possibly," said the AC.

"Now, Philip Lombard. Lombard has been mixed up in some very curious shows abroad. He's sailed very near the law once or twice. Got a reputation for daring and for not being overscrupulous. Sort of fellow who might do several murders in some quiet out of the way spot.

"Then we come to Blore." Maine hesitated. "He of course was one of our lot."

The other man stirred.

"Blore," said the Assistant Commissioner forcibly, "was a bad hat!"

"You think so, sir?"

The AC said:

"I always thought so. But he was clever enough to get away with it. It's my opinion that he committed black perjury in the Landor case. I wasn't happy about it at the time. But I couldn't find anything. I put Harris onto it and *he* couldn't find anything but I'm still of the opinion that there was something to find if we'd known how to set about it. The man wasn't straight."

There was a pause, then Sir Thomas Legge said:

"And Isaac Morris is dead, you say? When did he die?"

"I thought you'd soon come to that, sir. Isaac Morris died on the night of August 8th. Took an overdose of sleeping stuff—one of the barbiturates, I understand. There wasn't anything to show whether it was accident or suicide."

Legge said slowly:

"Care to know what I think, Maine?"

"Perhaps I can guess, sir."

Legge said heavily:

"That death of Morris's is a damned sight too opportune!"

Inspector Maine nodded. He said:

"I thought you'd say that, sir."

The Assistant Commissioner brought down his fist with a bang on the table. He cried out:

"The whole thing's fantastic—impossible. Ten people killed on a bare rock of an island—and we don't know who did it, or why, or how."

Maine coughed. He said:

"Well, it's not quite like that, sir. We do know *why*, more or less. Some fanatic with a bee in his bonnet about justice. He was out to get people who were beyond the reach of the law. He picked ten people—whether they were really guilty or not doesn't matter—"

The Commissioner stirred. He said sharply:

"Doesn't it? It seems to me—"

He stopped. Inspector Maine waited respectfully. With a sigh Legge shook his head.

"Carry on," he said. "Just for a minute I felt I'd got somewhere. Got, as it were, the clue to the thing. It's gone now. Go ahead with what you were saying."

Maine went on:

"There were ten people to be—executed, let's say. They *were* executed. U. N. Owen accomplished his task. And somehow or other he spirited himself off that island into thin air."

The AC said:

"First-class vanishing trick. But you know, Maine, there must be an explanation."

Maine said:

"You're thinking, sir, that if the man wasn't on the island, he couldn't have left the island, and according to the account of the interested parties he never was on the island. Well, then the only explanation possible is that he was actually one of the ten."

The AC nodded.

Maine said earnestly:

"We thought of that, sir. We went into it. Now, to begin with, we're not quite in the dark as to what happened on Soldier Island. Vera Claythorne kept a diary, so did Emily Brent. Old Wargrave made some notes—dry legal cryptic stuff, but quite clear. And Blore made notes too. All those accounts tally. The deaths occurred in this order. Marston, Mrs. Rogers, Macarthur, Rogers, Miss Brent, Wargrave. After his death Vera Claythorne's diary states that Armstrong left the house in the night and that Blore and Lombard had gone after him. Blore has one more entry in his notebook. Just two words. 'Armstrong disappeared.'

"Now, sir, it seemed to me, taking everything into account, that we might find here a perfectly good solution. Armstrong was drowned, you remember. Granting that Armstrong was mad, what was to prevent him having killed off all the others and then committed suicide by throwing himself over the cliff, or perhaps while trying to swim to the mainland?

"That was a good solution—but it won't do. No, sir, it won't do. First of all there's the police surgeon's evidence. He got to the island early on the morning of August 13. He couldn't say much to help us. All he could say was that all the people had been dead at least thirty-six hours and probably a good deal longer. But he was fairly definite about Armstrong. Said he must have been from eight to ten hours in the water before his body was washed up. That works out at this, that Armstrong must have gone into the sea sometime during the night of the 10th-11th—and I'll explain why. We found the point where the body was washed up—it had been wedged between two rocks and there were bits of cloth, hair, etc. on them. It must have been deposited there at high water on the 11th—that's to say round about 11 o'clock a.m. After that, the storm subsided, and succeeding high water marks are considerably lower.

"You might say, I suppose, that Armstrong managed to polish off the other three *before* he went into the sea that night. But there's another point and one you can't get over. *Armstrong's body had been dragged above high water mark.* We found it well above the reach of any tide. And it was laid out straight on the ground—all neat and tidy.

"So that settles one point definitely. *Someone* was alive on the island *after Armstrong was dead.*"

He paused and then went on.

"And that leaves—just what exactly? Here's the position early on the morning of the 11th. Armstrong has 'disappeared' (*drowned*). That leaves us three people. Lombard, Blore and Vera Claythorne. Lombard was shot. His body was down by the sea—near Armstrong's. Vera Claythorne was found hanged in her own bedroom. Blore's body was on the terrace. His head was crushed in by a heavy marble clock that it seems reasonable to suppose fell on him from the window above."

The AC said sharply:

"Whose window?"

"Vera Claythorne's. Now, sir, let's take each of these cases separately. First Philip Lombard. Let's say *he* pushed over that lump of marble on to Blore—then he doped Vera Claythorne and strung her up. Lastly, he went down to the seashore and shot himself.

"But if so, *who took away the revolver from him?* For that revolver was found up in the house just inside the door at the top of the stairs—Wargrave's room."

The AC said:

"Any fingerprints on it?"

"Yes, sir, Vera Claythorne's."

"But, man alive, then—"

"I know what you're going to say, sir. That it was Vera Claythorne. That she shot Lombard, took the revolver back to the house, toppled the marble block on to Blore and then—hanged herself.

"And that's quite all right—up to a point. There's a chair in her bedroom and on the seat of it there are marks of seaweed same as on her shoes. Looks as though she stood on the chair, adjusted the rope round her neck and kicked away the chair.

"*But that chair wasn't found kicked over.* It was, like all the other chairs, neatly put back against the wall. That was done *after Vera Claythorne's death*—by *someone else*.

"That leaves us with Blore and if you tell me that after shooting Lombard and inducing Vera Claythorne to hang herself he then went out and pulled down a whacking great block of marble on himself by tying a string to it or something like that—well, I simply don't believe you. Men don't commit suicide that way—and what's more Blore wasn't that kind of man. *We* knew Blore—and he was not the man that you'd ever accuse of a desire for abstract justice."

The Assistant Commissioner said:

"I agree."

Inspector Maine said:

"And therefore, sir, there must have been *someone else* on the island. Someone who tidied up when the whole business was over. But where was he all the time—and where did he go to? The Sticklehaven people are absolutely certain that no one could have left the island before the rescue boat got there. But in that case—"

He stopped.

The Assistant Commissioner said:

"In that case—"

He sighed. He shook his head. He leaned forward.

"But in that case," he said, "*who killed them?*"

A MANUSCRIPT DOCUMENT SENT TO SCOTLAND YARD BY THE MASTER OF THE *EMMA JANE* FISHING TRAWLER

From my earliest youth I realized that my nature was a mass of contradictions. I have, to begin with, an incurably romantic imagination. The practice of throwing a bottle into the sea with an important document inside was one that never failed to thrill me when reading adventure stories as a child. It thrills me still—and for that reason I have adopted this course—writing my confession, enclosing it in a bottle, sealing the latter, and casting it into the waves. There is, I suppose, a hundred to one chance that my confession may be found—and then (or do I flatter myself?) a hitherto unsolved murder mystery will be explained.

I was born with other traits besides my romantic fancy. I have a definite sadistic delight in seeing or causing death. I remember experiments with wasps—with various garden pests ... From an early age I knew very strongly the lust to kill.

But side by side with this went a contradictory trait—a strong sense of justice. It is abhorrent to me that an innocent person or creature should suffer or die by any act of mine. I have always felt strongly that right should prevail.

It may be understood—I think a psychologist would understand—that with my mental makeup being what it was, I adopted the law as a profession. The legal profession satisfied nearly all my instincts.

Crime and its punishment has always fascinated me. I enjoy reading every kind of detective story and thriller. I have devised for my own private amusement the most ingenious ways of carrying out a murder.

When in due course I came to preside over a court of law, that other secret instinct of mine was encouraged to develop. To see a wretched criminal squirming in the dock, suffering the tortures of the damned, as his doom came slowly and slowly nearer, was to me an exquisite pleasure. Mind you, I took no pleasure in seeing an *innocent* man there. On at least two occasions I stopped cases where to my mind the accused was palpably innocent, directing the jury that there was no case. Thanks, however, to the fairness and efficiency of our police force, the majority of the accused persons who have come before me to be tried for murder, have been guilty.

I will say here that such was the case with the man Edward Seton. His appearance and manner were misleading and he created a good impression on the jury. But not only the evidence, which was clear, though unspectacular, but my own knowledge of criminals told me without any doubt that the man had actually committed the crime with which he was charged, the brutal murder of an elderly woman who trusted him.

I have a reputation as a hanging judge, but that is unfair. I have always been strictly just and scrupulous in my summing up of a case.

All I have done is to protect the jury against the emotional effect of emotional appeals by some of our more emotional counsel. I have drawn their attention to the actual evidence.

For some years past I have been aware of a change within myself, a lessening of control—a desire to act instead of to judge.

I have wanted—let me admit it frankly—*to commit a murder myself*. I recognized this as the desire of the artist to express himself! I was, or could be, an artist in crime! My imagination, sternly checked by the exigencies of my profession, waxed secretly to colossal force.

I must—I must—I *must*—commit a murder! And what is more, it must be no ordinary murder! It must be a fantastical crime—something stupendous—out of the common! In that one respect, I have still, I think, an adolescent's imagination.

I wanted something theatrical, impossible!

I wanted to kill ... Yes, I wanted to kill ...

But—incongruous as it may seem to some—I was restrained and hampered by my innate sense of justice. The innocent must not suffer.

And then, quite suddenly, the idea came to me—started

by a chance remark uttered during casual conversation. It was a doctor to whom I was talking—some ordinary undistinguished GP. He mentioned casually how often murder must be committed which the law was unable to touch.

And he instanced a particular case—that of an old lady, a patient of his who had recently died. He was, he said, himself convinced that her death was due to the withholding of a restorative drug by a married couple who attended on her and who stood to benefit very substantially by her death. That sort of thing, he explained, was quite impossible to prove, but he was nevertheless quite sure of it in his own mind. He added that there were many cases of a similar nature going on all the time—cases of deliberate murder—and all quite untouchable by the law.

That was the beginning of the whole thing. I suddenly saw my way clear. And I determined to commit not one murder, but murder on a grand scale.

A childish rhyme of my infancy came back into my mind—the rhyme of the ten little soldier boys. It had fascinated me as a child of two—the inexorable diminishment—the sense of inevitability.

I began, secretly, to collect victims ...

I will not take up space here by going into details of how this was accomplished. I had a certain routine line of conversation which I employed with nearly every one I met—and the results I got were really surprising. During the time I was in a nursing home I collected the case of Dr. Armstrong—a violently teetotal Sister who attended on me being anxious to prove to me the evils of drink by recounting to me a case many years ago in hospital when a doctor under the influence of alcohol had killed a patient on whom he was operating. A careless question as to where the Sister in question had trained, etc., soon gave me the necessary data. I tracked down the doctor and the patient mentioned without difficulty.

A conversation between two old military gossips in my Club put me on the track of General Macarthur. A man who had recently returned from the Amazon gave me a devastating résumé of the activities of one Philip Lombard. An indignant mem-sahib in Majorca recounted the tale of the Puritan Emily Brent and her wretched servant girl. Anthony Marston I selected from a large group of people who had committed similar offences. His complete callousness and his inability to feel any responsibility for the lives he had taken made him, I considered, a type dangerous to the community and unfit to live. Ex-Inspector Blore came my way quite naturally, some of my professional brethren discussing the Landor case with freedom and vigour. I took a serious view of his offence. The police, as servants of the law, must be of a high order of integrity. For their word is perforce believed by virtue of their profession.

Finally there was the case of Vera Claythorne. It was

when I was crossing the Atlantic. At a late hour one night the sole occupants of the smoking room were myself and a good-looking young man called Hugo Hamilton.

Hugo Hamilton was unhappy. To assuage that unhappiness he had taken a considerable quantity of drink. He was in the maudlin confidential stage. Without much hope of any result I automatically started my routine conversational gambit. The response was startling. I can remember his words now. He said:

"You're right. Murder isn't what most people think—giving some one a dollop of arsenic—pushing them over a cliff—that sort of stuff." He leaned forward, thrusting his face into mine. He said, "I've known a murderess—known her, I tell you. And what's more I was crazy about her ... God help me, sometimes I think I still am ... It's hell, I tell you—hell. You see, she did it more or less for me ... Not that I ever dreamed. Women are fiends—absolute fiends—you wouldn't think a girl like that—a nice straight jolly girl—you wouldn't think she'd do that, would you? That she'd take a kid out to sea and let it drown—you wouldn't think a *woman* could do a thing like that?"

I said to him:

"Are you sure she did do it?"

He said and in saying it he seemed suddenly to sober up:

"I'm quite sure. Nobody else ever thought of it. But I knew the moment I looked at her—when I got back—after ... And she knew I knew ... What she didn't realize was that I loved that kid ..."

He didn't say any more, but it was easy enough for me to trace back the story and reconstruct it.

I needed a tenth victim. I found him in a man named Morris. He was a shady little creature. Amongst other things he was a dope pedlar and he was responsible for inducing the daughter of friends of mine to take to drugs. She committed suicide at the age of twenty-one.

During all this time of search my plan had been gradually maturing in my mind. It was now complete and the coping stone to it was an interview I had with a doctor in Harley Street. I have mentioned that I underwent an operation. My interview in Harley Street told me that another operation would be useless. My medical adviser wrapped up the information very prettily, but I am accustomed to getting at the truth of a statement.

I did not tell the doctor of my decision—that my death should not be a slow and protracted one as it would be in the course of nature. No, my death should take place in a blaze of excitement. I would *live* before I died.

And now to the actual mechanics of the crime of Soldier Island. To acquire the island, using the man Morris to cover my tracks, was easy enough. He was an expert in that sort of thing. Tabulating the information I had collected about my prospective victims, I was able to concoct a suitable bait for each. None of my plans miscarried. All my guests arrived at Soldier Island on the 8th of August. The party included myself.

Morris was already accounted for. He suffered from indigestion. Before leaving London I gave him a capsule to take last thing at night which had, I said, done wonders for my own gastric juices. He accepted unhesitatingly—the man was a slight hypochondriac. I had no fear that he would leave any compromising documents or memoranda behind. He was not that sort of man.

The order of death upon the island had been subjected by me to special thought and care. There were, I considered, amongst my guests, varying degrees of guilt. Those whose guilt was the lightest should, I decided, pass out first, and not suffer the prolonged mental strain and fear that the more cold-blooded offenders were to suffer.

Anthony Marston and Mrs. Rogers died first, the one instantaneously the other in a peaceful sleep. Marston, I recognized, was a type born without that feeling of moral responsibility which most of us have. He was amoral—pagan. Mrs. Rogers, I had no doubt, had acted very largely under the influence of her husband.

I need not describe closely how those two met their deaths. The police will have been able to work that out quite easily. Potassium cyanide is easily obtained by householders for putting down wasps. I had some in my possession and it was easy to slip it into Marston's almost empty glass during the tense period after the gramophone recital.

I may say that I watched the faces of my guests closely during that indictment and I had no doubt whatever, after my long court experience, that one and all were guilty.

During recent bouts of pain, I had been ordered a sleeping draught—Chloral Hydrate. It had been easy for me to suppress this until I had a lethal amount in my possession. When Rogers brought up some brandy for his wife, he set it down on a table and in passing that table I put the stuff into the brandy. It was easy, for at that time suspicion had not begun to set in.

General Macarthur met his death quite painlessly. He did not hear me come up behind him. I had, of course, to choose my time for leaving the terrace very carefully, but everything was successful.

As I had anticipated, a search was made of the island and it was discovered that there was no one on it but our seven selves. That at once created an atmosphere of suspicion. According to my plan I should shortly need an ally. I selected Dr. Armstrong for that part. He was a gullible sort of man, he knew me by sight and reputation and it was inconceivable to him that a man of my standing should actually be a murderer! All his suspicions were directed against Lombard and I pretended to concur in these. I hinted to him that I had a scheme by which it might be possible to trap the murderer into incriminating himself.

Though a search had been made of everyone's room, no search had as yet been made of the persons themselves. But that was bound to come soon.

I killed Rogers on the morning of August 10th. He was chopping sticks for lighting the fire and did not hear me approach. I found the key to the dining room door in his pocket. He had locked it the night before.

In the confusion attending the finding of Rogers' body I slipped into Lombard's room and abstracted his revolver. I knew that he would have one with him—in fact, I had instructed Morris to suggest as much when he interviewed him.

At breakfast I slipped my last dose of chloral into Miss Brent's coffee when I was refilling her cup. We left her in the dining room. I slipped in there a little while later—she was nearly unconscious and it was easy to inject a strong solution of cyanide into her. The bumble bee business was really rather childish—but somehow, you know, it pleased me. I liked adhering as closely as possible to my nursery rhyme.

Immediately after this what I had already foreseen happened—indeed I believe I suggested it myself. We all submitted to a rigorous search. I had safely hidden away the revolver, and had no more cyanide or chloral in my possession.

It was then that I intimated to Armstrong that we must carry our plan into effect. It was simply this—*I* must appear to be the next victim. That would perhaps rattle the murderer—at any rate once I was supposed to be dead I could move about the house and spy upon the unknown murderer.

Armstrong was keen on the idea. We carried it out that evening. A little plaster of red mud on the forehead—the red curtain and the wool and the stage was set. The lights of the candles were very flickering and uncertain and the only person who would examine me closely was Armstrong.

It worked perfectly. Miss Claythorne screamed the house down when she found the seaweed which I had thoughtfully arranged in her room. They all rushed up, and I took up my pose of a murdered man.

The effect on them when they found me was all that could be desired. Armstrong acted his part in the most professional manner. They carried me upstairs and laid me on my bed. Nobody worried about me, they were all too deadly scared and terrified of each other.

I had a rendezvous with Armstrong outside the house at a quarter to two. I took him up a little way behind the house on the edge of the cliff. I said that here we could see if any one else approached us, and we should not be seen from the house as the bedrooms faced the other way. He was still quite unsuspicious—and yet he ought to have been warned—if he had only remembered the words of the nursery rhyme. "A red herring swallowed one . . ." He took the red herring all right.

It was quite easy. I uttered an exclamation, leant over the cliff, told him to look, wasn't that the mouth of a cave? He leant right over. A quick vigorous push sent him off his balance and splash into the heaving sea below. I returned to the house. It must have been my footfall that Blore heard. A few minutes after I had returned to Armstrong's room I left it, this time making a certain amount of noise so that someone *should* hear me. I heard a door open as I got to the bottom of the stairs. They must have just glimpsed my figure as I went out of the front door.

It was a minute or two before they followed me. I had gone straight round the house and in at the dining room window which I had left open. I shut the window and later I broke the glass. Then I went upstairs and laid myself out again on my bed.

I calculated that they would search the house again, but I did not think they would look closely at any of the corpses, a mere twitch aside of the sheet to satisfy themselves that it was not Armstrong masquerading as a body. This is exactly what occurred.

I forgot to say that I returned the revolver to Lombard's room. It may be of interest to someone to know where it was hidden during the search. There was a big pile of tinned food in the larder. I opened the bottommost of the tins—biscuits I think it contained, bedded in the revolver and replaced the strip of adhesive tape.

I calculated, and rightly, that no one would think of working their way through a pile of apparently untouched foodstuffs, especially as all the top tins were soldered.

The red curtain I had concealed by laying it flat on the seat of one of the drawing room chairs under the chintz cover and the wool in the seat cushion, cutting a small hole.

And now came the moment that I had anticipated—three people who were so frightened of each other that anything might happen—*and one of them had a revolver*. I watched them from the windows of the house. When Blore came up alone I had the big marble clock poised ready. *Exit Blore* . . .

From my window I saw Vera Claythorne shoot Lombard. A daring and resourceful young woman. I always thought she was a match for him and more. As soon as that had happened I set the stage in her bedroom.

It was an interesting psychological experiment. Would the consciousness of her own guilt, the state of nervous tension consequent on having just shot a man, be sufficient, together with the hypnotic suggestion of the surroundings, to cause her to take her own life? I thought it would. I was right. Vera Claythorne hanged herself before my eyes where I stood in the shadow of the wardrobe.

And now for the last stage. I came forward, picked up the chair and set it against the wall. I looked for the revolver and found it at the top of the stairs where the girl had dropped it. I was careful to preserve her fingerprints on it.

And now?

I shall finish writing this. I shall enclose it and seal it in a bottle and I shall throw the bottle into the sea.

Why?

Yes, why? ...

It was my ambition to *invent* a murder mystery that no one could solve.

But no artist, I now realize, can be satisfied with art alone. There is a natural craving for recognition which cannot be gainsaid.

I have, let me confess it in all humility, a pitiful human wish that someone should know just how clever I have been ...

In all this, I have assumed that the mystery of Soldier Island will remain unsolved. It may be, of course, that the police will be cleverer than I think. There are, after all, three clues. One: the police are perfectly aware that Edward Seton was guilty. They know, therefore, that one of the ten people on the island was not a murderer in any sense of the word, and it follows, paradoxically, that that person must logically be *the* murderer. The second clue lies in the seventh verse of the nursery rhyme. Armstrong's death is associated with a "red herring" which he swallowed—or rather which resulted in swallowing him! That is to say that at that stage of the affair some hocus-pocus is clearly indicated—and that Armstrong was deceived by it and sent to his death. That might start a promising line of inquiry. For at that period there are only four persons and of those four I am clearly the only one likely to inspire him with confidence.

The third is symbolical. The manner of my death marking

me on the forehead. The brand of Cain.

There is, I think, little more to say.

After entrusting my bottle and its message to the sea I shall go to my room and lay myself down on the bed. To my eyeglasses is attached what seems a length of fine black cord—but it is elastic cord. I shall lay the weight of the body on the glasses. The cord I shall loop round the door handle and attach it, not too solidly, to the revolver. What I think will happen is this:

My hand, protected with a handkerchief, will press the trigger. My hand will fall to my side, the revolver, pulled by the elastic, will recoil to the door, jarred by the door handle it will detach itself from the elastic and fall. The elastic, released, will hang down innocently from the eyeglasses on which my body is lying. A handkerchief lying on the floor will cause no comment whatever.

I shall be found, laid neatly on my bed, shot through the forehead in accordance with the record kept by my fellow victims. Times of death cannot be stated with any accuracy by the time our bodies are examined.

When the sea goes down, there will come from the mainland boats and men.

And they will find ten dead bodies and an unsolved problem on Soldier Island.

Signed:
Lawrence Wargrave.

NOTES

📖 CHAPTER 1

p.5 1 smoking carriage 喫煙車 1 Mr. Justice Wargrave ウォーグレイヴ判事 2 lately retired from the bench 少し前に判事の座を退いた 3 *The Times*『タイムズ』紙（英国の有力新聞） 5 Somerset サマセット州 7 went over in his mind ひとつひとつ思い浮かべてみた 10 yachting ヨット遊び 10 account of... ～に関する説明 11 little island off the Devon coast デヴォン州の海岸沖にある小さな島 13 bad sailor 船酔いするたちの人 13 subsequent その後の 14 glowing 称賛に満ちた 16 bald statement そっけない記述 20 free from all publicity マスコミから逃れて 20 *Busy Bee*「忙しいミツバチ」（コラムの名前）

p.6 1 hinted delicately それとなくにおわせた 1 adobe for Royalty 王族の住まい 2 *Mr. Merryweather*「ミスター・メリーウェザー」（コラムの名前） 4 surrendered to Cupid キューピッドの愛の矢に射ぬかれた 4 *Jonas*「ジョーナス」（コラムの名前） 4 knew for a *fact* 事実として知っていた 5 Admiralty 海軍省 5 with a view to... ～をするために 6 hush-hush 極秘の 9 practically illegible ひどく読みにくい 12 *enchanting* とても魅力的な 13 *communion with nature* 自然との交わり 13 *bask in sunshine* 日差しを浴びる 14 *Paddington* （ロンドンの）パディントン駅 15 correspondent 手紙を書く人 15 with a flourish 麗々しく 17 cast back in his mind 過去を振り返った 21 *contadini* 農民 21 proceeded to... ～まで足をのばした 23 bedouin（遊牧民の）ベドウィン 26 in gentle approval of his logic 自分の考えに納得した

p.7 7 third-class carriage 三等車 11 holiday post 学校が休みの間のアルバイト 12 looking after a swarm of children 大勢の子どもの世話 12 secretarial 秘書の 14 agency 職業紹介所 14 hadn't held out much hope あまり期待を持たせなかった 20 *take up your duties* 仕事を始める 22 £1 notes 1ポンド札

p.8 1 there had been nothing else in the papers 新聞はその話題で

288

もちきりだった 5 the last word in luxury これ以上ないほどの豪華さ 6 strenuous 非常に骨が折れる 7 games mistress 体育教師 8 isn't much of a catch 理想的とは言えない 9 *decent* まともな 12 Coroner's Inquest 検死審問 13 acquit me of all blame 私には何の責任もないと無罪を宣言した 14 complimented 称賛した 14 presence of mind 冷静沈着さ 18 shivered 身震いした 20 *bobbing up and down* 浮いたり沈んだりしている 22 in easy practised strokes 熟練した泳ぎ方で 23 cleaving her way through the water 水を切って進んでいる

p.9   2 light eyes set rather close together 薄い色の目と目の間が狭い 3 arrogant ふてぶてしい 3 cruel 冷酷 11 summing up the girl opposite in a mere flash of his quick moving eyes すばやく目をちらっと向けただけで向かいの席の若い女性を品定めして 13 schoolmistressy 教師風 14 cool customer 平然としている人 15 hold her own 引けを取らない 16 take her on 彼女の相手をする 17 cut out all that kind of stuff そんな余計なことは考えるな 21 take it or leave it いやならいやでかまわない 21 Captain Lombard ロンバード大尉 23 *guineas* ギニー（イギリスで用いられていた金貨） 25 he was literally down to his last square meal あと一回まともな食事をしたら財布が空っぽになる 26 fancied... ～ではないかと思った 27 not been deceived だまされていない

p.10 1 damnable いまいましい 5 bald 髪のない 6 positively きっぱりと 7 the matter rests there これ以上話せることはない 8 a good man in a tight place ピンチに強い男 9 empowered to... ～する権限を与えられている 12 motored to... ～まで車で送られる 13 motor launch モーターボート 14 hold yourself at the disposal of my client 私の依頼人の指示に従う 15 abruptly 突然 19 undertake 引き受ける 19 illegal 違法の 20 darted a very sharp glance at the other 相手に鋭い視線を向けた 22 Semitic ユダヤ人の 22 gravely まじめくさって 23 be at perfect liberty to withdraw 身を引くのはまったく自由である 25 smooth 口先のうまい 25 brute ひどいやつ 27 legality 合法性 27 *sine qua non* (ラテン語) 必須条件

p.11 2 By Jove まったく 2 sailed pretty near the wind 限度ぎりぎりの

ところにいった 3 got away with it 何の罰も受けないですんだ 4 drew the line at 一線を引いて〜しない 12 as was her custom いつものように 13 lounging ゆったりとくつろぐこと 13 of the old school 昔かたぎの 14 particular about ... 〜についてうるさい 14 deportment 立ち居振る舞い 15 lax だらしない 16 carriage 身のこなし 17 righteousness 高潔さ 17 unyielding principles ゆるぎない信念 19 triumphed over ... 〜に打ち勝った 21 injections 注射 23 allowed their figures to slop about anyhow 体をさらすことにまったく無頓着で 26 lips set closely 唇をきゅっと結んだ 26 make an example of ... 〜を見せしめにする

p.12 3 mentally 心の中で 11 *opening* チャンス 12 *good plain cooking* 素朴でおいしい料理 13 *nudity* 裸 13 *gramophones* 蓄音機 22 impatiently いらいらして 23 illegibly 判読できないように 25 two summers running 二夏続けて 27 Canon 司教座聖堂参事会員

p.13 9 disadvantages 不便 11 *at any rate* とにかく 13 dividends 配当 14 take into consideration 考慮に入れる 23 as the crow flies 直線距離で

p.14 1 *cronies* 仲間 5 fighting shy of him 彼を避けている 6 owing to ... 〜のせいで 9 brooding くよくよ考えている 11 queerly 奇妙に 14 War Office 陸軍省 15 Air Force 空軍 18 every mortal luxury ありとあらゆる贅沢 25 Salisbury Plain ソールズベリー平野 26 penalties 代償 27 consulting room 診察室

p.15 1 correctly apparelled きちんとした服装で 2 appliances (医療)器具 4 venture 冒険的事業 8 accurate diagnosis 正確な診断 10 word had got about うわさが広まった 12 put his finger on the trouble 問題を突き止めた 13 The ball had started rolling. ボールが転がりだした 14 arrived 成功した 19 vague 漠然とした 20 accompanying 同封されている 20 cheque 小切手 20 whacking fee びっくりするような報酬 24 wouldn't hear of ... 〜 (という忠告) を聞こうとしない

p.16 2 boredom 退屈 6 putting right 回復させること 8 medicine was mostly faith-healing だいたい医療というものは、信じれば治るもの

だ　**9** inspire hope and belief 希望と信じる気持ちを与える　**11** pull himself together 立ち直る　**12** it had been a near thing あのときは本当に危なかった　**13** going to pieces めちゃくちゃになる　**14** cut out drink 酒をやめた　**16** devastating 衝撃的な　**16** ear-splitting 耳をつんざく　**19** hedge 生垣　**20** a near shave 間一髪

p.17　**5** let out スピードを出す　**6** heaps of... たくさんの〜　**8** fizzing 信じられないような　**11** rich and stinking 超大金持ち　**11** rather good at nosing people like that out そういう人間をかぎ出すのがうまい　**13** chap 男　**15** fellows who'd made their money and weren't born to it 金持ちの家に生まれたのでなく、自分で財を築いた人間　**16** pity 残念なこと　**22** admiringly ほれぼれと　**23** well-proportioned 均整のとれた　**24** intensely blue eyes 深みのある青い目　**26** errand boys 使い走りの少年　**27** latter 後者

p.18　**1** triumphal 勝利の　**7** seafaring 船乗りの　**8** bleary eye 涙でかすんだ目　**14** C.M.G. 聖マイケル・聖ジョージ勲章　**14** D.S.O. 殊勲従軍勲章　**14** manservant 男性の召使い　**17** slumbering 寝ている　**18** had one over the eight 酔っ払っている　**19** conscientiously 慎重に　**21** ruminated 思いめぐらせた　**22** slip up へまをする　**23** scrutinized じっくり観察した　**24** of a slightly military cast 軍人風の　**27** Major 少佐

p.19　**1** gent (gentleman) 紳士　**1** spot... 〜を見破る　**4** travel folder 旅行案内　**6** colonials 植民地住民　**7** a man of means 金持ち　**7** he could enter into any society unchallenged どんな場所でも怪しまれることはない　**10** smelly 臭い　**10** gulls カモメ　**13** whims 気まぐれ　**16** soothingly なだめるように　**17** hiccuped しゃっくりをした　**17** plaintively 悲しそうに　**18** squall 突風　**23** pacifically 穏やかに　**26** thish (this is) ここ　**26** fumbled with the window おぼつかない手つきで窓を開けようとした

p.20　**3** The day of judgment is at hand. 審判の日は近い　**5** collapsed 倒れこんだ　**6** recumbent position 横たわった姿勢　**7** with immense dignity 威厳をこめて　**10** subsiding 腰かけながら

▸ *CHAPTER 2*

p.21　**2** momentary 一時的な　**2** uncertainty とまどい　**2** porters 赤帽

6 gave assent 同意した 7 surreptitious こそこそした 10 party 一行 19 suggestion of command 命令調 20 occupied a position of authority 人に指図するような仕事に就いていた

p.22 　3 stiffly 堅苦しく 12 with due legal caution 判事らしく当たりさわりのない言葉を選んで 16 distinguished 上品な 20 inquired 尋ねた 25 unacquainted with... ～に不案内な

p.23 　2 decisively きっぱりと 7 stuffy 風通しの悪い 10 trying つらい 11 conventionally 月並みに 13 treacherous （天候が）当てにならない 21 imperceptibly かすかに 22 assured 自信に満ちた 26 taken ill 病気になった 26 wired 電報を打った 26 substitute 代役

p.24 　8 fascinating 魅力的な 11 keen on... ～に夢中になっている 13 awkward 気まずい 15 wasp スズメバチ 22 drawn-out 長くのびた 25 soldierly 軍人らしい 26 clipped close 短く刈りこんだ 27 neatly trimmed きれいに手入れした

p.25 　1 staggering よろめいて 3 competent 有能な 6 shrewd 抜け目のない 6 sized up 品定めした 14 plunged 飛びこんだ 14 a maze of cross-country lanes 迷路のような田舎道 14 steep 険しい 21 luscious-looking 豊かそうに見える 22 critically 批判的に 23 shut in 狭苦しい 27 disparagingly つまらなさそうに

p.26 　10 a mere cluster of cottages 小さな家がいくつかかたまっているだけの村 13 jutting up out of the sea 海から突き出している 19 faint resemblance to... ～にどことなく似ている 20 sinister 不吉な 22 inn 旅館 23 hunched 背中を丸めた 23 figure 人の姿 25 bluff ぶっきらぼうな 26 might as well... ～したほうがよさそうだ

p.27 　1 Natal （南アフリカの）ナタール州 1 natal spot 出生地 2 breezily 明るく 4 malevolence 敵意 7 a little nip 軽く一杯 7 embark 乗船する 8 hospitably 愛想よく 9 proposition 提案 13 curious 奇妙な 13 constraint ぎこちなさ 16 paralysing 麻痺させる 17 beckoning 招き寄せる 17 detached 離れた 19 rolling ゆらゆらと揺れる 19 gait 歩き方 19 proclaimed 明らかに示した 20 weather-beaten 深いしわを刻んだ 21 evasive あいまいな

p.28 　1 jetty 桟橋 4 persuasively 説得力を持って 6 as easy as winking とても簡単な 11 swell （波の）うねり 13 followed suit 先例にならっ

た　**14** fraternizing 親しい交わり　**15** puzzled 当惑している　**16** cast loose（ボートを岸から）解き放す　**19** fantastically とてつもなく　**19** superlatively きわめて　**20** apparition 亡霊　**27** something more than mortal 人間よりすばらしい何か

p.29　**7** a queer lot 風変わりな連中　**9** classy 上品な　**9** togged up 着飾った　**18** his Missus 彼の奥さん　**20** prompt 早い　**27** summed them up 彼らを評価した　**27** dispassionately 冷静に

p.30　**1** old maid オールドミス　**1** sour 気難しい　**2** tartar 始末におえない女　**5** cheery 陽気な　**7** lean やせた　**10** the pictures 映画　**24** churned 水面を波立たせて　**26** shelved 緩やかに傾斜して

p.31　**3** nosed ゆっくり進んだ　**4** inlet 入江　**8** southeasterly 南東風　**12** domestic problems 家事の問題　**13** grated against the rocks 岩をこすった　**14** alight 降りる　**15** made the boat fast to ... ～にボートを係留した　**19** felt uneasy 不安感を覚えた　**20** ascended 登った　**21** their spirits revived 彼らは元気を取り戻した　**22** correct butler ちゃんとした執事　**23** gravity 重々しさ　**23** reassured 安心させた　**27** lank ひょろりと背が高い　**27** respectable きちんとした

p.32　**4** rum 奇妙な　**4** None of *his* lot! 彼と同じ人種はひとりもいない　**21** uttered a quick exclamation of pleasure 歓声をあげた

p.33　**3** monotonous 単調な　**6** eyes that shifted the whole time from place to place 落ち着きなくキョロキョロと動く目　**9** frightened of her own shadow 自分の影におびえている　**11** in mortal fear ひどく恐れて　**21** flickered 細かく動いた　**24** extraordinary 奇妙な

p.34　**15** disturbed 困惑した　**17** ghostlike 幽霊のような　**18** oddly assorted party 不思議な取り合わせの一行　**24** gleaming ぴかぴかの　**24** parquet floor 寄せ木張りの床　**25** tinted 色のついた　**26** mantelpiece マントルピース（暖炉の上の飾り棚）　**26** bare of ornaments 装飾品がない　**26** save for ... ～を除いて

p.35　**1** inset はめこまれた　**2** parchment 羊皮紙　**4** nursery rhyme 童謡　**8** *choked* 窒息した　**10** *sat up very late* 遅くまで起きていた　**11** *overslept* 寝坊した　**16** *chopping up sticks* 薪を割っている　**17** *in halves* 半分に　**19** *hive* ミツバチの巣　**22** *going in for law* 法律を志している　**23** *Chancery* 大法官庁　**26** *red herring* 燻製のニシン

(注意を他へそらす謎のヒントなど)

p.36 5 *frizzled up* パリパリに焦げた 8 *hanged himself* 自分で首を吊った 14 vast expanse of blue water 青い海の広がり 14 rippling さざ波を立てている 17 depths (海の) 底 17 drowned 溺れた

p.37 3 ill-informed よく知らない 14 keep his nose to the grindstone あくせく働く 20 lost touch with the world 浮世離れしている

p.38 3 tortoise-like カメのような 5 given evidence 証言した 8 jury 陪審員 8 make their minds up for them 彼らを思いどおりに操作する 9 any day of the week どんなときでも 10 convictions 有罪判決 10 hanging judge 極刑を科すことが多い判事 18 witness-box 証言台 21 suave 慇懃な 22 personage 人物 23 grunted うなるように言った

p.39 1 decidedly 明らかに 1 reptilian 爬虫類に似た 6 state of affairs 事態 13 of no consequence まったく重大ではない 18 reflected on ... ~についてじっくり考えた 18 the subject of ... ~というテーマ 19 undependable 信頼できない 21 tight-lipped 口がかたい 22 cold-blooded 冷酷な 22 hussy ふしだらな女

p.40 11 luxuriated ゆったりと楽しんだ 12 limbs 手足 12 cramped こわばっている 14 a creature of sensation 感覚の人間 17 dismissed everything from his mind 頭の中を空っぽにした

p.41 1 cordial 友好的な 2 eyed each other 互いの様子をうかがっていた 4 bungle しくじる 7 neat touch 気が利いている 11 foresee the future 未来を予知する 17 deuced ひどく 19 for two pins すぐにでも 19 make an excuse 口実をつくる 21 mainland 本土 24 Not straight. 堅気じゃない

p.42 3 gong どら (銅鑼) 6 beast of prey 肉食獣 19 *heathen* 異教徒たち 21 *executeth* (executes) 執行する 21 *the wicked* 悪人 21 *snared* 罠にかかる 26 cairngorm 煙水晶

🕯 *CHAPTER 3*

p.43 1 drawing to a close 終わりに近づいている 2 waited 給仕をした 5 intimacy 親密さ 6 mellowed くつろいだ 6 port ポートワイン 7 caustic 痛烈な 7 fashion やり方 9 mutual friends 共通の友人

294

16 quaint 風変わりでおもしろい　18 china figures 陶器の人形

p.44　18 drawing room 客間　18 French windows ガラス格子の開き窓　19 murmuring ざわめき　23 flushed 赤くなった　24 composedly 落ち着いて　25 agreeable 心地のよい

p.45　2 servants 使用人　12 embroidery 刺繍　26 strolled ぶらぶら歩いた　27 naïve 単純そうな　27 statuette in brass 真鍮の小さな彫刻

p.46　1 bizarre 奇妙な　1 angularities ごつごつした形　6 *Punch*『パンチ』（イギリスの週刊風刺漫画雑誌）　13 replete 満ちた　15 inhuman 冷酷な　15 penetrating よく通る　20 *indictments* 告発

p.47　3 *guilty of . . .* ～の罪を犯した　6 *deliberately* 故意に　14 *bar* 被告席　14 *have you anything to say in your defense* 何か申し開きができるか　21 petrified 恐怖ですくみ上がった　22 resounding 鳴り響く　24 thud ドスンという音　26 flung it open 勢いよく開けた　26 lying in a huddled mass 丸くなって倒れている

p.48　3 sprang 飛んでいった　7 fainted 気を失った　7 She'll be round in a minute. すぐに意識が戻る　16 spluttered out しどろもどろに言った　17 practical joke 悪ふざけ　19 shoulders sagged 肩をがっくり落とした　23 comparatively 比較的　23 unmoved 平然としている　24 In both cheeks was a spot of hard colour. 両頬に真っ赤になっているところがあった　25 habitual pose いつもの格好

p.49　1 alert 油断のない　13 adjoining room 隣り合った部屋　14 swift すばやい　20 erect 背筋を伸ばして　26 unobtrusively 目立たないように　27 bored through the wall 壁に穴を開けてあった

p.50　6 obeyed 従った　8 disgraceful 恥ずべき　13 stroked さすった　17 who the devil . . . いったい誰が～　24 moaning うめき声を出している　27 Pull yourself together. しっかりしろ

p.51　3 urgency 切迫感　6 nasty turn ひどいめまい　11 fluttered ぴくぴくした　18 spirit 強い酒　18 did her good 効いた　22 Fair made me drop that tray. 思わずお盆を落としてしまった　25 had the effect of stopping him in full cry 大声をあげる彼を黙らせる効果があった

p.52　6 dryly 冷淡に　10 earnestly 誠実に　23 remarkable 驚くべき

p.53　10 broke out suddenly だしぬけに大声を出した　11 preposterous

ばかげている　12 slinging accusations about あちこちに言いがかり をつけて　16 interposed 言葉を挟んだ　24 tottered よろよろ歩いた

p.54　3 forage （食べ物を）探す　8 burden 荷物　9 dispensing 配る　10 stiff whiskey 強いウイスキー　11 stimulant 刺激剤　14 sedative 鎮静剤　18 took charge of the proceedings 進行を引き受けた　19 impromptu 即席の　19 court of law 法廷　21 get to the bottom of this 真相を探る

p.55　2 there was a faint stir かすかにざわついた　6 engaged 雇われた　9 established 定評のある　9 volunteered 自ら話した　16 in order 整っている　17 dusting ほこりを払うこと　21 afternoon post 午後 の郵便　22 detained 足止めされている

p.56　2 headed Ritz Hotel リッツ・ホテルのレターヘッドがついている　2 typewritten タイプライターで打ってある　6 twitched 引っ張った　8 no defects 欠陥（文字が欠けたところ）がない　9 the most widely used make 一番よく使われているタイプ（の紙）　10 fingerprints 指紋　14 Christian names 洗礼名　15 mouthful 発音しにくい語　16 with a slight start ちょっと驚いて　17 obliged 感謝している　18 suggestive 示唆に富む　19 thrusting his neck forward 首を突き出して　21 pool our information それぞれが持っている情報を出し合う

p.57　1 spoke with decision 意を決したように話し始めた　2 peculiar 奇妙な　4 purported to be ... ～だと称する　23 old horse あいつ

p.58　1 acquaintanceship 交際　3 colleague 同僚　5 verisimilitude 本当らしさ　6 presume 推定する　6 momentarily out of touch しばらく連絡が途絶えていた　25 fell for it まんまとだまされた

p.59　4 disembodied voice 姿の見えない人の声　4 by name 名指しで　5 precise 正確な　5 accusations 告発　12 sulkily 不機嫌に　13 cat's out of the bag 秘密がばれてしまった　18 false name 偽名　23 suspicious 疑い深い　25 clenched 握りしめた　26 swine 卑怯者　27 set his square jaw 四角いあごをこわばらせた

p.60　1 got me wrong 私を誤解している　2 credentials 身分証明書　2 ex-CID man ロンドン警視庁犯罪捜査部の元刑事　7 handsome かなりの金額の　7 money order 為替　13 my foot ばか言うな　16

296

appreciatively 感心しているように   17 justified 正統な根拠がある   19 surname 姓   19 scrawl なぐり書き   22 by a slight stretch of fancy 少し想像力を広げれば   23 UNKNOWN 無名の人   25 mad ばかげている

p.61　2 madman 狂人   3 homicidal lunatic 殺人狂

☛ CHAPTER 4

p.62　1 dismay うろたえ   2 bewilderment ろうばい   2 took up the thread once more 話の先を続けた   12 incoherent 支離滅裂の   16 emerges 明らかになる   17 *enticed* 誘った   20 epistolary 書簡の

p.63　2 whereabouts 居所   10 babel ざわめき   12 slander 誹謗中傷   14 iniquitous 不当極まりない   15 hoarsely しわがれ声で   19 calmed the tumult 混乱を静めた   22 accuses 告発する   24 trial 裁判   26 ably defended 巧みに弁護された

p.64　3 passing sentence of death 死刑を申し渡す   3 concurred 同意した   4 verdict 評決   4 an appeal was lodged 上訴が申し立てられた   4 on the grounds of ... ~を理由に   5 misdirection 不当説示   6 duly 予定どおりに   6 executed 死刑が執行された   7 conscience 良心   7 perfectly clear まったくやましいところはない   8 convicted 有罪判決を下された   14 acquittal 無罪判決   15 dead against 激しく反発している   15 turned the jury right round 陪審員を誘導して気を変えさせた   18 he had a private down on the fellow あの男に個人的なうらみがあった   21 impulsively 衝動的に

p.65　6 nursery governess 家庭教師   6 forbidden 禁じられていた   10 exonerated 疑いが晴れた   13 broke down 平静を失った   17 Got a bee in his bonnet! 奇妙な考えに取りつかれている   17 got hold of the wrong end of the stick 勘違いしている   19 squaring his shoulders 肩を怒らせて   23 officers 将校   24 reconnaissance 偵察   24 natural course of events 自然な成り行き   25 resent 憤慨する   25 slur on ... ~に対する誹謗   26 Caesar's wife どこに出しても恥ずかしくない妻 (「シーザーのような公人の妻は疑われるようなことをしてはならない」ということわざから)

p.66　2 cost him a good deal かなりこたえた   5 natives 先住民   9 self-preservation 自己防衛　12 sternly 厳しく　15 *pukka sahib* 本物の紳士　23 horrified ショックを受けている　27 Beastly bad luck. ひどく運が悪かった

p.67　1 acidly 批判的に　7 had my licence suspended 免許停止になった　7 nuisance やっかいなこと　9 speeding スピードの出しすぎ　13 can't get up a decent pace まともなスピードを出せない　22 moistening 湿らせている　23 deferential 敬意を表した

p.68　6 she was taken bad 体調を崩した　9 devoted to . . . 〜に誠心誠意尽くしていた　16 hearty 力強い　16 bullying 弱いものいじめをするような　19 came into a little something at her death 彼女が死んで、いくらかのものを相続した　20 drew himself up 背筋をピンと伸ばした　21 legacy 遺産　21 faithful services 忠実な勤務

p.69　1 bank robbery 銀行強盗　4 it didn't come before me 私が裁いた事件ではない　5 convicted on your evidence あなたの証言で有罪になった　9 penal servitude for life 終身刑　12 crook 悪党　13 The case was quite clear against him. あの男の有罪は明らかだった　15 able handling 有能な処理　22 law-abiding 法律を守る　23 Myself excepted. 私を除いて　25 distaste 嫌悪　25 drew herself away 身を引いた　27 master of himself 克己心がある

p.70　1 good-humouredly 上機嫌に　2 at a loss to understand まったくわからない　10 surgeon 外科医　14 *nerves all to pieces* 全身の神経がバラバラで　15 *sober* しらふ　16 *loyalty* 忠誠心　17 *held her tongue* 黙っていた　17 *Pulled me up.* おかげで目が覚めた　24 covertly ひそかに　25 expectation 期待

p.71　6 You reserve your defense? 申し開きは見合わせますか　8 acted in accordance with the dictates of my conscience 良心に従って行動した　10 reproach 非難する　12 swayed by . . . 〜に左右される　13 unyielding ゆるぎなく　23 not sane in the accepted sense of the word とても正気とは思えない

p.72　13 dissentient 異議　15 unsporting フェアでない　15 ferret out 捜し出す　16 detective story 探偵小説　22 The legal life's narrowing! 法律を守るばかりの生活は窮屈だ　22 I'm all for crime! Here's to it. ぼくは犯罪に大賛成、犯罪に乾杯しよう　23 drank it off at a gulp 一気に飲みほした 24 his face contorted 顔をゆがめた

🖤 *CHAPTER 5*

p.73 1 it took every one's breath away 誰もが息をのんだ 2 stupidly 呆然と 3 crumpled 倒れこんだ 7 awe-struck 畏敬の念に打たれた 9 They didn't take it in. Not at once. 誰もすぐにはのみこめなかった 10 Norse God 北欧の神様 10 in the prime of ... 〜の盛りのとき 11 Struck down all in a moment. 一瞬で倒れた 16 sniffed at ... 〜のにおいをかいだ

p.74 3 asphyxiation 窒息 5 dregs グラスの底に残った酒 9 choking fit むせる発作 12 In the midst of life we are in death. 生の最中にわれら死のうちにあり 13 brusquely ぶっきらぼうに 20 cyanides シアン化物 20 distinctive smell 独特のにおい 20 Prussic Acid 青酸 21 Potassium Cyanide 青酸カリ 21 acts pretty well instantaneously 即効性がある

p.75 9 suicide 自殺 9 That's a queer go. それは妙なことだ 17 immortal 不死の 22 untampered with 細工されていない 24 It followed therefore that ... ゆえに〜ということになる

p.76 11 inert 動かない 20 clung to each other's company for reassurance 互いにしがみついて安心感を得ようとした 25 I haven't cleared yet まだ片づけていない 26 curtly そっけなく

p.77 9 turn in 床につく 11 a slow unwilling procession 一列になって重い足取りで進む人々 12 creaking きしむ 14 the essence of modernity モダンそのもの 16 flooded with ... 〜があふれている 18 concealed 隠された 21 upper landing 階段を上ったところ 23 almost without conscious thought ほとんど考えもせずに

p.78 4 garments 衣類 8 straightforwardness 率直さ 10 for the Crown 検察官 11 overvehement やっきになりすぎている 11 prove 証明する 12 for the Defense 弁護人 13 His points had told. 有効な指摘をした 13 cross-examinations 反対尋問 14 deadly 非常に効果的 15 masterly 見事な 16 ordeal 辛い経験 18 impressed 感心した 19 everything had been over bar the shouting 勝負はつき、あとは喝采を浴びるだけだった 24 appreciating じっくり吟味して 24 tabulating 列挙して

p.79 1 defending counsel 弁護人 2 summing up 最終弁論 3 false teeth 義歯 5 predatory 肉食動物のような 6 hooding his eyes 目を半開きにして 7 cooked Seton's goose シートンの計画を台無しにした 8 rheumatic リューマチの 18 That's a rum go! 奇妙な状況だ 24 tossed from side to side 落ち着きなく寝返りを打った

p.80 2 capricious 気まぐれな 3 turn up her nose ばかにする 3 pronounce dull 退屈だと宣言する 8 ragged からかった

p.81 1 leave 休暇 3 brisk きびきびした 4 hypocrite 偽善者 5 murderous rage 殺意に満ちた怒り 9 inequalities of temper 気分のむら 9 accounted for 正当化された 10 men's nerves were continually snapping under the strain ストレスにさらされて男たちは常に神経を張り詰めていた 13 perceptions 洞察力 23 colossal blunders 大きな失敗 23 sacrificed 犠牲にした

p.82 4 found her out 彼女の秘密を知った 7 double pneumonia (両肺が炎症を起こす) 肺炎 13 shooting and fishing 狩猟と釣り 15 David putting Uriah in the forefront of the battle ダビデがウリヤを戦いの最前線に送ったこと (旧約聖書から) 19 talking about him behind his back 彼の陰口をきいている 23 withdrawn into himself 自分の殻に閉じこもった 25 purposeless 無益なこと

p.83 1 taken to shunning... ~を遠ざけるようになった 6 Kept a stiff upper lip? 感情を表に出さないでいたか? 7 betrayed the right amount of feeling 状況にふさわしい感情を見せた 7 indignation 憤り 8 discomfiture 困惑 10 far-fetched ありそうもない 12 Idiotic! ばかげている 15 the Regiment 連隊 16 pious 信心深い 17 hand and glove with... ~と密接な関係で 17 parsons 牧師

p.84 27 stout かっぷくのいい 27 whining 不平を言っている

p.85 8 decorous 礼儀をわきまえた 14 *I've not got a penny.* ぼくは文なしだ 14 *It's all I can do to keep myself.* 自分一人が暮らすだけでせいいっぱいだ 19 come into everything すべての財産を相続する 21 *I hadn't built on it* あてにしていたわけじゃない 21 *knock* ショック 24 rancour 憎しみ 25 puny 体が小さい

p.86 **2** irritating いらいらさせる **2** whiney 哀れっぽい **10** if *I* were doing away with myself 私が自殺するなら **10** overdose 過剰投与 **11** veronal ベロナール（睡眠薬の商品名） **12** shuddered 身震いした **13** convulsed けいれんした **15** doggerel こっけいな詩

☞ CHAPTER 6

p.87 **4** clammy 汗で湿った **5** scalpel 手術用メス **10** unwieldy 大きくて扱いにくい **10** spare ほっそりした **10** meagre やせた **17** operating table 手術台 **20** probationer 見習い看護師

p.88 **3** malicious 悪意のある **8** anaesthetic 麻酔薬 **8** ether エーテル **10** Châteauneuf-du-Pape シャトーヌフ・デュ・パプ（ワイン） **17** with a start ハッとして **26** efficient 効率のよい

p.89 **14** 'er 'eart (her heart) 彼女の心臓 **19** rheumaticky リューマチの気がある **20** attending her 彼女を診ている

p.90 **1** evaded 避けた **11** cascara カスカラ（下剤に使用される植物） **11** glycerine of cucumber きゅうり化粧水 **12** Elliman's エリマンズ（マッサージ・クリーム） **13** dressing-table 鏡台 **14** chest of drawers たんす **15** sleeping draughts 睡眠薬の水薬 **24** summons 招集 **25** pacing 行ったり来たりしている **26** desultory とりとめのない

p.91 **14** pursed up his mouth into a whistle 口をすぼめて口笛を吹いた **16** it will come on to blow 風が強くなる **18** squally 嵐になりそうな **25** do himself in 自殺する **26** hung back 後ろのほうにいた

p.92 **2** motive 動機 **2** well-off 裕福 **17** shortcomings 不十分なこと **18** single-handed 一人で **27** took the hint 言外の意味を読み取った

p.93 **2** by mutual consent 互いに同意の上で **2** tabooed 禁止された **5** reappearance 再登場 **5** Loch Ness monster ネス湖の怪獣 **7** cleared his throat importantly 意味ありげに咳払いをした **13** ejaculations 突然の叫び **18** cause of death 死因 **20** offhand すぐに **21** autopsy 検死 **22** certificate 証明書 **23** state of health 健康状態 **26** heart failure 心不全

p.94 **17** brought home 痛感させられた **20** adopt 受け入れる **21** exact knowledge 正確な知識　**22** cardiac 心臓の　**24** Act of God 神の行為　**26** carrying things a bit far 度を超している

p.95 **2** regard it as impossible 不可能と考える　**2** sinner 罪人　**3** struck down by the wrath of God 神の怒りにふれて打ち倒される　**6** ill-doing 悪事　**6** Providence 神　**7** conviction 有罪の決定　**7** chastisement 懲罰　**8** fraught with... 〜に満ちた　**27** sheer moonshine まったくのたわごと　**27** plain lunacy ただの変人

p.96 **1** Allow for the moment that it's true. あれが本当のことだと考えてみてください　**2** polished off 消した　**7** annoyed むっとして　**9** resumed 再び口を開いた　**10** That's as may be. あるいはそうかもしれない　**12** spills the beans 秘密を漏らす　**13** cracks 精神的にまってしまう　**13** hung over her 彼女にぴったりくっついて離れなかった　**14** coming round 意識が戻るとき　**15** solicitude 気遣い　**15** like a cat on hot bricks そわそわして　**19** raked up 蒸し返された　**19** ten to one 十中八九　**20** give the show away 秘密をばらす　**21** brazen it out どこまでも白を切る　**22** straight face 澄ました顔　**23** till kingdom comes いつまでも

p.97 **3** snorted 鼻先で笑った　**14** sentiment 情緒

p.98 **3** explosively 激情的に　**21** nigh on ほぼ　**23** part and parcel of... 〜の本質的な部分　**24** bound up together 相互に結びついている

p.99 **15** obliquely さりげなく　**16** loose rocks 浮石　**20** barmy 気が狂った　**24** ex-Inspector 元警部　**25** send me off my head 正気を失わせる

p.100 **11** after a moment of indecision 少し迷ってから　**18** working 引きつっている　**20** restraint 控えめな態度　**21** taken aback びっくりさせられた　**24** frenzied ひどく興奮した

p.101 **4** jerked out いきなり言った　**11** talking in riddles 謎めいた話し方をしている

CHAPTER 7

p.103 **3** acquiesced 仕方なく従った　**4** crests 波頭　**9** bay 湾

p.104 **7** easily taken in 簡単にだまされる　**8** absurd ばかげている　**10** mechanically 無意識に　**11** takes things for granted いろいろなこ

とを当然と思いこむ 21 gazed 見つめた 26 Everything goes to support the idea. そう考えると何もかもつじつまが合う

p.105 1 it didn't ring true 真実味がなかった 6 haunted 悩まされていた 8 nursery 子供部屋 9 *Be sure thy sin will find thee out.* 遅かれ早かれ罪を償うことになる 11 scrambled to her feet よろよろ立ち上がった 18 chaotic 混沌とした 20 perplexedly 当惑して

p.106 7 in his public capacity 公人として 8 ex-Scotland Yard man ロンドン警視庁の元刑事 11 not a fit subject to discuss before gentlemen 紳士方の前で話すようなことではない 14 serenely 落ち着いて 15 in service with... ～の使用人だった 18 sheerest hypocrisy まったくの偽善 19 loose girl with no morals 道徳心のかけらもないふしだらな娘 21 in trouble 妊娠している

p.107 1 immorality 不道徳 6 on her conscience 心にのしかかって 6 committed a still graver sin さらに重い罪を犯した 19 hardness 厳しさ 19 drove her to it 彼女を（自殺に）追いこんだ 22 modest つつましい 25 uneasiness 不安 25 self-righteous 独善的 27 encased in her own armour of virtue 自前の美徳のよろいで身を固めている

p.108 1 spinster 未婚女性 3 terrible 恐ろしい 10 placidly 落ち着いて 15 speculatively 探るように 17 acute 鋭い 17 wavered 迷った 19 at this juncture 今ここで 26 out of earshot 聞こえないところ

p.109 13 feasible ありそうな話 13 taken alone それだけを考えれば 25 enlightening 物事をはっきりさせる 26 amyl nitrate 硝酸アミル 27 ampoule アンプル（注射液が入った容器）

p.110 1 inhaled 吸入した 2 withheld 与えられなかった 2 consequences 結果 2 fatal 命にかかわる 7 administer 投与する 7 negation 何もしないでいる 13 that explains a good deal いろいろなことの説明がつく 18 perpetrators 悪事を行う人 20 strictly within the law 完全に法律の範囲内で 24 stiletto 細くとがった小剣

p.111 4 *safe as houses* とても安全だ 6 hence それゆえ 16 lost her nerve おじけづいて 16 took an easy way out 安易な解決法を選んだ 22 *too* much to swallow やすやすと受け入れられない 24 precious little brains ほとんど空っぽな頭 24 got the wind up 怖く

なった　25 mowed down ひき殺した　27 get hold of 手に入れる

p.112　2 waistcoat ベスト　3 line of country 専門分野　7 ardent 熱心な

p.113　21 Fits too damned well to be a coincidence! 偶然にしてはできすぎている　23 with a vengeance 猛烈に

p.114　2 at large 野放しになっている　14 isolated 隔絶した　16 raving maniac 錯乱した狂人　21 bare rock むき出しの岩　23 Esq. (Esquire) 殿　24 warningly 警告するように

p.115　3 rope in 誘いこむ　5 ga-ga もうろくしている　6 forte 得意分野　6 masterly inactivity 見事なまでに活動しないこと

☞ CHAPTER 8

p.116　3 makes all the difference 話はまったく変わってくる　6 by proxy 代理人を通じて　8 racket 大騒ぎ

p.117　3 dose 一服分　7 concerned elsewhere 他に注意を向けていた　25 young arsenal ちょっとした兵器庫　26 dagger 短剣

p.118　3 unassuming つつましい　14 the cliffs fell sheer to the sea below 崖は海から垂直に切り立っていた　14 their surface unbroken 表面はなめらかだった　19 narrowly scanning the least irregularity in the rock 岩にでこぼこしたところがないか細かく調べた　22 skirting the water's edge 水際を歩いて　26 horizon 水平線

p.119　1 his oblivion of ... 彼が～にまったく気づかないこと　4 gone into a trance 神がかり状態になった　7 conversational tone くだけた口調で　9 He cast a quick look over his shoulder. 肩越しにチラッと見た　11 insist 要求する　13 genially 愛想よく　20 retreated 後ろへ下がった

p.120　16 bonfire たき火　18 that's all probably been provided for そうすることは承知で、すでに手を打っているだろう　21 be marooned 孤立状態にされる　23 wager 賭け　25 dubiously 疑わしそうに

p.121　13 clambered down はい下りた　25 recess へこみ

p.122　2 on the face of it 一見したところでは　6 mass themselves together 集まってひとかたまりになる　16 aversion 嫌悪　22 impudently 生意気に　23 beyond the reach of pity or terror 哀れみも恐怖も届かないところにいる

p.123 **1** dock 被告席 **4** pronounce sentence 刑を宣告する **6** extreme end 最先端 **10** apprehension 懸念 **10** intently 一心に

p.124 **13** worked spasmodically 引きつったように震えた **15** musingly 物思いにふけるように **20** gay 陽気

p.125 **3** regrets 後悔 **3** Serves him damned well right! 自業自得だ **8** distressed 心を痛めている **25** unconscious of... ～意識していない

p.126 **3** coiled ぐるぐる巻きにした **8** carelessly ぞんざいに **16** grimly 険しい様子で **17** *What price Macarthur?* マッカーサーはどうだ **19** incredulously 信じられないといった様子で

p.127 **7** Keep a lookout for a sudden strain on the rope. ロープが突然引っ張られないか気をつけていてくれ **14** mountaineering 登山 **18** cove やつ **21** He's a wrong 'un! あいつは悪党だ

p.128 **2** be kept pretty dark 秘密にしておく **13** the strain relaxed ロープが緩んだ **16** out of the way places 人里離れた場所 **17** primus プリマス・ストーブ（屋外用の小型調理コンロ） **17** bug powder 虫よけパウダー **23** thorough 徹底的な **24** futile 無益な **25** perspiration 汗 **26** We're up against it. 手詰まりになった

p.129 **4** outbuildings 納屋 **5** yard measure 物差し **8** devoid of concealments 隠れられる場所はない **9** ground floor 一階 **10** mounted 上がった **15** impassive countenance 冷静な表情

p.130 **2** cisterns 貯水槽 **5** furtive こそこそした **5** footfall 足音 **7** admonitory 警告的な **17** stealthily こっそりと **25** stopped dead ぴたりと止まった

p.131 **10** guest chambers 客室 **14** sheeted シーツをかけられた **27** I feel it in my bones... ～という確かな予感がする

p.132 **8** assumed 想定した **10** cavernous 洞窟のような **11** torch 懐中電灯 **13** festooned with cobwebs クモの巣にまみれて

☛ *CHAPTER 9*

p.133 **3** superstition 迷信 **6** the argument holds あの考え方は間違っていない **6** hang it all ちくしょう **20** embarrassed きまりが悪い

p.134 **1** grew a little deeper in hue 色が少し濃くなった **1** blurting out the words 思わず言葉が口をついて出てきたように　3 dope 薬物　11 mild dose 少量　11 trional トリオナール（鎮静薬）　12 preparation 調合薬　14 not to mince matters はっきり言うと　24 on purpose わざと　26 keep our heads 冷静さを保つ

p.135　1 sullenly 不機嫌に　4 mirthless smile 作り笑い　10 went white 顔面蒼白になった　12 offensive 無礼な　14 perjury 偽証

p.136　5 run into a spot of trouble トラブルに巻きこまれる　10 holding out on... ～に隠していた　10 persisted しつこく聞いた　25 shut up like a clam 貝のように口を閉じた　26 hard up 金に困っている

p.137　2 eloquent 雄弁な　4 eventuality 起こりうる事件　4 lay low 目立たないようにして　5 noncommittal 当たりさわりのない　6 shrewdly 抜け目なく　15 take my oath 誓う　20 pealed 鳴り響いた

p.138　5 stores are holding out (食料の) 蓄えはもっている　6 tinned 缶詰の　7 larder 食糧貯蔵室　18 ball of wool 毛糸の玉　18 rewinding 巻き直して　21 white horses 白波　23 measured tread 慎重で注意深い歩き方　24 occupants 部屋にいる人

p.139　24 gusts of wind 突風

p.140　1 discourse 会話　5 old salts 老練な水夫　12 as by common accord 考えが一致したかのように

p.141　3 storm broke 嵐がやってきた　3 borne in 運びこまれた　9 deserted 無人の　26 examination 診察

p.142　13 life preserver 護身用こん棒　25 overt activity 目立った動き　26 assumed command 指揮を執った　26 with the ease born of a long habit of authority 長年、人の上に立っていた者らしい自然な態度で　27 presided over the court 裁判長を務めた

p.143　8 doubtless 間違いなく　9 namely... すなわち～　14 loony 変人　17 main preoccupation 最大の関心事　27 scheme 計画

p.144　1 execution of justice 裁きを行うこと　1 offences which the law cannot touch 法律では裁けない犯罪　15 grave danger 深刻な危機　19 beyond suspicion 疑いをかける余地がない　20 bogus 偽の

p.145　7 possessed by a devil 悪魔に取りつかれている　20 scornfully あざ

けるように　23 succinctly 簡潔に　25 corroborate 裏づける

p.146 5 there is only one course of procedure to adopt われわれがとるべき手順はひとつしかない　7 eliminate from suspicion 容疑からはずす　7 on the evidence which is in our possession われわれが握っている証拠に照らして　12 arrested 阻止した　23 assert that... ～と断言する　24 subject to... ～にさらされる　25 irritably いらいらして

p.147 4 physically capable of... ～をする身体的能力がある　7 instrument 凶器　8 rubber truncheon ゴム製のこん棒　8 cosh こん棒　9 undue exertion of force 過度な力の行使　11 wriggled よじった　14 dispute 異を唱える　15 compassed 達成される　19 weighing humanity in the balance 人をはかりにかけること　21 specimen 標本　24 measured tones 慎重な口調

p.148 13 character or position 人格または地位　15 unblinkingly 毅然と　18 ruled out 除外された

p.149 6 less long in the tooth もっと若い　7 dealing out crazy justice 狂った正義を行う　10 hearsay 伝聞　11 conspired 共謀した　15 mentally unhinged 精神が錯乱した　19 qualify 条件を備えている

p.150 5 as regards... ～については　17 uncalled for 余計なこと　20 compelling 注目せずにはいられない

p.151 19 outrageous とんでもない　20 remorseless 無慈悲な　24 common humanity 常識的な思いやり　24 criminal offence 犯罪　26 establishing facts 事実を立証している

p.152 1 doctored 細工した　8 jubilant 歓喜にあふれる　17 acquiescent 黙従する　22 obediently 従順に

p.153 10 fast asleep ぐっすり眠っている　11 under the influence of... ～の影響を受けて　13 in all likelihood おそらく　13 certainty 確実なこと　14 prescribed 処方した　17 idiosyncrasy 特異体質　20 suits your book あなたには好都合だ　25 recrimination 非難

p.154 1 probability value is not high 確率は高くない　4 occasioned no surprise 驚きをもたらさない　25 valid 有効な　26 meditating on the singular position 異常な状況について熟考している

p.155 4 unobserved 気づかれないで　11 bear me out 私の言い分を裏づ

けてくれる　**19** turned crimson 顔を真っ赤にした

p.156　**5** heliographing 日光反射信号を送ること　**16** evenly 冷静に

p.157　**4** readily 進んで

p.158　**3** summoned before the court 法廷に呼び出された　**9** have any bearing upon . . . ～と関係がある　**19** to the best of our ability できる限り　**20** implicated 関係している　**22** complicity 共謀　**22** reiterate 繰り返して言う　**24** insane criminal 精神障害の犯罪者　**26** at the present juncture 現時点では

p.159　**6** be upon his or her guard 警戒する　**8** unsuspicious 疑っていない　**9** Forewarned is forearmed. あらかじめの警戒はあらかじめの武装と同じ　**12** the court will now adjourn これにて閉廷する

☞ CHAPTER 10

p.160　**6** cocked his head 首を傾げた　**16** grimace しかめ面

p.161　**15** excepting our two selves われわれ二人を除外して　**18** level-headed 冷静な　**19** stake my reputation on your sanity あなたが正気であることに私の評判を賭ける　**21** wry smile 苦笑い　**26** you don't hold human life particularly sacred あなたは人の命をとくに尊いものだと思っていない

p.162　**1** dictated 口述した　**4** solely for what I could get out of them 自分にとって何か利益がある場合だけ　**4** mass clearance 大量殺人　**8** nothing to go upon 何の根拠もない　**8** plump for . . . ～を選ぶ　**14** played God Almighty 全能の神を演じた　**15** go to a man's head 人をうぬぼれさせる　**17** snap プツッと切れる　**18** Executioner 死刑執行人　**19** Judge Extraordinary 絶対の審判者

p.163　**11** have a lot of strain ストレスが多い　**16** hared down there and back again 大急ぎで走っていってすぐに戻ってきた

p.164　**1** contradict 反論する　**14** lad 若者　**15** 'is lordship 閣下　**16** fiend in 'uman form 人の姿をした悪魔　**18** shrewdly 抜け目なく

p.165　**16** profess to be . . . ～であることを主張する　**18** plight 苦境　**25** take every possible precaution against . . . ～を未然に防ぐために可能な限りの予防策をとる

p.166 1 tenacious of life 生きることに執着がある　2 marvelled at... ~に驚嘆した　3 junior to... ~より若い　4 vastly inferior 大きく劣っている　8 *clichés* 陳腐な決まり文句　8 commonplace ごく普通の

p.167 18 *convinced* 確信している　24 filmy かすんでいる　24 straggled drunkenly ふらふらと動き出した

p.168 5 scored through 線を入れて消した　6 unevenly scrawled characters なぐり書きされた不ぞろいな文字　16 listlessly 無気力に

p.169 4 skeins 毛糸の玉　5 rattle and clink of china 陶器がカタカタ鳴る音　18 vanished 消えた　26 oilsilk オイルシルク（防水加工をしたシルクの布地）　26 it went with... ~とマッチしていた

p.170 5 what of it? たいした問題ではない　11 the pall of fear had fallen anew 新たな恐怖のとばりが降りてきた　19 the strain was almost too great to be borne 緊張は耐えがたいほどだった

p.171 3 bolts being shot 掛け金が下ろされる

p.172 7 eye lingered on... ~にじっと視線を注いだ　8 plaque of looking glass 鏡の飾り板　21 seen to that うまく取り計らった

📖 CHAPTER 11

p.173 1 daybreak 夜明け　3 abated 弱まった　15 tousled 乱れた　16 his eyes were still dim with sleep まだ寝ぼけている　17 affably 愛想よく　18 Sleeping the clock round? 一日中寝ているつもりか　18 got an easy conscience やましいことがない　20 shortly そっけなく

p.174 11 It's a case of echo answers where. こちらが聞きたい　15 there's no kettle on やかんが火にかかっていない　17 swore under his breath 小声で悪態をついた　27 ascertained 確認した

p.175 1 untenanted 無人の　18 mackintosh レインコート　23 exceedingly 非常に　27 look out 見張り

p.176 13 coffee urn コーヒー沸かし　15 athletic たくましい　16 wince 顔をしかめる　26 washhouse 洗濯小屋

p.177 1 chopper 斧　2 a heavy affair 重いもの　3 stained a dull brown くすんだ茶色に汚れていた　3 it corresponded only too well with... ~と一致していることは明らかだった　14 flour sifter 粉ふるい　22

fragile-looking ひ弱そうに見える　23 wiry strength 細くても頑丈な人の力　24 unsuspected strength 思いがけない力

p.178　7 uncomprehendingly 事態が飲みこめていない様子で　16 I know the whole thing by heart 私は全部暗記している　21 struck her a flat blow on the cheek 彼女の頬を平手で打った

p.179　14 sensible 分別がある　16 firewood 薪　19 rind 皮

p.180　9 A light touch was incomprehensible to him. ユーモアをきかせた会話など彼には理解できなかった　22 laconically 手短に　25 neat and prim 取り澄ましている

p.181　1 as mad as a hatter まったく気が狂っている　9 ploddingly のろのろと　9 perseveringly 根気よく　18 take jolly good care to be rolled up in bed snoring ベッドでいびきをかいている（ところを見られる）ようにする　21 innocent 無実

p.182　1 shamefacedly 恥ずかしそうに　9 I take my hat off to ... ～に脱帽する　12 stiffs 死体　12 you did indulge in that spot of perjury 君が偽証したという話は本当だろう　16 Doesn't seem to make much odds now. 今となってはどうでもいいことかもしれない　18 squared 賄賂を渡した　18 got him put away for a stretch 彼を刑務所に送った　21 made a tidy bit out of it かなりの金額を稼いだ

p.183　9 betting man 賭けをする人　17 sitting target 無防備な標的　18 can make rings round you 君を悠々と負かすことができる

p.184　7 prided herself on ... ～を誇りに思っていた　8 levelheadedness 冷静さ　13 current 潮の流れ　16 *sang-froid* 困難な状況下での冷静さ　24 sizzling fat ジュージューいう脂

p.185　2 make a fuss 騒ぎ立てる　5 repressed 抑圧された　10 gimlet 小さな錐（きり）　11 solid congealed mass 凝固したかたまり　16 unflinchingly 毅然として　16 upright 道徳心のある　20 *Thou shalt not be afraid for the terror by night; nor for the arrow that flieth by day.* あなたは夜の恐ろしい物をも、昼に飛んでくる矢をも恐れることはない　27 impious 神を敬わない

p.186　7 came to herself with a start ハッとわれに返った　18 outwardly self-possessed and normal 外見上は冷静沈着で正常な　24 *that's the ticket* まさしくそれだ   **27** *can't get the hang of it* 理解できない

CHAPTER 12

p.188   **3** authoritative 権威ありげな   **4** advisable 賢明である   **20** giddy めまいがする

p.189   **4** exploding shell 爆発する砲弾   **5** It took every one aback. 誰もが面食らった   **14** domestic 家庭的   **20** drowsy 眠たい   **25** bumble bee マルハナバチ

p.190   **3** honey in the comb 巣の中のはちみつ   **3** strain 濾す   **4** muslin bag 綿モスリンの袋   **14** wet dank smell 濡れてじめじめしたにおい   **14** nostrils 鼻腔   **16** prick ちくりと刺される痛み   **17** bee sting ハチ刺され   **27** inquiringly 問いかけるように

p.191   **3** author of these deaths これまでの殺人事件の犯人

p.192   **4** remorse 自責の念   **6** unmoved 冷静   **8** hearts as hard as flints 金剛石のような心（旧約聖書から）   **8** envy 嫉妬   **12** conclave 秘密会議   **18** demeanour ふるまい   **21** saw nothing amiss とくに変わった様子は見えなかった   **24** suffused with blood 充血した

p.193   **10** riveted 釘づけになった   **13** hypodermic syringe 皮下注射器

p.194   **2** touch of local colour 地元色の演出   **3** playful beast いたずら好き   **4** nursery jingle 童謡   **5** shrill 甲高い   **6** seasoned 年季の入った   **7** hazards 危険   **7** dangerous undertakings 危ない仕事   **7** given out だめになった   **11** reasoning powers 推理力   **16** fastened on ... ～に釘づけになった   **17** hostile 敵意を持った   **24** verify 正しいことを証明する

p.195   **20** sulphonal スルホナール（睡眠薬）   **21** bromide ブロマイド（鎮静剤）   **21** bicarbonate of soda 重曹   **25** lethal 命にかかわる

p.196   **5** firearms 銃器   **7** of our persons and of our effects 身体（検査）と持ち物の（検査）   **14** outcome 結果   **19** resist 抵抗する   **21** snarl 歯をむき出してうなる   **22** got it all taped out すべて理解している

p.197   **8** recoiled 後ずさりした   **15** stripped to the skin まる裸になった   **16** meticulously 念入りに   **24** bathing dress 水着

p.198 3 rucked ひだがついた

p.199 6 cumbersome 面倒な 15 dint くぼみ

p.200 7 devise 工夫する 27 By all means. もちろん

p.201 3 cellars 地下室

▶ CHAPTER 13

p.202 7 veneer 見せかけ 9 instinct 本能 11 reverted to more bestial types 野生の獣に返った 14 coarser and clumsier 以前より粗野でぎこちない 14 build 体つき 15 padding そっと歩く 16 mingled ferocity and stupidity 残忍さと愚かさが混ざり合った 17 beast at bay 追い詰められた獣 17 charge 突撃する 17 pursuers 追っ手 18 senses seemed heightened, rather than diminished 感覚が鈍るのではなく鋭くなっているようだ 20 lithe しなやかな

p.203 5 dazed 呆然としている 7 crouches うずくまる 8 immobility 静止 9 pitiable 哀れな 11 stubbed them out もみ消した 12 inaction 何もしないこと 12 gall いらだたせる 14 torrent ほとばしり 21 fitful gusts 断続的な突風 21 pattering パタパタ音を立てている 23 tacit consent 暗黙の了解 23 plan of campaign 作戦

p.204 2 raft いかだ 4 cackle 甲高い笑い声 19 abnormal 異常な 19 feverish 熱っぽい 19 diseased 病的な

p.205 9 *hearse* 霊柩車 17 burst 破裂する 22 do the trick うまくいく

p.206 13 siphon ソーダ・サイフォン 13 nailed up case 釘で留めた箱

p.207 9 unbearable 耐えられない 10 temples こめかみ 18 stood stock still 呆然と立っていた 25 tide out 潮が引いた

p.208 2 horrid ひどく不快な 2 spoilt 甘やかされた 7 draught すきま風 25 desperate 絶望した

p.209 2 restoring her sanity 正気を取り戻して 14 seaweed 海藻 22 faintness 失神 25 aeons of time 非常に長い時間

p.210 2 warning note 警告音 12 you've got your wits about you あなたは冷静な判断力を持っている 19 basin 洗面台 19 swaying 揺れて 19 clutching しっかりとつかんで 22 resentfully 怒ったように

p.211 4 tampered with … 〜を細工した 8 corkscrew コルク栓抜き 10

deception ごまかし　**11** tin foil アルミホイル

p.212　**2** did not commit himself はっきりとは言わなかった　**3** subject 対象者　**10** ruddy いまいましい　**10** block 頭

p.213　**15** onlookers 見ている人々　**16** robed in scarlet 深紅のガウンをまとっていた　**19** reeling よろめいて　**25** felt for the pulse 脈を探した　**27** expressionless 無表情な

p.214　**24** outburst どなり出したこと

☞ CHAPTER 14

p.217　**5** doublecross だまし打ち　**5** planted こっそり仕掛けられた　**6** it worked just as it was intended to 計画どおりにいった　**8** caught the old boy off his guard 油断したおやじを襲った

p.218　**6** dead beat 疲れ果てている　**21** farce 笑劇　**26** barricaded バリケードの中に閉じこもった

p.219　**9** rattled 不安にさせた　**23** summon the courage 勇気を奮い起こす

p.220　**11** pestering しつこく悩ませている　**22** good egg いい人　**22** lark 楽しい冒険

p.221　**4** untruthful 正直でない

p.222　**4** red-rimmed and bloodshot 赤く充血した　**5** a wild boar waiting to charge 突進しようと待ち構えているイノシシ　**7** inclination to . . . 〜したいという気持ち　**8** menace 脅威　**9** sagacity 賢明さ　**9** astuteness 抜け目のなさ　**10** gone the way of the rest ほかの人たちと同じ目にあった　**12** geezer じじい　**14** smug 独りよがりの　**15** He'd got his all right. 彼は当然の報いを受けた　**23** brow furrowed 眉をひそめて　**24** creased and puckered しわがより、細くなった

p.223　**1** went so far as to . . . 〜までした　**4** painstakingly 細心の注意を払って　**4** as he had been wont to do いつもしていたように　**9** disquieting 不安にさせる　**10** a thousand age-old fears 昔から人を悩ませてきたありとあらゆる不安　**11** struggled for supremacy 覇権をめぐって戦った　**12** mockery あざけり　**15** spectacled めがねをかけた　**20** mug まぬけ　**27** feature 造作　**27** distinct 鮮明な

p.224　**2** a thin slip of a woman ほっそりした女性　**19** with two strides 大

またで二歩歩き 24 scalp 頭皮 27 assailed 襲った

p.225 2 prowling うろついている 7 rigid 硬直して 9 dogged 頑固な 16 stairhead 階段を上ったところ 24 tiptoed つま先で歩いた 27 flex 電気コード 27 ebonite エボナイト（硬質ゴム）

p.226 2 sprinted 大急ぎで走った 3 precaution 用心 11 illuminated 照明で照らした 13 had an instantaneous glimpse of a figure 人影をちらりと見た 15 in pursuit 追跡して 18 to lure him out of the house 彼を家からおびき出すため 23 ascertain 確かめる

p.227 20 pigeon 目指す相手 21 I don't take anything on trust. 何事も頭から信用してかかることはしない 23 rapped トントンたたいた 27 inserted 差しこんだ 27 gingerly 慎重に

p.228 24 The hunt's up! 追跡開始だ 27 chuckled くっくっと笑った

p.229 3 latch 掛け金 17 I suppose I'm asking for it. 自ら災難を招くようなものだ 21 pluckily 勇敢に 22 undefined はっきりしない 22 tinged with the supernatural 超自然的な色合いがある

p.230 6 wedged 押しこまれた 9 intent on . . . ～に没頭している 9 cunning 巧妙さ 10 employ 使う 11 reflecting on the means he might employ 彼がどのような手段を使うか考えて 15 mortally wounded 瀕死の重傷を負った 20 having previously laid a trail of petrol あらかじめガソリンをまいておいて

p.231 3 stiffened to attention ハッとして動きを止めた 10 had their origin in her own imagination 彼女自身の想像の産物 12 concrete nature はっきりした 14 decided 明白な

p.232 14 conjuring trick 手品 20 as clear as day 昼間のように明るい 22 doubled back 引き返した 26 vamoosed ずらかった

p.233 5 pane ガラス板

☞ CHAPTER 15

p.234 3 thing of the past 過去のこと 14 bright lad 利口な少年 18 merriment 陽気な騒ぎ 20 Morse モールス符号

p.235 4 Terrific swell on! 波が高くなっている 17 quietus とどめ

p.236 12 come now これこれ 15 blockhead ばか者

p.237 **8** lay claims to ... 〜と主張した　**10** stolidly 感情を抑えて　**13** at your mercy あなたの言いなりだ　**25** pot 撃つ

p.238 **13** meaning 意味ありげな

p.240 **6** haze もや　**7** weaved in a gigantic swell 大きくうねっていた　**8** abortive 実を結ばない　**12** her breath coming with a slight catch in it 少し息をつまらせながら

p.241 **10** obstinately 頑として　**23** don't relish the idea of ... 〜をとくに望んでいない

p.242 **5** lion's den 危ない場所　**15** jumpy 不安な　**23** feeding time 餌の時間　**23** regular in their habits 規則正しく習慣を守る

p.243 **21** bunkum ナンセンス　**22** escaped inmate of Broadmoor ブロードムア（精神病院）から脱走してきた犯罪者

p.244 **4** touching 感動的な　**13** nerves 神経過敏　**19** Supreme Court 最高裁判所　**20** Absolute Justice 絶対的な正義　**24** heavenly visitants ほかの世界から来た訪問者

p.245 **9** lassitude 脱力感　**9** weariness 疲労　**23** Please yourself. 好きにすればいい　**27** innocuous 無害な

p.246 **2** made a cautious circuit of the house 用心しながら家を一周した　**3** spreadeagled 大の字になっていた　**4** mangled 潰された

p.247 **3** went over the place with a fine-tooth comb あの家を徹底的に調べた　**12** Priest's Hole 司祭の隠れ場　**12** manor houses 領主の館

p.248 **26** raucous 耳障りな

p.249 **9** enveloped 包みこんだ　**12** have a bathe 泳ぐ　**19** bather 泳ぐ人

▶ CHAPTER 16

p.251 **20** precisely そのとおり

p.252 **10** menacing 脅迫的な　**18** acceptance 受け入れる気持ち　**19** rebellion 反抗　**23** sneered 嘲笑った

p.253 **11** tugging at ... 〜を引っ張って　**13** panted 息を切らした　**16** high water mark 最高水位線

p.254 **1** pick my pocket ぼくから（ピストルを）すり取る　**13** lull her into security 彼女を油断させる　**17** argumentatively 説得するように　**20** feline ネコのような　**22** leaping body stayed poised in mid-spring 飛び上がった体が空中で動きを止めた　**24** warily 用心深く

p.255　**3** exquisite このうえなく美しい　**5** steeling of her nerves 神経を研ぎ澄ませること　**19** principally 主に

p.256　**5** peril 危機　**5** quick-wittedness 頭の回転の速さ　**6** adroitness 抜け目なさ　**6** turned the tables on... 〜と形勢を逆転した　**6** her would-be destroyer 彼女を殺そうとした犯人　**9** streaked 筋になっている　**22** wouldn't care to... 〜したいと思わない

p.257　**5** behind the times 時代に遅れている　**14** clasped 強く握った　**27** pile carpet パイル織のカーペット

p.258　**14** *rope with a noose* 先が輪になったロープ　**20** unheeded 気づかれず　**20** fender 暖炉の格子　**21** automaton ロボット

p.259　**1** sleepwalker 夢遊病者

☞ *EPILOGUE*

p.260　**1** Assistant Commissioner 副警視総監　**7** not a living soul 生きている者はひとりもいない　**18** chloral クロラール

p.261　**11** provisioned 用意した　**19** savoury 健全な　**20** share-pushing fraud 証券詐欺事件　**26** third party 第三者

p.262　**2** financial angle 金銭的な角度　**4** wangle figures 数字をごまかす　**5** chartered accountant 公認会計士　**5** wouldn't know if he was on his head or his heels 何が何だかわからない　**7** covered his employer's tracks 雇い主のために証拠を消した　**17** smell a rat あやしいと思う　**27** gloomily 憂鬱そうに

p.263　**4** illuminating 物事を明らかにする　**14** run a boat ashore ボートを岸につける　**16** there was a big sea on 海が荒れていた　**20** big breakers inshore 沿岸は波が高かった

p.264　**3** c/o... 〜気付　**4** hitherto unacted play これまで上演されていない芝居　**5** typescript タイプライターで打った文書　**7** subject matter 主題　**18** funny business 不正行為　**19** neglect 世話を怠ったこと　**25** beyond any shadow of doubt 疑いの余地なく

p.265 **1** vindictive 恨みを抱いた　**6** carried out to sea 沖へ押し流された　**11** aboveboard 公明正大な　**15** peritonitis 腹膜炎　**17** op (operation) 手術　**21** turned out 追い出された

p.266 **5** let off with a fine 罰金だけで釈放された　**9** killed in action 戦死した　**17** sailed very near the law 違法すれすれのことをした　**18** daring 大胆な　**18** not being overscrupulous あまり几帳面ではない　**22** our lot われわれの仲間　**24** forcibly 力強く　**25** bad hat 悪人

p.267 **2** committed black perjury 偽証した　**12** barbiturates バルビツール酸塩　**18** sight too opportune タイミングがよすぎる

p.268 **13** to be executed これから処刑される予定の　**15** spirited himself off that island 島からひそかに姿を消した　**15** into thin air 跡形もなく　**18** vanishing trick 消失の奇術

p.269 **2** not quite in the dark まったく見当がつかないわけではない　**4** cryptic 謎めいた　**5** All those accounts tally. どの記述も内容は一致している　**14** granting that ... 仮に〜だとしても

p.270 **5** deposited 打ち上げられた　**5** high water 満潮時　**7** subsided おさまった　**7** succeeding その後の

p.271 **13** man alive 驚いた　**27** inducing 誘導して

p.272 **6** abstract justice 抽象的な正義

A MANUSCRIPT DOCUMENT SENT TO SCOTLAND YARD BY THE MASTER OF THE EMMA JANE FISHING TRAWLER
（トロール漁船〈エマ・ジェーン〉の船長よりロンドン警視庁に送付された手書きの文書）

p.273 **1** my nature was a mass of contradictions 私の性格は矛盾に満ちていた　**2** incurably 救いがたく　**7** confession 告白　**10** or do I flatter myself それともこれは私のうぬぼれだろうか　**11** hitherto unsolved murder mystery これまで未解決だった殺人事件　**12** traits 性格　**15** pests 害虫　**18** sense of justice 正義感　**18** abhorrent 忌まわしい　**20** right should prevail 正義が勝つべきである

p.274 **2** mental makeup 精神構造　**5** crime and its punishment 罪と罰　**8** ingenious うまくできた　**11** wretched 惨めな　**11** squirming もがいている　**11** dock 被告席　**12** doom 恐ろしい運命　**16** palpably 明らかに　**25** unspectacular 見栄えのしない　**27** the crime with which he was charged 彼が告発された罪　27 brutal 残酷な

p.275　3 strictly just 絶対に公正　3 scrupulous 良心的　10 lessening of control 自制心の弱まり　15 exigencies 差し迫った必要　16 waxed secretly to colossal force ひそかにふくれあがって巨大な力になった　19 stupendous 途方もない　21 adolescent 青年　24 incongruous 釣り合わない　25 restrained and hampered 抑制され、妨害されていた　25 innate 生まれつき備わっている

p.276　3 GP (general practitioner) 一般開業医　9 withholding of a restorative drug 回復させる薬を与えなかったこと　10 stood to benefit very substantially かなりの金額の遺産をもらえることになっていた　21 inexorable 止められない　22 diminishment 減っていくこと　22 inevitability 避けられないこと　25 routine line of conversation いつも変わらない一連の会話

p.277　1 nursing home 老人ホーム　2 teetotal 絶対禁酒の　4 recounting 順を追って話す　14 mem-sahib 女主人　15 Puritan 宗教・道徳に厳格な人　18 callousness 冷淡さ　20 unfit to live 生きている価値がない　22 brethren 仲間　25 integrity 高潔さ　25 perforce believed 必然的に信頼される　25 by virtue of ... 〜のおかげで

p.278　4 assuage 静める　6 maudlin confidential stage 感傷的になり、心のうちを誰かに打ち明けたくなる段階　8 conversational gambit 会話を始める糸口　11 dollop 少量　13 murderess 女の人殺し

p.279　3 reconstruct 再現する　5 shady いかがわしい　6 dope pedlar 麻薬の売人　10 maturing 熟している　10 coping stone 笠石（最後の仕上げ）　18 protracted 長引く　20 blaze of excitement 興奮の炎　21 mechanics どのように実行されたか　23 cover my tracks 自分の行動の形跡を隠す　25 prospective victims 犠牲になる見込みの人々　25 concoct 作り上げる　26 bait 餌

p.280　3 indigestion 消化不良　4 done wonders 驚くほどよく効いた　5 gastric juices 胃液　6 a slight hypochondriac 自分の健康にちょっと神経質になっている人　7 compromising documents or memoranda 人に見られては困る書類やメモ　9 order of death 死の順番　9 subjected by me to special thought and care とくに慎重にじっくり考えた　11 varying degrees of guilt 罪の重さがそれぞれ違う　14

offenders 犯罪者　**18** amoral 道徳心がない　**19** pagan 信仰を持たない　**24** putting down wasps スズメバチの退治

p.281　**4** bouts of pain 疼痛の発作　**5** Chloral Hydrate 抱水クロラール（催眠剤）　**18** ally 協力者　**19** gullible 信じやすい　**21** inconceivable 想像もつかない　**21** standing 地位　**25** trap the murderer into incriminating himself 殺人犯を罠にはめて自ら有罪を立証させる

p.282　**6** In the confusion attending ... 〜の混乱にまぎれて　**7** abstracted 盗んだ　**14** strong solution of cyanide シアン化物の強い溶剤　**16** I liked adhering as closely as possible to my nursery rhyme. できる限り童謡のとおりにしたかった　**20** rigorous 厳しい　**22** intimated 知らせた　**23** carry our plan into effect 計画を実行する

p.283　**2** plaster of red mud 赤い泥を塗ったもの　**15** rendezvous 会う約束　**26** vigorous 激しい　**27** heaving sea 大きくうねる海

p.284　**15** masquerading as ... 〜のふりをする　**20** bottommost 一番下の　**22** adhesive tape 粘着テープ　**25** foodstuffs 食料　**25** soldered はんだ付けされた　**27** chintz 更紗

p.285　**7** *Exit Blore* ... ブロア、退場　**9** resourceful 機知に富む　**10** she was a match for him and more 彼女は彼より上手だった　**12** psychological experiment 心理学実験　**13** consciousness of her own guilt 彼女自身の罪の意識　**14** consequent on ... 〜の結果として生じる　**15** hypnotic suggestion 催眠暗示

p.286　**2** It was my ambition to *invent* a murder mystery that no one could solve. 誰も解けない殺人ミステリーを考案することが私の夢だった　**5** craving for recognition 認められたいという願望　**6** cannot be gainsaid 否定できない　**16** paradoxically 逆説的に　**21** hocus-pocus ごまかし　**25** inspire him with confidence 彼に信頼させる

p.287　**1** brand of Cain カインの烙印（旧約聖書から。カインは弟のアベルを殺した）　**3** entrusting 託して　**5** a length of fine black cord 一本の細い黒ひも　**6** elastic cord ゴムひも　**11** trigger 引き金　**12** recoil to the door ドアのほうに跳ね返る　**12** jarred by the door handle ドアのノブにぶつかって

　　　　　　　　　　　　　　（後註執筆・星野真理／翻訳家）

KODANSHA ENGLISH LIBRARY

そして誰(だれ)もいなくなった
And Then There Were None

2016年11月17日	第1刷発行
2025年3月6日	第4刷発行

著 者	アガサ・クリスティ
発行者	清田 則子
発行所	株式会社講談社
	〒112-8001　東京都文京区音羽2-12-21
	販売　東京 03-5395-5817
	業務　東京 03-5395-3615
編 集	株式会社講談社エディトリアル
	代表　堺 公江
	〒112-0013　東京都文京区音羽1-17-18 護国寺SIAビル
	編集部　東京 03-5319-2171
本文DTP	ギルド
印刷所	大日本印刷株式会社
製本所	株式会社国宝社

落丁本・乱丁本は購入書店名を明記のうえ、講談社業務宛にお送りください。送料小社負担にてお取り替えいたします。なお、この本についてのお問い合わせは、講談社エディトリアル宛にお願いいたします。本書のコピー、スキャン、デジタル化等の無断複製は著作権法上での例外を除き禁じられています。本書を代行業者等の第三者に依頼してスキャンやデジタル化することはたとえ個人や家庭内の利用でも著作権法違反です。

定価はカバーに表示してあります。

©1939 Agatha Christie Limited
Printed in Japan 2016
ISBN 978-4-06-250086-9